I0666476

THE PLAN

BY:

RAVEN H. PRICE

SelfPubBookCovers.Com

Artist: Petal65

RAVEN H. PRICE

Disclaimer/Copyright

The Plan

This book is Christian Fiction and based on the author's imagination and faith. No one is slandered or libeled in this work; resemblance to other persons living or dead is purely coincidental in nature and places where events take place are fake to the author's knowledge. No portion of this book may be reproduced, stored in a retrieval system, or transmitted in any form or by any means-electronic, mechanical, photocopy, recording, scanning, or other-except for brief quotations in critical reviews or articles, without the prior written permission of the author(s). No part of this book may be made into a movie without permission of the author(s). All rights reserved

Library of Congress Cataloguing-in-Publication Data

DEDICATION

I dedicate this book to my granddaughter, Thea Hansen. May she always know the truth about how much Jesus loves her. Without him, there is no true love anywhere or with anyone.

ACKNOWLEDGEMENTS

I would first like to acknowledge my husband, Ralph Price, III, who put up with me during this process and encouraged me through it all.

Second, I would like to acknowledge Jan Kane who proofed and helped edit this work.

Third, I would like to acknowledge my Father-in-law, Ralph Price, and Sister-in-law, Karen Wright, who believed in me enough to invest and support this work.

TABLE OF CONTENTS

PROLOGUE

For as-long-as I can remember, I have sensed a detachment from this world. I was aware of another realm or place from a very early age. At maybe three or four I started wondering about my life.

When my feelings were hurt one day, I escaped into my own thoughts outside in the sunshine. I seemed to be in a trance and something got my attention. I heard a soft voice ask, *"Little One, what is wrong? Why are you so sad?"* I responded without thinking. I said, "No one wants to be with me." The soft voice said to me. *"I'm here; I'll never leave or forsake you. You are so precious to me."*

From that day forward, my life was never the same. I craved hearing more of that same soft voice.

Before I go any further, my readers need to know about my beginning and why I was told by my new friend that a plan had been made for my life. He said the plan was developed just for me because of a prayer that God received from my mother. I was too young to understand it or what impact it would have when I got older.

The narration of this book will be in two different manners. Because the thoughts are from a baby's point of view, the first part of this book has been written in the third person. As time progresses, the story will be told in the first person.

So, get ready for an adventure.

IN THE BEGINNING

On November 20, 1954, God granted Emily and Jason Parody a baby girl. The baby was fully developed but was very small, only weighing an ounce over five pounds. She was named Rachel Eve Parody.

Problems began soon after Emily and Jason took little Rachel home. One night, Emily felt in her heart that she needed to check on Rachel one more time before she turned in for the night. When she turned on the bedside lamp, she noticed her little girl was blue. She began to scream, "Jason, call an ambulance!" "Rachel is not breathing!"

When the ambulance arrived and took little Rachel with her mother to the hospital the plan for Rachel's life began. During the ride to the hospital, Emily cried out to God. "Please Lord spare my child. I know that you gave her to me and that you have a good plan designed for her life. I'm trusting in you Lord to carry out your promise and keep her safe and healthy. I'm asking that you forgive me for thinking I could raise Rachel keeping her safe and healthy on my own. Lord, I should have dedicated her to you from the moment of her birth. I'm so sorry. From this moment on, I'm putting my trust in you and what you tell the doctors to do."

When the ambulance arrived at the hospital, Emily was not allowed in the examining room until the ER doctors looked over Rachel. When Jason finally arrived, Emily was peaceful amid the crisis.

He asked, "Is she okay? What is going on?"

Emily told him she did not know, but she felt that it would be all right because the doctors would know what to do. She did not tell him about her prayer, petitioning God for good doctors. Jason was not a strong Christian, he knew of Jesus and went to church with Emily occasionally, but that was all. She knew talking with him about her prayer would only cause doubt or fear to get started, and she didn't need that from him. So, she focused her conversation only with the help of the doctors. She needed Jason's support and strength at that moment and he had complete trust in a doctor's words.

Jason had been through rough times himself as a kid. Through the help of medicine, he became strong but very self-serving.

Emily and Jason found a corner of the emergency room's waiting area where they joined hands and waited for a staff member or a doctor to call them into Rachel's examining room.

*****

In heaven, God heard a wonderful call to Him for help. He looked at His son Jesus and said, "I'm hearing a mother giving us her daughter."

"Remember when Hannah gave us Samuel?" Jesus asked.

"Yes, and he turned out to be so helpful to our plan." God said, "This woman is putting her faith in us. The child is sick, and

11

the mother is counting on a promise she believes in from the Word."

Jesus said, "Father, what do you want to do? I know your promises never fail for those who believe in them."

"I know", God said. "I think I'm going to let you take care of this one, though, and the call I have on this little one is for a specific purpose. Make her your bride. Show her how love really is."

Jesus asked, "From such an early age?"

God's reply was, "Yes, woo her now by showing her true love from the beginning."

Jesus replied, "Okay, I'll show myself to her and teach her about the kingdom slowly until she is old enough to choose correctly. I know she can never depart from scripture, so I'll have to teach her in layman terms where she can understand."

"Great!" was God's reply.

Jesus went immediately to that emergency room and rebuked an evil demon of sickness that was trying to take little Rachel's life. In that examining room, He fell in love with the little baby. He said to her, *Little One, I'm here, I'll always be with you.*

As Rachel began to respond to Jesus' love, her breathing became normal again.

12

*****

At the same time, Jesus' enemy was still lurking in the shadows of that very room. Satan's messenger said to himself, "I knew that baby was trouble from the moment she was born. Her mother and grandmother are too goody, goody always talking about Jesus, Jesus, Jesus. Now, look. Here He is cooing over that brat. I'm going to have to keep watch over her and make sure she is destroyed when her attention is diverted. Time will tell."

"But first, I'm going to use the girl's father to get her destruction started. I'm going to make him trust in everything the doctor says. Keep him focused on fear and money rather than any plans that "He" has." Then he hissed as he slid off like the snake he came from so he could devise the trap.

*****

About an hour and a half after going to the ER, Dr. Ken Wright came into the waiting area to speak with Jason and Emily. He said, "Your baby seems to be very sick. I've started her on oxygen therapy and an IV to keep her hydrated for now. I'll run some blood tests tomorrow to see if we can determine why she stopped breathing. You can go in to see her, but there is really nothing you can do for her except watch over her. You need your strength, so I recommend you go home and get as much sleep as you can." Then Dr. Wright left.

A very sweet nurse led them into Rachel's little room. To keep the conversation light, she told them, "She is so small and lovely. I bet she was an answer to your prayers, wasn't she? I knew from the moment I saw her she was special. We'll take as much care with her as possible. I'm going to leave you alone with her for a while. Buzz me when you want something."

When the nurse left, Emily's heart broke. On that tiny bed, Rachel was hooked up to every kind of monitor and tube. She had a tent over her whole bed pumping oxygen into it for her to breathe. Even though the sight was awful, Emily knew what her mother had taught her, she needed to keep her eyes on Jesus; not on what was in front of her. Emily realized not focusing on Rachel's illness was one of the hardest things she had ever been faced with. Her little angel was so helpless, and it was hard to wrench her eyes away from that picture to trust in the prayer she petitioned just over two hours earlier. But she knew her baby's life depended on what her mother had taught on having faith in her God.

Emily never left the hospital, she slept as much as possible in a lounge chair that was provided by the staff. Jason would bring her a fresh set of clothes every night after work, along with something to eat and her cigarettes. Back then, hospitals allowed smoking, but Emily could not smoke in Rachel's room while oxygen was being administered. She had to go down the hall to a break area to get her cigarette fix every few hours.

Rachel's stay at the hospital continued: test after test, medicine trial after medicine trial, day after day. Still, the doctor was stumped. In his office, while looking over the latest set of tests done on the child, he said to himself, *"I can't find anything wrong with this child to clarify why she keeps losing her breath.*

14

Jason and Emily are going to think I've lost my mind, that I'm a quack making their daughter suffer through all this. Jason has a good job, though, so I know he'll be able to pay for this. I'll just bluff my way out of this one. I'm going to boost Rachel's immune system and tell her parents that it was malfunctioning. The treatments can't hurt her and will be very beneficial. I'll baffle them with medical speak because I really don't know what is wrong and I need to cover my butt."

All the while, the evil messenger from hell was working on making things hard on the Parody family's finances. He made it where Jason's mom was unable to support herself any longer. Jason would have to invite her to live with them. And with Emily not working, Jason would have to put in longer and longer hours on the job. Evil made it necessary for Jason to bring work home where he made phone calls and tried to collect past due debts owed to his company. Evil's plan was to wear Jason out, cause his temper to get the best of him, where he would become impatient with customers as well as with his family.

Evil also stole Jason's peace. When Jason learned, he didn't have long-term medical coverage on his family any longer, it would cause the medical bills for Rachel's care to grow to place a severe strain on things.

One night at the hospital, while Emily was taking a shower, Jason held little Rachel. It was then he felt a surge of disgust for his daughter. He was now responsible for a misfit, not deformed, but just as bad in his mind. She was the cause of the financial burden around his neck, the one causing all his plans to crumble. "Now how was he going to get the bigger house they needed or the land that he wanted to start a farm on?" He wanted to scream and cry all at the same time. "How could he tell Emily his feelings against their only child? She loved this baby with all her heart and if he expressed the thoughts he was having, she'd hate him. Emily was everything to him. He couldn't risk losing her because of this baby. So, he bottled his thoughts inside and tried to work through them alone.

*****

All the while, Evil was laughing at his plan taking the desired shape for Rachel's destruction. He said, "Just as I'd planned the father can't see past himself and his needs. Soon, he will completely hate this child if I can keep up the financial hardships. I'll keep taking from his wallet and he'll lose his cool altogether. I can't wait to see it."

*****

In heaven, God was seeing all of Evil's plans going forth and wasn't too happy with them. He called Jesus in for a meeting concerning the situation.

"What are you doing about Rachel?" God asked.

Jesus replied, "I'm comforting her and making sure that she receives good care."

"Are you aware of that stupid demon trying to cause havoc?" God asked.

"I know all about it," Jesus said. "Little does he know, but he is part of My plan as well.   It will be hard to watch what he does, but it will be necessary for our plan for Rachel to be effective. I'm just like you Father; I get jealous because I want all her attention. I don't think I'll be able to bear all of what he plans to do, but I know if we don't let it play out, we may lose her forever."

God's reply was, "Don't look into the future that far ahead, Son. Stay focused on the present.   Remember she is still under her father's authority so you will need to work around that issue for now."

God knew until Rachel was old enough to choose, her father was the one that would have the say not only in her natural matters but especially in her spiritual ones he knew nothing about. Her heart was at stake because of him, not just her physical well-being, and God knew this. He also understood how a broken spirit can dry up bones and make the person bitter. That was not part of His plans for her at all. She had such a pure heart from the day she was born and left up to Him; her heart was going to stay that way. So, God commanded Preservation to keep watch over little Rachel's life also. Preservation was to keep her alive and keep her heart from turning hard or bitter towards anyone while the plan for her life played out.   She might get her feelings hurt or be discouraged from time to time, but Preservation was not to let those feelings fester into hardness of heart. God said to Himself, "I still have a say in this plan even though I've given her over to my Son. I can't stand watching Evil throw nasty tricks on such a sweet baby."

*****

After Rachel was released from the hospital, Dr. Wright gave Jason and Emily strict orders if she stopped breathing to get her to the emergency room. If her breathing was just labored, they would only need to give her an injection to relax her lungs and open her airways.

Jason asked the doctor "Is the medicine we are to keep on hand very expensive?"

Dr. Wright said, "The medicine is not, but the immunization treatments I have to prescribe for her to take every three months is very expensive and she may need them indefinitely."

Jason thought to himself, "That is just great! More issues I have to keep up with costing me out the yahoo."

Now that Rachel was home, it seemed every few days Emily had to give her injections. Once, in the middle of the night, Emily felt a soft nudge waking her up. Little did she know, but Preservation had prompted her to wake up. Getting up she decided to check on Rachel. Rachel, again, had turned blue and was laboring hard to breathe. Emily didn't even change clothes. She threw on a coat and drove her baby to the ER as fast as she could. Once she got there she called home waking Jason up. She told him that in her panic, she didn't want to waste time trying to get him out of bed.

When Jason got to the hospital, Dr. Wright had just finished examining Rachel and placing her back under oxygen therapy. He sat Jason and Emily down and told them he thought Rachel was an acute asthmatic.

"What is that?" Emily asked.

"The tubes leading into her lungs become constricted and cause air to stop flowing properly. I feel it still has something to do with her immune system, but until we know what she is allergic to, we need to keep her on immunization injections and steroids." Dr. Wright answered.

*****

Evil was ecstatic watching the latest batch of tricks destroy little Rachel. Her parents were such fools! Little did they know but he was using their very own cigarette smoke to cause Rachel to stop breathing-not an allergy or her immune system.

He was having fun using her parents smoking habit along with Grandma's, who chained smoked from sun up to sun down, even waking up in the middle of the night to have a puff. He kept their house full of smoke all the time a grown person who didn't smoke would have a hard time breathing in their house for any length of time.

As time went on, Rachel's hospital visits were regular. The immunization injections caused her so much pain Emily couldn't even stand to watch the nurses give them to her. But Jason couldn't see her pain. All he could do was stew over the bills which made his attitude toward his little girl grow increasingly bitter.

Jason talked to himself about his attitude," I want to love Rachel; she is so sweet and cute." And when he held her, she looked at him as if she worshiped him. "Why can't I return her love?" What could he do? He was tired all the time and had no free time to just be himself.

Just before Rachel's second birthday, Emily went to Jason and told him she had some good news. "I'm pregnant again!" Jason couldn't believe it. He wanted to be happy, but fear gripped his heart like a steel vice.

"What if we have another baby like Rachel?" He said.

Hurt by his remark, Emily said, "We will just have to wait and see. I believe this baby is also a gift from God just like Rachel, so I will love it just as much no matter what."

Sensing that he had hurt Emily's feelings, Jason hugged her and told her he would love it too, even though in the back of his mind he was worried.

One good thing came out of Emily's pregnancy- she stopped smoking. The very thought of a cigarette made her sick, so she decided it was time to give them up. Because Rachel was

20

around her more than the other two during the day, Rachel's breathing got better. Emily noticed that at night, when Jason and Grandma were home after work, Rachel would have trouble getting a deep breath. She decided to do an experiment. She asked them to smoke outside for a while to see what would happen.

Low and behold, Rachel's breathing got better each day. Emily was on cloud nine. Her baby was getting well. But through her joy, she would tell everyone that it was the immunization shots and the help of Rachel's doctor that was healing Rachel. Never did she once give credit to the One who ordered Rachel's healing from the very beginning of this ordeal. This made God sad.

Even though God was sad, He and Jesus never broke their promises. The truth would someday be revealed. Rachel herself would one day declare the truth and then they would get the proper credit.

On March 20th Jason Lance Parody, Jr. was born (JL for short). He was a big, eight-pound, healthy baby with white hair and deep blue eyes just like his Daddy's. Jason fell head over heels in love with the child. He thought to himself, JL is the exact opposite of Rachel. She was dark haired, green eyed and let's don't mention, sickly.

While Jason worked double shifts, and brought work home, he still didn't have enough to make financial ends meet. His worry caused his old stomach problem to flare up again: Ulcers! When would these medical issues stop? The more he fretted over the bills; it seemed the deeper in debt he became. His childhood stomach issue of vomiting up blood was a secret he was hiding from Emily. He didn't want her to pressure him into going to the doctor. He knew what to do. He'd been through this before when he was younger.

He knew it was a stress issue causing his stomach to react. He would have to get a grip on himself and get things straight.

He had a bright idea, "Why not mortgage the house". It was paid for. He and his father had built the little house themselves and it would be worth something. So, he paid an adjuster to give him the appraisal value of the house and he went to the bank with that knowledge. "Wow," he thought. "This amount will pay off the medical bills incurred from Rachel as well as what the birth of JL cost." They would be able to afford things better if he consolidated with a mortgage loan. Being a loan officer himself, he knew what that meant, and he would be able to handle all the bills if he kept his job.

So, the self-made plan to mortgage the house went into effect and Jason got the temporary peace he needed from financial stress. His health issue improved or just lay low for now.

*****

Evil was hopping mad. How had he let this happen? Jason was happy and that certainly was not in his plan. He couldn't allow this happiness to develop into self-forgiveness where Rachel was concerned. He went away to consult with his master, so they could devise something more devious.

Satan told him, "Why not destroy the whole family instead of focusing on the girl. The new baby is the center of Jason's attention now, his pride and joy. Touch him and see the happiness crumble and the stress mount again when those finances scream pay me, pay me or lose everything."

Evil went back to the Parody family and started his new attack.

It was fall, just turning cooler, and people everywhere were getting the flu. "Here is my chance." Evil said to himself. He caused an issue with one of the family cars. It stalled out several yards from the house so the family, all five of them, got stuck out in bad weather drenching them with rain before they could get into the shelter of the house. Not only that, but he caused Jason to forget to buy gas for the heating season and it became cooler much sooner than usual. Evil was having fun making it a night where they all would suffer from the cold.

*****

The next day, little JL started coughing and running a temperature. By nightfall, he was extremely sick. So, sick with fever, Emily feared the worst. Calling Dr. Wright at home she asked. "What do you recommend, doctor? JL's temperature is almost 103 and he is coughing so much."

23

Dr. Wright, remembering Rachel's problems, told her "Emily, get your little boy to the ER right now, I'll meet you and Jason there."

Fear struck Jason like a bat making him think, "His little boy, not his little boy!" Expecting the worst, they took off as Jason's let his mouth run on and on with complaint and fear as it's steering wheel.

JL had pneumonia and was put under an oxygen tent. Two days later, Rachel also developed pneumonia and was put in the same room with JL, but in her own bed under an oxygen tent. Jason was crazy with fear. Two babies sick! Hadn't he just risked a mortgage to get their debt under control? What was this going to cost?

The babies got well and were sent home, but the bills kept growing. Every month things got tighter until they had to sell one of the cars. Now they were down to one car to meet the needs of three adults. Two had daily jobs with different schedules. Talk about stress - Jason's was soaring.

THE MEETING

God's plan now is to communicate directly with Rachel to hear her speak and tell her side of life. She is now old enough to talk and understand so, it's only right for her to speak. Not a baby any longer, He would listen to her as well as to her parent's opinions.

I told my Grandma one Sunday morning, "I'm a big girl now! Mama said that I don't have to go to baby and toddler school at church anymore. In my new class, we will learn songs and have lessons like big kids."

"That's great," Grandma said.

Thinking to herself, Grandma was glad Emily was taking the kids to church. It was Emily's only activity outside of the house, and she needed friends.

God thought, "Grandma really didn't have a clue to Emily's needs. It was not friends that Emily was seeking, it was His peace that only He could give. Emily's mother had taken her to church as much as possible and it was at the family church where she learned to accept my Son, Jesus. She did learn that He was the way to eternal life and through Him, hell would not be an issue. She just wasn't taught at the church attended that she could have a good life now. All they taught her was the sweet by and by. They never taught her much past eternal life and repentance."

He saw that Emily felt guilty all the time and forgiveness is what she needed more than friends. He watched her go to her little church, repenting about everything she could think of and casting her cares on Jesus but leaving there just as confused as when she went. The benefits of salvation were not being offered through the pastor's teaching, so she didn't know that by her faith she could really count on all scripture said.

It was just a fluke that through her panic over Rachel's life-threatening problem when she was a baby, that she could make her appeal to me, He thought. But that simple cry for help from her heart is all it took to get my attention. He could see in her mind, the problems were still there, Rachel was alive, yes, but her health issues and Jason's lack of sympathy were awful and her faith wavered.

Jesus was preoccupied on the sidelines watching Rachel.

"In my class, I learned the song 'Jesus loves me'. It is my favorite song. I sing it all the time," Rachel told Grandma.

Hearing her little voice made Jesus happy. He loved the little mistakes she'd sometimes make while trying to remember all the words. It was precious. He wanted so much to introduce Himself to her, but He had to wait until her little heart needed Him.

*****

Evil had another bright idea to destroy the family; he'd take Emily away as much as possible. So, he arranged one day for Emily to get a call from her old boss. He would tell her he really needed her to work for him again a few hours each week. She could

26

schedule her appointments around her family's needs if she could start seeing patients again. Evil knew that Emily wanted to work and help Jason with the bills. She was skilled as a registered Dental Hygienist and loved helping people before her babies were born. Now he would use Dr. Neal's growing business as a weapon to keep her away from the family.

Evil could also use Jason's mother. She's starting her retirement process and only working three days a week with Saturday being one of them. It would make it possible for Emily to work two and half days each week while Jason's mom was at home. He'd make it seem that Grandma could take care of the babies and Emily would be able to help bring funds back into the household again.

Evil was having fun making plans for the Parody family. He decided he'd work on Jason some more while making plans for the women. He would cause their work schedules to get confused, making both unavailable for the kids. This left Jason as their only solution for a babysitter. He was the only one who didn't have personal contact with people on the job every day and could work around the kids and Evil knew this would never do.

That day came when Evil made things work out, so Jason was forced into the issue of babysitting. He laughed when Jason grumbled as he took JL and Rachel to work with him. Wasn't it all Jason needed to cause him interruptions where he couldn't make those much-needed collection calls. Now he'd have to keep his eyes on the kids and that would make his attitude even viler towards them, especially Rachel.

*****

I was so happy. I was getting to go to work with Daddy. I must really be a big girl I thought until I saw JL was going with us. Why couldn't I have time alone with my Daddy? I wanted him to show me what he did at work but now he'd have to hold JL and make sure he didn't get into trouble.

Just like I thought, Daddy held JL in his lap while he talked on the phone. But he did give me a notepad and several different colored pens to draw with. I loved to draw and make pictures but every time I wanted to show Daddy one of my pictures he would nod and tell me to make another one.

As the day progressed, I had to use the toilet badly. I didn't use a diaper anymore, but I needed help. I didn't know where the toilet was so, I tried to get Daddy's attention. "Daddy, I need to potty real, bad," I told him. He said, "Wait just a minute." I tried to wait, really, I did, but my bowels wouldn't hold.

Smelling the poop, Daddy started yelling at me. "You are not a baby! Why didn't you go to the restroom?" He screamed. "Now we have to go home! You are a pain in my neck!" While he arranged for us to leave, I cried softly to myself. I didn't want Daddy to yell at me again. I was a big girl. It was an accident. I would have tried to go by myself if I had known where to go.

When we got home, Daddy cleaned me and put fresh clothes on me. He still was angry at me, though. I tried to love him, but it didn't help. With disgust, Daddy pushed me aside gently and told me to go play outside. My chest was hurting so bad. All I wanted was for Daddy not to be mad at me anymore. I started mumbling to myself once I got outside.

"I love the sunshine," I thought to myself, "It makes me feel like I'm being hugged by some large person." But today I want to be hugged by Daddy. It was then that I said to myself. "I wish I had someone to talk and play with. No one wants to be with me."

Jesus thought to himself, "Finally our time for meeting each other has come."

I heard a soft voice say to me, *"Little One, what is wrong? Why are you so sad?"*

I was startled but not afraid, so I replied, "No one wants to be with me."

Jesus replied, *"I'll never leave you or forsake you."*

At those words, I was curious, so I asked, "Where are you? I hear you but I don't see you."

"I know you can't" Jesus replies. *"You'll need to find me,"* He said.

"Do you want to play hide and seek?" I asked happily.

"Yes, but you'll find me with your eyes closed. Can you do it that way for me?" Jesus said.

29

I asked confused, "What do I do when I close my eyes?"

"You'll need to think of a special place in your head and picture me there. Can you do that?" Jesus asked.

"Oh, yes," I said. "I know the perfect place I want us to play."

I thought about the field Daddy had taken the family to see last week. He told us he wanted to buy this field and move the family there to live. It was so lovely. It had wildflowers everywhere and was so pretty.

I focused so hard on the place in my head that suddenly, a bright light began to shine in my mind. I saw a figure of a man coming towards me. He was tall and it looked like he was glowing.

"I see you!" I said in delight. "Do you see me?" I pleaded.

"I sure do," Jesus told me.

Then He asked me, *"What would you like to play?"*

"I don't know. What do you like to play?" I asked Him back.

He said, *"Let's play find the ants."*

"Find the ants?" I asked. "What kind of game is that?" I thought to myself. "It doesn't matter. It's a game. I may like it. " So, I told Him, "Okay, let's find the ants."

As we lay on our stomachs looking at the ants, my new friend began telling me all about them. I was fascinated and wanted to know more. So, we located another bug and He started telling me all about it. "This is fun," I told Him.

We'd been together for what seemed to be a long time when I got up my courage to ask His name. I asked very shyly, "What is your name? I don't know what to call you."

Moved by her shyness, Jesus said to her, *"Why don't you give me a name that will be our special secret."*

"I'd love too," I said excitedly. "Can I call you Sunny?" I asked.

"Why that name?" Jesus asked me curiously.

"Oh, when you came to me today, you looked like the sun," I exclaimed.

"I was just thinking to myself that the sunshine made me feel like I was being hugged. I really needed a hug and there you came looking like sunlight to me. Is that name okay?" I asked Him.

He said, *"It sure is Little One, because I am light, I'll be Sunny just for you."*

It was then I heard Mama calling me to come inside. When I turned around, Sunny had disappeared and I was at home again in my backyard. I ran into the house and told my Mama that I had a new friend. She just nodded and said, "That's great, honey."

31

Being tired from work, Emily assumed Rachel was talking about an imaginary friend. Someone she had made up because she was lonely. She'd have to ask Jason after dinner if they could get Rachel a dog or cat to play with.

*****

Evil was worried now; Jesus and Rachel had met. "What was he going to do?" He thought to himself. "I'm going to need help fast. I can't allow love and trust to develop between them."

He asked for a meeting with Satan, and the two of them agreed that more help from other evil demons was needed. Jesus had finally made Himself known to the child as her ultimate friend. One she could call on anytime. "That friendship must never fully develop." Evil told his master. "It makes me sick to watch them."

Satan said to the Evil. "I know what we can do. Didn't you say Emily thought Rachel was lonely? We need to influence Jason when Emily asks him to allow the kid to have a pet. We'll make sure the pet becomes her ultimate friend, so she can't think of Him."

That very night when Emily spoke to Jason about Rachel being lonely, he agreed to get a pet. He was tired from work that evening and he didn't want a discussion about anything. He just agreed to whatever Emily was asking without thinking it through.

DISTRACTIONS

"Mama, Mama!" I yelled, "Grandma is going to show me how to make colored pears."

"What?" Emily asked.

"You know the pink ones, the green and blue ones that are in jars," I said.

"Pickled pears?" Emily asked.

"Yes, those! I love them, and Grandma wants my help this morning." I told her.

Emily said, "Great honey, I love them too. Make a lot of them so we'll have them all year long, okay."

So, for several days, Grandma and I made colored pears. I would put the color in the jars after she put the hot pears in them. They were so pretty, and I helped. I was proud of myself.

The last day of pear making Mama came in the kitchen with a huge smile on her face.

I asked, "Why are you so happy?"

"Come outside Rachel, I want to show you a surprise." She replied.

"A surprise!" I screamed with delight.

And I took off running to the back door. On the porch was the prettiest puppy I had ever seen.

"Is she mine?" I asked Mama.

"She is both yours and JL's. You'll have to be very careful with her though because she is a baby." She told me.

Unhappy that I had to share, I exclaimed, "JL is a baby too. He'll be too rough, I'll have to make sure that he is gentle with her." "Can I name her?" I begged.

"Sure, JL is too little to do it so you make up her name," Mama said.

I thought and thought. Then her name just popped into my head. I'd been playing in sugar all week with Grandma making colored pears, so I'd name her Sugar.

"I want to call her Sugar," I told Mama.

Mama thought that Sugar was a sweet name for our new baby.

Sugar is so much fun. But because she is still a baby she makes accidents for me to clean up every now and then. I hate that, but Mama said if I wanted to keep her I must clean up after her and take her outside a lot until she got used to making poopy outdoors. Now I know why Daddy got so mad at me when I had an accident in my pants. It was yucky and smelly. I almost lost my breakfast this morning when I stepped in Sugar's poop and had to clean up the mess and my shoe.

Sugar was growing so fast, but I was promised that she would never get too big for me to pick up. She was a small dog by nature and would stop growing when she got to be about ten or twelve pounds. Every day, Grandma would let me, and Sugar go outside and play. We would play until lunchtime, then again until Mama got home. The weather was so nice and sunny, and we had fun running and playing fetch. We loved each other so much.

At night Mama lets Sugar sleep in between JL's crib and my bed on her own little mat. I can let my hand down easy to pet her and make sure she is still in the room. I couldn't have her going off and making a mess for Daddy to find. He'd be so mad at me.

Last Saturday, Daddy woke up and searched for his house shoes but couldn't find one of them. He asked if I would help him look for it. I saw Sugar had it in the living room. She had been chewing on it. Boy, was Daddy mad when he came in the room and saw her. He spanked her good with the shoe then looked at me and told me, "You'd better not cry, Rachel." I shook my head and left the room and cried. I didn't like seeing my baby get a spanking. She didn't know it was Daddy's shoe.

After that, I kept a close watch on where Sugar went in the house. She has eaten holes in my socks, but I hid them or threw them in the wastebasket so Mama wouldn't find them and spank her. Sugar was my responsibility. JL was too little to do anything but play with her. He could barely talk so she didn't respond to anything he ever said. Mostly she'd follow me around because JL was always pulling her tail.

I was so happy. I had the best friend in the world. Sugar loved me so much and we were inseparable.

*****

Evil couldn't stand Rachel being happy. The child's very existence made him miserable. He knew that the pet was supposed to keep her away from Him, but he didn't want the child to be happy either. He couldn't help himself. He had to mess up her happiness. He wanted her heart to break. Destroy her from the inside.

So, one fall afternoon, as Rachel and Sugar were playing outside, Evil decided to take the dog from her. "But how?" he thought. Then he said to himself, "I'll make her Daddy give the dog away. It will break the child's heart and cause her to hate her father. She'll never get over it. That dog is everything to her."

How was he going to make Jason give the dog away? He knew that Jason didn't have a problem with the animal and it kept Rachel entertained. The only way he could make Jason do it was to affect his wallet again. Make it appear the dog had caused Rachel to get sick. She hadn't been sick in a long time and now was the time to throw a sickness on her, big time. Evil thought.

*****

The leaves were piled high in the backyard and it made a fun hiding place for Sugar. She would get in the leaves and jump out at me making me scream. It was so much fun. When we were tired from playing, I noticed that Sugar was covered in yellow dust, so I tried to wipe it off her fur. When I wiped at the dust clinging to Sugar's coat, the dust would poof up into my eyes and up my nose. It made my eyes water and my nose tingle. The more I wiped them with my hand the worse I felt.

I ran inside for help because I was miserable. That is when I realized I couldn't talk. My throat had swollen shut. I tried to tell Grandma, but she didn't notice that I was in trouble. I shook her dress until she looked down at me. I swear I saw her face go white. She grabbed me and started washing my face and hands. She put her head to my chest and started swearing. I'd never heard my Grandma say those kinds of words before; I guess she was scared or mad at me. I didn't know.

She called my Daddy at work and told him to get Mama and come home or she was going to have to call an ambulance. By the time, they got home, I was really struggling to breathe. Mama gave me a shot, but that didn't help much. So off we went to the hospital.

Dr. Wright looked me over and put a mask on my face after he gave me two more shots. I was getting tired of being poked. He asked my parents to follow him into another room, so they could talk while I rested.

In the waiting area, Dr. Wright asked my Mama what had caused the episode. That's when they told him I had been playing with our dog, Sugar. He told Mama and Daddy that he needed to do some blood work on me to see if I was allergic to something. He would let them know soon.

In his office, Dr. Wright studied the results of Rachel's blood work. "Nothing," he said to himself. 'So, what caused the child to react so adversely? I'm going to have to tell them something. They look up to me for all the answers concerning Rachel's health. Most children with asthma are allergic to a lot of things, but Rachel's blood work doesn't show anything. The test should be showing allergies of all kinds but there is nothing."

During his rounds at the hospital, when Dr. Wright arrived at Rachel's room, he was ready for Emily's and Jason's questions. He told them, "I feel Rachel's asthma attack was a seasonal thing. I recommend that she not go outside to play right now or be allowed to play with her dog until this season has passed. She is going to be fine and I'm going to let her go home tomorrow."

Evil had his fingers in Jason's ears, so he wasn't allowed to hear correctly what the Dr. said. All he heard was not let Rachel outside or play with the dog. To him, her playing outside and the dog were the cause of her asthma. That night, when he and Emily got home, he demanded the dog be given away or taken to the pound. He would not allow the animal to cause Rachel to get sick all the time.

Emily was heartbroken over Jason's demand, so she called the dog's prior owner to see if they could take Sugar back. Thank God, they said yes. They told her they understood and wanted a good home for the animal.

So, the next day, before Jason and Emily went to pick up Rachel from the hospital, they loaded up Sugar, her bed, and all her playthings to take back to her Mama at the place where she was born.

*****

Preservation was ready. He was not going to allow Evil's plan to break Rachel's, heart. He was going to tell Emily exactly what to tell the little girl so that she could accept it and eventually be okay with their plan.

On the way home from the hospital, Mama told me that she needed to tell me something. Guided by Preservation, she started by asking me a question, "Honey if I were to need you with me really badly wouldn't you want to be with me?" I told her, "I'd want to be with you anytime." That's when she responded, "I know honey, but it is important that you understand what Mama is trying to tell you now, okay. I don't want you to cry or be upset, but Sugar's Mama needed her to come home. So, Daddy and I let her go back home to be with her Mama."

I couldn't help it. I started to cry but asked, "Is she coming back?"

Mama hugged me and whispered to me, "No, darling her Mama really needed her to stay and look after her."

My heart felt like it was about to burst out of me. I didn't even get to hug her bye but I was so proud of my little Sugar. She took care of me for a long time. She was good at making us happy. She'd be good company for her Mama.

When we got home, I asked if I could go outside. Mama told me that I could sit on the swing, but that I was not allowed to play. I needed to remember my little Sugar. I needed my friend so bad.

Being in the sun reminded me of another friend.

"Sunny!" I called.

"Here I am Little One." I heard him say softly.

I whispered, "I need you."

He said, *"Remember how to find me; close your eyes and think of our place."*

And just like before, I saw Him, and He was so beautiful. His smile was so overwhelming that I relaxed enough to stop crying.

"Tell me what is wrong Little One." He urged.

Then from my heart I just started talking, "I don't have Sugar anymore and she was my best friend. I miss her so much. But I want her to be happy."

"You love animals, don't you?" He asked me.

"Yes, but I don't think I'll ever love another one like her," I explained.

40

That is when He told me, *"Where I am you can be with all my animals. Look around us, what do you see?"*

That's when I saw squirrels, rabbits, puppies, kittens, horses, goats, and pigs. I was so excited I jumped into His arms and hugged Him. "Can I play with all these?" I asked.

"Sure, if we are together whatever is mine is yours." Was His reply.

So, all that afternoon, even though I was sitting quietly on my swing at home, I was playing with Sunny and His animal friends in our secret place.

When Mama came outside to get me, I was happy. Seeing that I appeared to be happy made her feel better. I told her in time I'd get to see Sugar again. Hearing me say that made her think to herself. "Rachel's got a grip on the hereafter. She thinks she'll see Sugar again one day in heaven." She didn't know it was Sunny who told me Sugar and I were going to be together with Him someday. I would just have to wait awhile.

Months went by and everyday Sunny and I played together with His animals. Grandma thought I was swinging on my swing outside because I wasn't allowed to run and play.

One day, butterflies came and flew all around me. All sizes and varieties. They were so beautiful. Sunny told me they were His friends also and they liked me. I reached out my hand towards them and some perched on my fingers and looked at me. Their little eyes seemed to be staring at me curiously.

41

I asked Sunny, "Are they trying to speak to me? They seem to be saying something."

He laughed at me then told me, *"They think you are beautiful, too, and are telling you that."*

Right then my life was so full. I hadn't been sick in a while and I felt wonderful.

In 1960 I would be starting first grade but not in Belmont where we lived. Daddy bought the land that he wanted, and it was in another county close to Wellington, about ten miles from Belmont. From now on, we were going to be living at my secret place.

I asked Sunny, "When we move, do I still have to close my eyes when I want to see you or will you just be there? Are all the animals going to be there when we move?" My little mind could not comprehend how our secret place was going to stay secret if my family was going to live there.

He told me, *"Our secret place will still be our secret, but you'll need to find me the same way. And yes, where I am my animals will be there with me. You don't have to worry about your family spoiling our secret."*

The move was fun. JL and I still had to share a room because Grandma was moving with us. I didn't mind. JL could be fun now that he was talking and walking better. We would play out in the yard and I showed him the ants. We called them our little soldiers because they looked like they were marching off to war.

I wanted to play outside so Mama told me not to leave the yard. Daddy bought a bull and if I went over the fence, the bull would run at me and she was afraid I'd get hurt. I wasn't afraid of animals because none of Sunny's were mean. They would come up to me and let me pet them. So, when she told me not to leave the yard I had to push my luck a bit. I didn't leave the yard, but I stood up on the fence to watch the big bull, hoping he'd see me and come up for a pat. Yeah, he saw me all right, that big fellow started running towards me. I jumped down just before he rammed the fence hard. He looked like he wanted to kill me.

That was the first time I felt my heart pound in my chest from fear. I was so scared I had to sit down on the grass several yards from the fence to get a hold of myself.

I closed my eyes and called Sunny, "What happened?" I asked Him.

"You were not with me when you approached the animal. Remember, I said you needed to be with me where all my animals were yours to play with." He replied. *"Animals outside of our secret place are unpredictable and can harm you. But with me, they respect my friends and love them as I do."* He told me.

From then on, I knew better than to approach anything when I was told not to. If I told Mama what happened she would want to put a protective leash on me. If Daddy finds out, he might spank me for getting too close and daring the bull. Either way, nobody but Sunny was going to know what happened.

The following Sunday, we started going to another church. I was put in a class with bigger kids. In their class, we learned about Jesus. He was our Lord! I thought to myself, "Lord? What is that?"

So, I raised my hand and ask my teacher, "What is a Lord?"

She grinned and said, "It is someone who has rule over you and sees after your wellbeing."

"Wow! Someone has the job of looking over the whole world. He must be wonderful." I thought. "I'd like to know Him. He must be so strong and powerful. Big like Superman." I was guessing.

We learned that He loved all the little children, red and yellow, black, and white. Just like in my favorite song, "Jesus loves me." My song made more sense to me now. I understood it was talking about the Lord. God was His Daddy and He made everything. If we asked the Lord, we could talk with His Daddy, the teacher told us. "I'd like to do that," I told her. She just smiled at me saying that was nice.

When I got in the car with Mama to go home from church, I showed her a picture book that we could color in and bring back next Sunday. Each page had a verse on it and we were supposed to learn one before going back. I couldn't read yet, so I asked Mama if she could help me.

I told her "It won't be too much longer Mama before I can read it. I start school tomorrow."

EARLY SCHOOL DAYS

"Why can't this brat just die?" The evil spirit of sickness told his companion. "I scared that bull into hating her so much it charged her the other day. I've made her Daddy's responses to her indifferent. A normal child would be in a warped frame of mind, but not her." He exclaimed.

The companion named Fear, responded, "Scaring is not in your line of work. That's mine. Instead of scaring animals and turning her Daddy against her, let's make her afraid. Didn't you hear how fast her heart pounded the other day? Music to my ears. I could smell her fear. I'd like to make her scared of everything. So scared, she'll have problems with people as well as animals. In fact, she'll be afraid of her own thoughts."

*****

On the first day of school, Mama gave me a new outfit and new shoes to wear. She brushed my hair until I thought it was all going to come out on the brush. She seemed to be acting funny, so I asked her, "Mama why are you so jumpy with me this morning?"

"I didn't know I was honey. I was just thinking this will be the first time that you'll be away from us all by yourself." She said.

That made me think a little, I had always been with at least one of my family members every day. Her fear was making me a little scared but I didn't want to make Mama worry more.

46

I asked her, "Mama will I know anyone at school?"

She replied, "I really don't know, let me think. Yes, you'll know Chuck, Mr. Charlie's little boy. The two of you get along okay when they come over to our house or when we go over to theirs."

"Great!" I thought to myself, Chuck. He'd be no fun, he was a boy and all he wanted to do was boy-stuff. But I guess having just one person there would be enough until I met more people.

When we got to the school, there were kids everywhere. When Mama and I got to my classroom, there was Chuck sitting in one of the desk chairs crying. Then Mama squatted down to my eye level and said, "Rachel, you are a big girl now. I must go to work. This is your teacher Mrs. Lane. She will be with you and the others today. If you need me, tell her and she will get a message to me. But, don't have her call me unless you are sick or hurt. Okay?"

Then a tightening grabbed my chest, my heart started pounding and I started to shake. I said, "Mama I'm scared to be here. Look at Chuck. He is crying and all by himself."

Mama went over to Chuck and asked him, "What is the matter?"

He said to her crying, "I want my Mama."

That is when she told him the same thing she told me. That his Mama had to work, but Mrs. Lane was there for us during the day and we'd be all right in her class.

After Mama left, Chuck started crying even more. So much more he got sick on the floor. Mrs. Lane had to call his Mama to come and get him from school. I wasn't much better. My hands were shaking so bad I had to hold them together. And my chest hurt. Mrs. Lane showed all the kids to their assigned seats and I was told to sit near the back of the room.

We were given paper and pencils in a little tote bag. They were ours to keep and we needed to bring them back every day. She took a piece of chalk and started to write on the blackboard but what she was writing was strange to me. I could barely see it from my seat. But I didn't tell her that. I wanted to be a good girl and not cause problems.

She had all the kids tell their names and ages, and their birthday. That's when I noticed that I was five and all the other kids were six. "Had Mama and Daddy put me in school too young?" I thought to myself. These kids are going to think I'm a baby. I was too little to understand that my birthday was only a few more months away making me six. Most of the other kids had already had a birthday before September making them six when school started.

48

Evil focused on Rachel's thoughts to find a weakness. She didn't like being made fun of and it scared her to be alone. So, he played with the other kid's emotions to make them want to pick on a little girl.

*****

Just as I feared, one of the boys in my class picked on me at recess. His name was Bud. Bud kept telling me, "Five-year-old kids aren't allowed in school. Why are you here? Didn't your Mama and Daddy want you at home anymore?" He was so big, bigger than the other kids in my class and it scared me when he acted mean to me. When he started picking on me it caused other kids to do it too. There was not one kid in my class that wanted to play with me. It seemed none of them liked me or they were afraid to say so because of Bud.

At lunchtime, we were led into the lunch room to eat. We walked to our tables and stood behind a chair which had a tray with food and a carton of milk. I had a sliced apple, half of a peanut butter sandwich and half of a cheese sandwich. It was good, but I was too nervous to eat much. I felt everyone was watching me.

We were all shown the washrooms again after we ate and were told if we needed to use the toilet during class time that we had to raise our hands to be excused. We didn't have to wait for recess before we went like we did this morning.

When classes were finished, Mrs. Lane took all the kids that were to ride home in buses to the bus line. We walked in what she called a single file, so no one would get lost. When we got there, I saw the big yellow trucks. I'd never seen a bus, so to me, they looked like trucks. She showed each kid which bus to ride and she told us that every day we were to get on the same one.

I got on my bus and sat down by myself. I was fine until we went to another school to pick up bigger kids. I didn't have a seat alone for long because this big boy pushed me over and told me to move so he could sit next to the window. I moved so he could sit leaving me very little space.

Fear, heat, heightened emotions will play into my plan so well, Evil said to himself. Rachel will hate her life so much she'll make her parents miserable. The little brat will vomit her way into everyone's misery.

*****

The ride to my house was long and hot. When we got to our house I was sick the moment I got off the bus. Everything was spinning so I sat down on the ground for a few minutes after the bus left until I heard Grandma calling me. "Rachel, where are you? Come on in the house, you'll need to change clothes and shoes."

When I went in the house, I was so dizzy and sick that I thought to myself. "I don't want to go to school anymore I don't like it."

When Mama got home she started asking me about my day. "What did you do after I left? Did you and Chuck find other friends?"

I was ready to tell her everything I felt. I was a little mad at what had happened, so I emphatically replied. "Chuck had to go home, and all the kids were mean to me. They called me a baby because you made me go to school too little. Then a big boy on my bus pushed me and made me sit on the edge of my seat. Then I threw up when I got off the bus. I'm not going back to that place until I'm six." I'd let all my frustrations come out in one breath. Mama was stunned.

Evil's plan that night was for Rachel to hear her parents talking and laughing in their room and she would be the topic of their laughter. He wanted to make her very angry as she heard them making fun of her. She didn't think any of it was funny and Evil knew this. He'd make her night miserable, so she would cry until she fell asleep from exhaustion.

✱✱✱✱✱

In the morning, when Mama woke me up the weather outside was bad. As I ate my breakfast I was hoping that I didn't have to go to school. Hadn't I made myself plain about needing to wait? To my disappointment, though, Mama came and told me to go pick out what I wanted to wear that day. I had several dresses and a few skirts and blouses to choose from, but because I wasn't going to school that day, (so I thought) I put on my jeans.

"What are you doing Rachel?" Mama asked me when she saw that I had put on jeans and a t-shirt.

"I thought I didn't have to go to school today since the weather was bad so I put on my play clothes," I told her.

"I'm sorry, Rachel. Even though you don't want to go back to school yet, you must go. You will go every day except Saturday and Sunday even if it is raining outside." Mama told me.

In those days, schools didn't allow little girls to wear pants, so I had to choose one of my dresses or skirts and blouses. I had a yellow jacket with a hat to wear on rainy days and a pair of rain boots to go over my shoes that I wore to church on rainy days. So, Mama got them out for me to wear that day also.

Mama and I sat in the car until my bus came that morning. She told me to sit behind the driver so that big boy wouldn't have a chance to push me around. She said the driver wouldn't let someone pick on me if she could see me.

✶✶✶✶✶

Evil overheard the conversations between Rachel and her mom so, he would make it hard for Rachel to have any kind of confidence. When the bus finally came, she would be shocked to see that it would be full already and she couldn't find a seat close to the driver anywhere. She would have to search for one and hope that it wouldn't be with a big kid who was mean.

*****

When I got on the bus it was already packed with kids. I had to go all the way to the back to find a seat. I finally was allowed a place with another girl who was nice enough to let me sit with her but I still didn't have much room. Again, I felt hot, cramped and uncomfortable.

When we got to school, my stomach felt sick like it had the day before so I told Mrs. Lane. She said, "Take off your rain suit and boots. You are probably too hot." When I got to my book closet, I couldn't get the buttons undone on my jacket because I felt so bad, so, I went back to Mrs. Lane for help. After we got the jacket off I went back to my closet to take off my boots. Frustrated by this time, because everyone was waiting on me, I pulled off shoes with boots and just walked around in my socks until Mrs. Lane saw me.

"Rachel, where are your shoes?" She asked.

I told her, "I couldn't get them out of my rain boots and I didn't want to be late."

Everyone started laughing at me. I was so embarrassed I started crying. Mrs. Lane went and got my shoes and told me not to be afraid to ask her for help next time.

All day I was stressed. I had problems seeing what Mrs. Lane wrote on the blackboard and needed her help, my stomach still felt sick, and nobody wanted to be my friend.   When it was time to go home, Mrs. Lane had to help me back into my jacket and boots and told me to practice getting them on and off with Mama until I could do it by myself.

When I got on the bus, I found a seat closer to the driver this time, but still not right behind her.   The ride home on the bus was just as long as yesterday and I got hot again, and when I stepped off the bus I was sick. I threw up two times before I could get into my house.

Grandma noticed that I didn't feel good and asked me, "Honey, are you sick again?" Then she helped me put on play clothes and told me to lie on the sofa until Mama got home.

*****

This torture was fun Evil said to himself.   I'm going to scare her even more in this new place. Plus, I'm going to blind her Daddy from seeing her fear and worry and make him appear uncaring towards her needs.

*****

The weather got worse as night came and in our new house, I heard all kinds of sounds that terrified me. I was especially scared in my bedroom when it rained. It sounded like something was trying to come through the roof, scratching the walls and banging on the windows. I couldn't sleep so I got up and turned on my closet light. Daddy noticed the light was on when he went by our room, so he came in and turned it off. After he left, I got up again and turned the light back on thinking if I could focus on it then I could pretend I was in the sunlight and maybe go to sleep. That was the wrong thing to do. Daddy came back in and gave me a swat.

"You are going to keep your grandmother and brother up if you keep turning this light on. If you touch it again, I'm really going to spank you. Don't move from that bed again until morning. Do you hear me?" He said.

"Yes sir" I cried.

I was afraid to move. I was scared from the noises and now I feared making Daddy mad. I needed Sunny. It was dark, and I couldn't feel the sun, so I wasn't sure he could come to me. He had never come in my house before and I didn't want Daddy to be mad that I was having company at night. I lay in bed a long-time hearing all the thunder and lightning outside with all the sounds that scared me. I couldn't sleep nor was I supposed to move. What was I going to do? I thought.

Finally, I couldn't stand it any longer. Softly I said, "Sunny, I need you."

In a flash, faster than lightning, He was there.

"Little One, I told you I would never leave you, remember? No matter where you are I'll come to you when you need me. We don't have to be outside or even in the sunlight." He told me.

55

"I'm scared, all these noises are keeping me awake, plus I'm not supposed to move," I told Him.

"I'll lie here with you until you go to sleep. Is that all right?" He asked me.

"Please, I'm tired and afraid," I told Him.

He told me, *"I will show you tomorrow what is making all of the sounds you are hearing so you won't be afraid the next time the wind blows or when it rains."*

He stretched out beside me on my little bed. I laid my head on His shoulder and He placed His other arm around me until I went to sleep.

The next morning, He was gone. I had rested after all.

The third day going to school I was sick again after the bus ride and I still couldn't see the blackboard when Mrs. Lane tried to show us how to write. Grandma met me at the bus stop and again I got sick after I got off the bus. So far, my school experiences were not fun. It took a while for my stomach to straighten up before I wanted to play, but after I felt better I couldn't wait to go outside and be with Sunny.

*****

God told Jesus, "I'm going to bless Jason so that the family will have two cars again. Rachel doesn't need to be sick from her bus rides every day. One less problem for her will help."

*****

"**I** should have expected they would step in to help their precious. I was making progress keeping the kid sick and giving the other kids a chance to make fun of her all the time. I'll have to think of other ways to tear her down and stay ahead of them." Evil thought.

*****

That day, Daddy came home all excited. During dinner, I heard he was going to get a car from work to use and Mama would be able to have the other car. That was a big deal to him. He said not everyone at work got a business car to use.

The next Monday, Mama told me I wasn't going to ride the bus to school anymore. She was taking me and picking me up from now on. She and Daddy had talked it over after he got his new car and decided they needed to help me. They could see I was getting motion sick from the bus rides, so they needed to drive me to school. I liked this idea a lot.

It wasn't long before Mrs. Lane, scheduled an appointment with Mama to discuss my lessons in school. Apparently, I wasn't seeing the blackboard very good, so she thought Mama needed to know how it was affecting my work.

Within the next week, I was wearing glasses.

It's time to cause more insecurity in Rachel's mind," Evil said to his friends. "I'm going to cause her to be made fun of and ridiculed because of her eyes. I'll cause her Daddy to make her feel unattractive. She'll overhear him say she wasn't pretty."

*****

I picked out glasses with sparkles that made me feel pretty, but the boys in my class made fun of me. My Daddy couldn't believe Mama approved them either. He said I looked stupid. My feelings were hurt so I took them off as much as I could, even at home. I didn't want to look stupid. I wanted to be pretty.

Sunny would come to me even at school when I needed Him. It was great that nobody knew He was with me. He told me during the day I could talk with Him in my mind and He would hear and answer me the same way. Even though I felt better when He was with me at school, I still wanted friends my age to play with.

In the second grade, I finally found a girlfriend. She was a girl that I knew in my Sunday school class. We were friends at church each Sunday. Kathy was her name. We sat next to each other in class and played together at recess. There was only one problem: she was athletic, and I had no athletic ability. I'd been kept away from sports by my parents, so I hadn't developed enough strength to play on the equipment outside. My muscles were weak compared to hers and she would get frustrated with me when I wouldn't play on the giant stride with her. I was afraid to try it. It looked hard and when they ran, it would lift them up high. I was also very afraid of heights.

As I watched, I thought of Sunny and I asked Him if He could help me play like other kids.

"There is nothing to be afraid of Little One. When you try, just remember that I'm there with you. I will give you the strength to do it and if you keep your thoughts on me being with you even going high will be fun." He said.

When they stopped, I got up and took one of the grips.

I said, "Let's go."

I wasn't talking to the kids on the ride with me, but they didn't know it. I was talking to Sunny in my mind. I ran and jumped with the other kids and the ride got faster and faster then, we started going up off the ground. I held on so hard that my hands burned but Sunny was right there with me, just like He promised. I focused my thoughts on telling Him that I was having fun while we played and thanked Him for staying. I was so happy I was playing like the other kids.

Kathy and I were best friends and she understood when some days I'd have to take it easy if my breathing got hard. But as time went on, I didn't need much medicine. I felt good most days and was getting stronger.

I was also getting good at some games. Every day after school I would practice hoops with my little brother so by the time I got to the fifth-grade I wanted to try out for junior basketball.

59

*****

The evil spirit of sickness and his companion fear were not happy. It seemed that every time they came at the girl, their plans failed. Now she was getting good at a sport and was liked at school. They needed other forces involved so they asked the spirit of infirmity to join them. They had developed a plan, so she wouldn't be allowed to excel in anything. Her mind and emotions were to become totally warped and confused so it would affect her actions and body. Their plan needed to start soon.

*****

One afternoon I stayed after school to practice with other girls who were going to try out for the junior basketball team. During tryouts, I was placed with a girl named Dana who was going to play offense to my defense during the practice. As Dana and I were doing the drills, I felt something in my knee pop. It hurt so bad I fell to the floor screaming in pain. When the coach came over to help me stand, I couldn't put any pressure on that leg. We noticed my knee would not support my weight. I could hardly stand much less walk.

I was taken to the emergency room again, where they x-rayed my leg. I didn't have any broken bones, but the knee had swollen to two times its normal size. Mama was told to take me home and keep ice packs on it until she could get me an appointment with an orthopedic doctor the next day.

All night my leg throbbed. I couldn't walk. I had to hop everywhere or use crutches. I hated crutches. I didn't know how to use them very well. The pressure under my arms was terrible and I kept tripping. It was easier to just hop around.

I had an appointment the next afternoon with Dr. Warner. He looked over the hospital's x-rays and agreed that nothing was broken. Looking at my leg, he told Mama he needed to remove fluid by inserting a needle in the joint. As if I wasn't even in the room with them, he told her that it would be very painful.

I freaked! I hated needles! All my life, it seemed, people tortured me with needles. But this needle was the daddy of all needles. It was about six inches long and the barrel on it was huge. When I saw that needle, I started screaming embarrassing Mama so much she put her hand over my mouth as she assisted the nurse. They had to hold me down while Dr. Warner shoved it in my knee. I wanted no part of this at all.

After three barrels, full of fluid had been pulled from my knee joint, I was a little bit calmer. My knee wasn't hurting as much so I started to relax. When we got in the car, Mama told me how much I had embarrassed her. Not once did she ask me if I felt better. She was too mad.

I was out of school for a week. Kathy and her mom were sweet enough to bring my homework each afternoon, so I could keep up. I could call Kathy if I needed help with homework and that was fun, being able to talk on the telephone to a friend.

My next visit to Dr. Warner was the following week. Because my actions last week had been uncalled for, Mama made me apologize to the nurse and doctor when they came in to check me. I did as Mama asked and told them both I was very sorry I hollered so loud.

The swelling was gone, but I still didn't have any stability in my knee. I had to wear a knee brace and stay on crutches to get around for two months. After my time on crutches, my knee felt steady, but I was not allowed to play sports anymore. I needed to be careful not to cause my joint to slip out again. My basketball plans were over, and I wasn't allowed to stay and watch the others practice after school. So, Kathy and I would talk a lot at night on the phone when she got home from practice. She made the team and would be a replacement if one was needed during a junior league game. It was fun hearing her talk about playing. I was just a little jealous that I couldn't play.

During one of the periodic evil meetings, Satan and his bunch had concerning Rachel, Loneliness and Gluttony expressed how they wanted a turn at making Rachel's life miserable.

Loneliness said, "I need a chance at her demise. I want to prevent her from being around her friends very much."

Gluttony pitched in also, "I'll increase her appetite and replace feeling lonely with a desire for unhealthy foods. Loneliness and I can work together."

✻✻✻✻✻

I was bored. After school, I was forbidden to play outside again. Mama and Daddy didn't want me to re-injure my knee. That was when I started eating a lot more after school. I stayed in my room listening to the radio while I did my homework and ate and ate. Cookies and milk were my passion. I had to have a dozen or so every day with a glass of milk to dunk them into. When I finished my homework, I'd get on the telephone and talk with Kathy. I had no physical activity except going to school, doing homework, and going to bed. So, I gained a lot of weight that year.

Grandma loved to cook so she kept JL and I supplied with goodies. She would also have a large dinner ready every night for the family. I would always brag on her cooking, so she cooked anything I asked for. The food was filling up my boredom.

Not only did Grandma cook, she sewed all my clothes. Sewing was what she knew best. After retiring, she didn't sew for people anymore, so she had time to make me pretty dresses. My weight gain was not an issue if my clothes came from Grandma. She would take in or let out as I needed things adjusted.

Kathy didn't care if I was fat. I was her best friend and she was mine. We shared all our plans with each other. At school, we studied together, at church we learned about Jesus. When we were twelve, we both gave our hearts over to our Lord.

One day I told her Heaven was where I wanted to go.

"Me too," she replied. "Both of us together, friends forever. We will get to be with Jesus and never die."

I didn't like thinking about dying or going to hell. We were taught if we didn't give our hearts to Jesus, we would not have our loved ones with us ever again. We would be taken to a place where we would be burned up.

Because of our decision to give our hearts to the Lord, we both had to talk to our pastor before we were to be baptized.

Brother Moore asked me, "Rachel, why do you want to be baptized?"

I told him, "I know Jesus is my way to heaven. I want to go there and have eternal life."

He asked me, "Rachel, do you love the Lord?"

"Yes," I told him.

The next Sunday night Kathy and I were baptized with several other people. It felt good knowing that I now had a place in heaven.

It had been a long time since I'd called Sunny. Kathy was my friend and being with her kept my attention occupied. I didn't feel like I was alone much anymore. It was when I felt lonely that I really needed Him. I was still too young to realize Sunny and Jesus were the same person. I wasn't being taught at church about having a personal relationship with Jesus. I learned about heaven and repentance; or the need to confess my sins only when I did something bad; or the need to forgive my trespassors. No one ever told me I could have Jesus as a friend.

Jesus was happy that Rachel had been baptized. At least she wanted eternal life with Him, even if she didn't know who He was yet. All she knew was she needed a master or a hero protecting and watching over her.

I'M FAT

One afternoon after school Mama overheard me talking on the phone to Kathy about boys and she asked me, "Rachel, do you like a certain boy at school?"

"No, Mama, I don't have a boyfriend, but Kathy does, and we were talking about him," I told her.

Little did I realize overhearing our conversation would cause Mama to worry about me. It wasn't long after we talked about Kathy having a boyfriend that Mama took me in her room and gave me a little book about the birds and bees.

She said, "Dr. Wright had several of these books in his office for parents to share with their kids when the time was right. I want you to read it so you'll understand about growing up."

I took my little book and looked through it, but Mama said she really wanted me to take time and read it. So, that night I read it after I did my homework and finally understood some things I had questions about concerning my body. I had recently started my monthly cycle and my breasts were growing and now I understood why I had some sensations and pains. I understood also that now I was fertile and could have a baby if I mated with a boy. Now I knew why Mama was concerned and what she meant about the time being right for me to know.

In junior high, I didn't have a boyfriend, but Kathy did, so we didn't spend as much time together. My afternoons and nights after school were lonely, too, because we didn't talk on the telephone as much. I told her one day at church that I missed our times together and she told me why we couldn't be together, "My time is limited on the phone and I want to be able to spend it talking with James, please don't be mad at me."

Of course, I understood if I had a boyfriend I'd want to talk with him every night before I went to bed. So, when we could, Kathy and I would share secrets about her love life. It made her happy to tell me that she was in love.

Mama never talked to me in detail about sex. She would tell me Christian girls must wait until marriage. Most of the girls were also taught in Sunday school that it was a sin to have sex before marriage and we needed to wait. It seemed all topics of conversations with grownups were based on boys or not having sex. I didn't know why it even mattered to them. I didn't have a boyfriend.

Evil said to the other companions, "I'm going to put it in Rachel's mind that she has to have a boyfriend to be somebody at school. It doesn't matter if she thinks he is cute or not, or if he is a good boy or not; just a boy so she can feel like she is not a misfit. Then I'm going to crush her spirit when she finds out that she is unappealing to the opposite sex. If any of you have any ideas on how to expound on this to make her miserable speak up."

I did think one boy was cute in my class, so I asked Kathy to find out if he thought I was cute also. I wish I hadn't bothered. What I found out was he thought I was fat and ugly.

That night I asked Mama, "Am I too fat?"

And she told me, "You're just pleasantly plump."

*****

Evil, using his old trick of letting Rachel hear her parent's conversations, could always get a reaction out of the girl. So, at night when she would go to bed he would enhance the sound waves, so Rachel could hear them talking about her.

*****

Sometimes I wish I couldn't hear through my bedroom walls. I overheard Mama and Daddy as they were talking about me again. I heard Daddy say, "She is fat. Every week she seems to be getting bigger and bigger and Mama isn't helping any by baking goodies all the time. If I was a boy her age, I'd be repulsed if she liked me. Why can't she be like JL, he doesn't eat everything Mama cooks like there is never going to be anything else. He's lean and fit for a kid his age. She is disgusting. I'm ashamed of her."

*****

"That trick was a good one," Evil said to the others. "Now she knows not only do boys think she is fat even her own father doesn't like the way she looks. They will keep her self-esteem so low no one will want to be around her. She'll be ugly inside and out." He laughed.

*****

My heart broke; my Daddy didn't even think I was pretty. "How could any boy like me if my Daddy didn't," I thought? That's when I remembered Sunny. Could I expect that He would still be my friend? It had been a year or so since I'd wanted to be with Him. Why would He even want to talk to me much less be with me, I sobbed.

I really needed a friend again; I needed to know that boys liked me and He was male. So, I closed my eyes while I lay in my bed and thought about Sunny. Just like always He was there.

Shyly I said, "Hi. I didn't know if you remembered me. I kind of snubbed you after I found a new friend, didn't I? I'm so sorry. I must have hurt Your feelings."

His answer was polite but firm. *"Yes, I do remember you and I was sad that I wasn't needed. But because I keep my promises, I never left you, I've always been near."*

"Wow! I said. "You've been with me all these years?"

"Yes," He replied. *"I've watched when you met Kathy, I saw when you got hurt and I was there when you began eating to calm down your boredom."*

69

"So, you know that I'm fat?" I asked Him.

"Little One, I love you no matter how you look. To me you are beautiful." He said.

That is when He told me what He had done for me.

He said, *"I made sure you had beautiful clothes, leather shoes to wear and from time to time I encouraged your parents to buy you nice jewelry. You are beautiful to me. I love you and want you to have the best I can offer."*

I didn't know what He was talking about; He had never bought me any clothes, so I asked Him to explain.

"Little One, you have a master seamstress to make your clothes. That is what your Grandma did when she worked before staying at home. Because your ankles and knees were weak, the doctor told your parents they needed to buy you good leather shoes to keep you supported. Good shoes. The best shoes were what I directed them to buy for you, so you wouldn't get hurt so easy. I even caused your Daddy to buy you a ring when he bought your mother one for Christmas. Few girls, your age have a diamond ring as large as yours to wear." He explained.

"You made all that happen for me? Why?" I asked.

"I love you." He said

That night, I allowed Him to lie on my bed with me like He did when I was little. I rested my head on His arm, so He could hold me with His other while He explained to me how precious I was to Him. It made me feel so special. I needed to hear that someone cared so much for me. Our reunion was wonderful and my mind soared. I got the best rest ever.

"No! No! No!" Evil shouted. He can't be allowed to restore her, He always interrupts my plans. I'm going to make things so hard on her from now on she'll never want to be around Him again. If He thinks all it takes to make her happy is a few sweet words, then I'm going to make sure they will be drowned out with insanity. I'm going to give her what she wants. She'll have a pretty face and a curvy body. But at the same time, I'm going to scar her with stretch marks from weight loss and give her dry skin so that she'll have bumpy arms and thighs. She'll be self-conscious about how her skin and hair looks and focused on hiding that while the boys will be looking at her body and wanting to mate with her. I'll get fear and shame involved so she'll be afraid to show off her new looks to anyone, confusing everything. We'll keep her from seeing and feeling how she really appears to the world."

When Jesus got alone with the Father, He told Him that His confession of love had been made to Rachel.

God said, "Now the war for her heart will intensify. Satan and his bunch will fight us now at every turn for her affections."

71

"I know. This is the time that I knew would come. I don't want this to happen to her but is it is necessary." Jesus replied.

"Remember to keep your jealousy under control Son as much as possible. She'll come around again." God told Him.

*****

It was the next week Mama had me in another doctor's office. This time it was to do something about my weight gain. I didn't know Daddy's remarks about me had also hurt her feelings. She blamed herself for allowing me to get out of control with my eating.

I can say one thing about my Mama, though; she didn't forbid me to eat any goodies until after I had my first doctor's appointment. I didn't even know about the doctor's appointment, so I wasn't stressed out about going at all. I was feeling beautiful inside because Sunny had made me feel so special.

Dr. Kelsey was nice. He told us, "I help a lot of girls lose weight and get strong. If you follow my eating plan you should lose weight fast and be able to keep the weight off afterward."

To start, he gave me a prescription to control my appetite and water pills to help me lose retained water. I was to eat meat, cheese, vegetables, and fruit as much as I wanted. But I couldn't eat pastries, cookies, pies, ice cream, bread, rice, or potatoes and nothing fried.

I was used to eating a lot so after my visit, I started focusing on the foods that I could eat all the time. I had to, to keep sane.

Even with the pills, I still wanted my cookies every afternoon. I compromised by eating something that I could have like hamburger patties. Grandma cooked them several times each week; they were now my favorite snack. I could have catsup, so I used it for something sweet. This diet was doable.

When I got lonely at night, I would call on Sunny and go to our secret place. Kathy was still too busy with her boyfriend in the evenings, so we still didn't talk much after school. Sunny never said anything about me dieting. He seemed to focus more on self-confidence. He would tell me that I needed to think of myself as a queen but not to act haughty or too good to be around others. Just to focus on the fact that I was very special.

Often when we were alone He would tell me with a very serious voice, *"Do not arouse or awaken love until it so desires."*

I really didn't understand what He meant by those words, so I didn't ask Him to explain. I assumed He was saying the same thing we were hearing in Sunday school about being good; which was the "no sex until marriage" speech.

I was keeping Grandma busy because I was losing weight fast. I never had clothes that looked too big to wear and now I was proud of my clothes since I knew that Sunny was the one responsible for me having them. He gave Grandma the desire to sew for me.

Evil had another plan; he'd asked Satan if he could cause the party spirit to approach the Parody's, especially Jason. He was feeling like an old man lately and needed to get out and party, so this would be the time to cause more problems in that household.

"Satan, Party here, wants to join in the fun and he said he's noticed Jason Parody has the itch. Can we lead them into drinking and partying, so they will want to leave their kids alone a lot?" Evil asked.

Satan responded, "You know that I don't have a problem with anything that causes divisions and indifference within a family. One of my main focuses is the destruction of the family."

It was the summer before I went into the ninth grade, that Daddy had a desire to join a club in town. He wanted a place where he and Mama could go out dancing. Plus, it also had a swimming pool where Mama would take me and JL swimming several times a week. It was at the club one evening that my parents met some new friends; the Rileys.

Mama and Mrs. Riley liked to sunbathe, so they became good friends and we'd meet with her and her kids at the pool a lot. The Rileys had three children, Fay, Linda, and Louis Jr. Fay was a year younger than I so we became fast friends. It seemed we were with the Riley family all the time. Daddy called them the beautiful ones because they all were lean and tan with blonde hair and blue eyes.

*****

Seeing that Jason really appreciated how beautiful the Rileys were, Evil had another tool to use in the destruction of Rachel's self-confidence. He would cause her to overhear how Jason thought the Riley girls were beautiful and appealing opposed to his own daughter's looks. He would use Jealousy again to make the girl self-destruct.

*****

That summer I lost weight fast because we were always at the pool. Fay and I loved to swim, and we'd often race. I was good at swimming; I think it is the only sport I truly love. Mrs. Riley didn't work so she would come and get me and JL, so her kids would have playmates at the pool while she lay out in the sun. I was having the best time playing so I didn't even think about eating. I was too busy.

Then I overheard Daddy make the comment to Mama one day that Fay and Linda were like two little goddesses, all bronze with blonde hair and blue eyes; every boy's dream. He even said that JL had a stupid look on his teenage face when he was around Fay. Those words made me feel sick. I never heard him say anything about me like that. What was wrong with me? Why wasn't I pretty? After that my summer was ruined I felt so ugly when I was around Fay and Linda that I didn't want to be seen in a bathing suit anymore.

BOYS

I was now in high school, a place for teenagers only. No little kids were even allowed on the campus.

That year Kathy and I didn't have many classes together, so I had to make other friends at school. We'd still be together on Sundays at church and could hang out with each other there, but we seemed to have drifted apart.

This year was going to be different, I was determined to be happy and proud of myself because I was skinny. I was finally in a small dress size and Mama and Grandma kept me in pretty things. When I got a new outfit, Mama would make sure I had shoes and jewelry to match. I really looked good and I did feel better about myself now that school had started, and I wasn't around Fay and Linda all the time. But even though I looked better, the boys in my school still thought of me as the fat girl that couldn't do anything. So, I still didn't have a boyfriend that went to Belmont High.

At night, I still would call on Sunny to assure me I was not some kind of freak. He would tell me I was beautiful. He'd say my hair reminded Him of long black wool;-thick and curly. He would say my eyes were lovely deep green pools that could reflect trust. I loved hearing those nice things, but I was at the age where I needed to hear those things from a boyfriend my own age, not from a man Sunny's age. He was an adult.

Didn't Sunny know that curly hair was not in fashion? Straight hair was the thing, so I had Mama iron mine often. My hair was bushy, and the other girls were always making comments about it and this too was a contention with me that kept me feeling unattractive. It was hard when I would put on makeup and dress up to feel anything like a queen. No matter how much Sunny told me I was one.

"It's working, Evil told the others, she is constantly focusing on minor issues and trying to change to make boys look at hair and clothes when all they'll see anyway is the body. She'll start acting goofy about her appearance even more by the time we get through."

That year, it seemed like various high school clubs were doing fundraisers every weekend. The fundraisers requested the most were dances. The dances were held every few weeks at the local Veteran's Clubhouse. And because they were highly chaperoned, Mama and Daddy let me go. I'd meet with other girlfriends and we'd stand around like wallflowers, waiting for some boy to ask us to dance. Some nights I danced once or twice others I'd never get asked I enjoyed the fellowship and fun anyway.

"It's time to call in Jealousy again and have him do a number on Rachel's and Fay's friendship. He can cause her to hate quicker

77

than any of us can and that will cause Rachel to burn before we can even get started." Evil shared with Fear and Shame.

✲✲✲✲✲

The next summer was much like the last, Mrs. Riley would come get me and JL and we'd hang out with Fay, Linda, and Louis. Fay was gorgeous; every boy at the pool went gaga over her. She didn't even notice how pretty she really was. Male attention didn't faze, Fay. When she and I were together I would have, boys, talk with me, but they weren't interested in me. They wanted to get to know her through me.

Because the two moms loved the sun so much, Daddy and Mr. Riley came up with the idea of us all going on vacation together. It was the first time our families went out of town anywhere, so we went to the beach for summer vacation. Daytona Beach, Florida was a great place to go.

Fay wanted to strut so she came up with a game for us. She said when we got there, "Let's pretend we are hot babes able to get any lifeguard we want." So, we tried by flirting with them as we walked up and down the beach. It was fun to have them notice. Our parents didn't want us to go off alone with the boys, but they would let us hang out with them if Linda, Louis, and JL could be with us. We had to endure it, and it was not fun.

JL would embarrass me so much; he knew just what buttons to push to make me mad or hurt my feelings. He would say things like, "She is a former fatty, and she weighed almost two hundred pounds last year." He thought it was funny when he made me feel stupid and ugly. But all it did was cause me to stay inside and hide from embarrassment.

When we got home from vacation that summer, Grandma let us know about her plans to move in with our Aunt Jane. She told Mama and Daddy, "Jane needs my help at her seafood shop in Mobile, so I'll be leaving soon." Aunt Jane planned to come get her in a few weeks.

I didn't know until much later that one of the reasons Grandma decided to move was because she was feeling bad about JL and I having to share a room as teenagers.

I loved my Grandma and was very sad when she left. I missed her very much. But I finally had privacy when I was given her room.

Before Grandma moved away, she made sure that I had a brand-new wardrobe for tenth grade. I never told her I would be made fun of because of them. By that time the trends were designer labeled clothes and with my new clothes Grandma made, I didn't fit in. Some of the more popular girls called me homemade girl.

Even at fifteen, I was glad I still had Sunny to talk with. I didn't call on Him much but when I needed Him, He was always there. I asked Him, "Why can't I ever fit in with the girls at school? There is always some issue that keeps me from being accepted by the popular girls."

He had a simple answer for me, "*Jealousy speaks Little One. They truly wish they had someone who cared enough to do for them. So, they are only lashing out at you for what they really want.*"

I laughed, and then I replied, "They are the popular ones, not me. Everyone looks up to them as if they are royalty. To them I'm just the dirt their lovely shoes walk on."

"*Not to me you're not,*" He said.

He tried to make me feel better. I asked Him, "What am I to do about my clothes? I don't want to be called the homemade girl anymore."

He told me not to worry things would always work out if I trusted Him. He reminded me, "*Do you remember when I said that I could make it possible for you to always have lovely clothes? I haven't broken my word, you must trust me.* "

"Yes, I remember," I told Him.

"*Wait and see.*" He assured me.

Mama knew that something was bothering me so she asked me one morning at the breakfast table, "Why are you so sad?" I told her about the girls making fun of my homemade clothes. She was very concerned and told me, "I'll be able to get you a few new things soon." Her compassion helped, and I went to school that day feeling a little better.

After Grandma left Mama still worked every day. She and Daddy had to hire a lady to come in and clean our house and be there when JL and I got home from school. After the family ate each evening, she and I would clean up the kitchen together and we would talk about things that interested me, like hairstyles, makeup, and clothes. I loved our time together each night because she really understood my feelings and it helped.

The next weekend, she and I went shopping together and she bought me so many new things. Things that came from the same stores the popular girls got their clothes and things from. I also had shoes to match with all my new outfits. By working Mama could have her own credit accounts and she told me, "Keep these purchases a secret from Daddy, okay. Let it be our secret only. Daddy would not understand me buying things for you after Grandma had made you new clothes before she left."

It was during the Christmas Holidays that same year, Kathy and I were invited by a friend at church to go the Shriners' Christmas dance. She and James had broken up, so she wanted to pal around again. We planned to go to the dance that was to be held at the Albany Lodge hoping to find some new guys to have fun with.

For the occasion, Mama bought me a new party dress and shoes, so I would feel special. I think that night was the first time I really felt I resembled a queen. The dress was green velvet with shoes to match and my whole family thought I looked beautiful, even Daddy.

At the dance that night, I met several new boys and two of the boys wanted my telephone number, so they could call me later. I was so happy I could hardly sleep that night when I got home. I was finally able to draw a boy's attention without someone else getting all their attention first. I couldn't wait to tell Sunny that feeling and looking like a queen made me act like one on the inside.

*****

Satan had a meeting, calling in all his servants. He told them, "I see the child, Rachel, is now old enough for delusion. I want you all to be on alert. She has been spending too much time in His presence and we can't have her falling in love with Him. He wants her to rely on every word He speaks, but we need to show her what it feels like to have physical attention. She will never want Him around after she knows physical desire."

That's when he called one of the molesting demons into the meeting.

"I want you to delude the child. Go to her at night like He does, but don't speak. She will know it is not Him if she hears another voice. Just show yourself as light and make her think her body is responding to touch. After desire is awakened in her, she'll never call on Him again." Satan said.

The molester said, "I'll do it for you but I'm liable to be destroyed when He sees me tempt her into it."

"You'll have to take that chance," Satan said.

Satan didn't care if that idiot messed up and got himself destroyed; he had many other molesters to call when he needed.

My favorite of the two boys called me the following Tuesday night. We talked about a half hour before Daddy made me get off the telephone. I went to my room so excited that before I went to bed, I played a few of the new hit love songs on my record player, fantasying about romance.

During sleep, a light appeared around me, so I just assumed Sunny was there in my dream. During the dream, I began to feel sensations like hands touching me and I saw the face of Sam the boy I'd talked with that night. As the dream progressed I was feeling his lips on my neck, but he wouldn't kiss my mouth. I wanted him to kiss me, but he wouldn't. The touching in my dream was wonderful and I kept thinking to myself even then, that I needed more of that pleasure.

Preservation had watched the whole scene and he was furious. He thought to himself, when this demon is finished he'll never touch another girl again. The molesting demon didn't stand a chance. The angel of Preservation was upon him the instant he left Rachel's side. His very look made the demon's body burst into flames.

All the other demon companions witnessed what happened to Molester. They knew then that a war was waging, and Evil must win. When they messed around with Rachel from now on, they had to be very careful.

*****

When I finally woke up, I was tingling all over. "What had happened to me?" I thought. Whatever it was felt terrific.

The whole day, I planned in my head to get alone with Sam. All I could think of was that I wanted him to kiss me. If the anticipation of his kisses were anything like they were in my dream, I couldn't wait.

The waiting that afternoon after school for him to call me was torture. When I finally got a call, it wasn't Sam. It was the other boy I didn't really like. His name was Donnie. Donnie was nice, but I was not attracted to him like I was to Sam. I talked with him a few minutes, so I wouldn't be rude, but I lied and told him, "My Daddy needs to use the telephone." My call from Sam didn't come that night.

Days went by and Sam didn't call me again. So, I agreed to go on a date with Donnie. We went to a movie and had a hamburger before he took me home. He tried to kiss me, but it was awkward and very unappealing. Instead of feeling all tingly, I felt disgusted. I told him, "Thanks for taking me to the movie and for my dinner." Afterward, I went inside not lingering at my front door.

That night I dreamed of Sam again, but it was not like the last dream. In that dream, I was chasing him begging him to come back to me.

At school the next Monday, I got with Kathy and begged her to call Sam for me. "I need to know if he still likes me," I stated. Her family knew his family well, so she knew how to get in touch with him. I was happy when she agreed; the suspense of not knowing kept me from focusing on my school work all day.

She called me after dinner with the news. Yes, she did ask Sam if he was still interested in me like I wanted. But what I heard from her lips were not the words I needed to hear.

She told me, "Rachel, Sam has another girlfriend, one that he really likes at his school in Wellington. All he wanted the night of the dance was a girl to have fun with. He didn't want a new girlfriend."

I told her, "Please forgive me but I don't feel like talking anymore. I'm so hurt and confused." So, after we hung up the telephone I went to my room to cry.

Donnie asked me out again the next weekend, but I couldn't stand the thought of going through the motions. So, I turned him down. All I did was stay home and think about the dream I had with Sam.

Mama knew something was going on with me, so she tried to help get my mind off my problems by teaching me how to drive her car. I was thrilled but Mama was petrified about it. She faced the situation and kept her promise and we went driving every day or so while I had my learner's license. This was fun and made me feel special.

INFATUATIONS

Some of my new girlfriends at school and I decided to go to the Valentine's Day Dance at the Veterans Clubhouse. We always had fun at the dances even if we didn't dance with the boys. The music was great, and we loved to just hang out. But that night, Julie my latest best friend, and I met two boys from Dukes, a town about twenty miles away. Tommy wanted to dance with her and his friend Steve wanted to dance with me. The four of us paired off and had great fun.

It wasn't until the next day, she and I learned that Tommy really wanted to date me, and Steve wanted to date her, and she and I were thinking the same thing about them. But before I could even go out with a guy they had to meet Daddy's standards. He was very strict about how the guys dressed when they wanted to take me out on a date. He had a rule that no boy could date his daughter wearing jeans.

He thought jeans were street clothes from the hood or gangster clothes and wouldn't allow me to go out with a guy if they came to our house dressed in them. He said it didn't show respect for me or him. They were to wear dress slacks, or they couldn't take me out anywhere. I was appalled when I had to tell Tommy how to dress for our date but was glad when he said it didn't matter because he could see Daddy's point of view.

In the darkness of the spiritual realm, evil made plans to confuse and torment every aspect of dating for Rachel. He would speak to the guys and acquire certain reactions from them by using their own natural desires as a weapon. Wasn't it man's need to mate; their pure animal instinct that drives them to be with women and a teenager was a prime target to use for this. Their base instincts will cause them to push for release too soon for an innocent to cope.

*****

Tommy and I really hit it off. He was cute, funny and he sure could kiss. Boy howdy, could he kiss!

Before each date ended, he would stop his car at the entrance of our driveway. Thank goodness, we had a very, very long driveway, away from prying eyes so we could make out before it was time for me to be at home. At first, it was sweet, and then the kisses became very passionate and demanding and I became confused and weary. I thought I wanted that kind of attention because I had fantasized about it, but all I could hear in my head was the bad girl speech.

Being so young, though, after a few dates, I thought I was in love with him. One night he asked me, "Do you want to be my girl and go steady?"

"Yes!" I told him excitedly.

He even let me wear his class ring. To me, that meant he really loved me. Wearing a guy's class ring meant you were someone special.

Months went by into spring, and we'd always park in my driveway after each date. Tommy's reactions to me when the passion would get a little intense was getting weird and he'd start trying to take advantage of me by moving his hands in places he shouldn't. Every time he tried, I would hear this voice say, "*Don't! Stop it.*" I'd make him stop, but I could tell he didn't like it much and he would say hurtful snide things like, "I thought you loved me? People who love each other touch each other and give them pleasure. You are being a cold fish."

Each date after would end in tension between us. I needed the attention that made me feel wanted. I needed his kisses, but in my mind, I was afraid of becoming one of those bad girls that the teachers in Sunday school would warn us we become if we had sex outside of marriage. So, I'd clam up and make Tommy mad. So, about four months into our relationship, Tommy broke up with me and I was devastated and cried for days.

"**We**'ve got her now, Evil laughed. She is desperate and hungry for love. We'll torture her into becoming pitiful and shameless, begging him to come back to her. She'd get so disgusting to him that she'll look stupid and unappealing."

*****

I'd make up excuses to call his house and talk with one of his sisters as if we were friends, so I could know what he was doing. I literally chased him. I think it was because I was bugging his sister so much that she finally told me the truth. I was pitiful and needy at this point.

She told me, "He got tired of you putting him off, didn't you understand that he needed to have sex with you, but you wouldn't let him. So, he moved on to another girl. He's had her before and knows she really likes sex; so, you need to get over it."

✳✳✳✳✳

Seeing what was happening Preservation knew he had his work cut out for him concerning Rachel's heart, especially after that last conversation. How was he going to keep her from losing hope in love? A new interest would help he thought to himself, "I'm going to cause one of the church boys to seek her attention, someone with a good upbringing that can show her respect; one of Father's children."

✳✳✳✳✳

That summer, I was busy. If I wasn't at Fay's house or swimming at the club swimming pool, I was at church with Kathy and some of my other friends. That was when I met Ed, a new boy at church who was very nice. He came to all our classes and to some of the functions we had during the week for teenagers.

90

Ed and I didn't really date we just paired off at the church functions. We'd hold hands and share food at the picnics but the passion my heart desired was not happening with him. When we kissed, it didn't give me any sparks or tingles. I considered him a good friend more than a boyfriend.

The next school year my brother and I were taken out of the public-school system. Several of my previous classmates were also. Kathy was one and because Ed was new to the area his parents started him in our new school as well. The school was very small but unbelievably, it had all twelve grades. Yes, it had first-grade kids in the same building with the twelfth graders.

There were kids from county areas all around who were bused into our new private school. There were new boys to meet, ones who would not remember me as being fat. I knew it was going to be fun starting fresh at this new school.

Ed and I were still close, even at the new school but I had to make sure that my new friends didn't think we were boyfriend and girlfriend. I wanted a chance to have more than one boy as a friend. Maybe even another steady one.

Friends were all the new boys became. Not one of them attracted me enough to make me want to date them. If I needed a boy to go to a function, I have good ole Ed. He was always willing to go with me places. We'd go then he'd bring me home giving me a sweet little kiss at my door; nothing special. My whole eleventh-grade year was lonely and boring in the romance department.

It was the next summer I would get to meet another new boy at church. This boy was the son of our youth music director, Daniel was his name. He didn't live with his parents and other siblings, though. He stayed with his grandparents in Morris where he grew up. When I enquired about him, his sister Anne told me that he was very good at football back at Morris County High and needed to stay in that school because he may be eligible for a college grant if he did well playing that coming year. His parents didn't want to risk the chance of his failing to get a free ride to a college with all expenses paid.

Daniel and I liked each other instantly but because he didn't live in Belmont with his parents it made it hard for us to see each other. He only came to see them about one weekend each month. So, in all, we got to see each other about three times that summer. We kept in touch through his sister, Anne.

"It's time we took her away from these church boys, all they seem to do is get in the way of our plans. Let's introduce her to someone who works with our plan. One who has a one-track mine for a boy his age and will try all the moves possible to get her to succumb to sexual desire." Evil said to the other demons.

"She's never been around any people who used drugs; let's tempt her with that as well. I see she tends to like the bad boys. So, bad we'll give her."

Also, that same summer Fay had a steady boyfriend she'd been dating for over a year, his name was Peter. Peter asked me one day, "Would you be interested in going on a date with one of my friends? Fay and I would like it if you would join us. We are planning to go to the Belmont Junior College dance and Charlie needs a date."

"I love dances, so yes, I'll go," I told him.

Charlie was gorgeous and being around him made me feel a little intimated, but he quickly made me relax by being funny. Plus, I had a security blanket by being with my other friends.

The way he smelled was so good and the way he held me during the dances was mesmerizing. I was getting those funny feelings again. We kissed several times that night and before they took me home he asks if he could see me again. Finally, I thought, I've met someone that brings excitement back into my life.

Charlie and I dated a lot that summer, especially with Peter and Fay. To my surprise, Daddy and Mama said I could invite Charlie to go on vacation with us to the beach that year. They told me that Fay's parents were letting Peter go so it would be nice if Charlie went so I wouldn't feel like a third wheel when hanging out with Fay and Peter.

When I got up the nerve to ask him, I phoned him and said. "Would you like to go with us to Daytona? Peter is going with Fay and I'd like to have you come with me."

He said, "I'm not sure my parents will let me. I'll ask them, and I call you back."

When he called me back, he said, "They made it very plain that I would have to work and save up for my part of the hotel room. They were not able to give me any money for a trip. How much do you think all this is going to cost me?"

I replied, "Daddy said to tell you that a room for you and Peter would be thirty-five dollars a night. Add up the amount then divide it by two. Your meals will be taken care of, but if you want anything else it's on you."

✻✻✻✻✻

"Now is our chance!" Evil screamed to his friends. "We have the opportunity to really do her some damage. We'll use the boy's own lust and his words of seduction to make her do things against her moral standards. At the beach, she'll be practically naked in her swimsuit so any grabbing he'll want to do then will only make things easier for him to manipulate her responses. She'll be pregnant before we know it and her Daddy will want to kill her. She'll ruin his precious reputation in town and it will make him so mad and disgraced, he will kick her out of their house."

✻✻✻✻✻

God overheard their wicked conversation and warned Preservation to be on guard. "She has had proper training on being chaste and knows what to do. But I'm giving you permission to make it a little easier for her to say no when the time comes. She is still a little shy and insecure about her body, so we will use those emotions in her favor. It is not the time for babies yet."

*****

I couldn't believe it; I was going to one of my favorite places in the world and with my boyfriend. I was in heaven, or so I thought.

*****

Preservation also had a plan, he'd cause her monthly cycle to show up late and cause her to be more self-conscience.

*****

When the day finally arrived to go, I was mortified when I woke up on my monthly cycle. I should have started the week before; it was just day 33. I could handle the mess ups around Fay, but if I had one around Charlie I'd be devastated. I'd just have to make the most of it and try not to worry, acting normal as much as I possibly could.

At the beach, our parents didn't pay a lot of attention to what we were doing. They only wanted us to check in with them from time to time. That first day we walked the beach and played in the surf, hugged, and kissed a lot while we played around.

Then I noticed Peter and Fay wanted to spend a lot of time in his room and it was during one of those times I found out they were sexually active. To my surprise, Charlie thought we were going to be doing the same. I felt like I had two heads; one constantly wanted to go all the way and the other was disgusted with the idea. I kept hearing "S*top!!!*" a lot in my head. The hollering won out each time. I don't know if it was a shock or my moral compass kicking in.

✵✵✵✵✵

Evil stomped around screaming. "No! No! No! What is it going to take to cause this kid to buckle, I know she must be in torment, having his hands roam all on her nakedness. I made sure she wanted to make an impression with a skimpy bikini, so what is the problem?"

Manipulation spoke up then and said," I'll cause Charlie to turn the circumstances around, he'll cause her to want to keep his attention, by giving him pleasure even if she doesn't want any. He'll make her fear losing him if she doesn't comply."

✵✵✵✵✵

One day, Charlie and Peter walked away from Fay and me for a while and when they came back they were stoned. Fay said, "Peter likes to have a little toke from time to time to loosen up so he and Charlie have gone off, so our parents wouldn't catch them."

"Are they crazy, if Daddy finds out there is going to be murder at the beach. He'll have all of our heads." I said freaking out.

I was surprised to learn when Charlie got stoned, he was rough or a little mean. It was also at those times he'd get to groping me too much and I'd have to make him mad with my rejections.

"Come on baby, it really feels good, what are you afraid of?" He'd say.

I thought that when I said I was on my monthly cycle he wouldn't try anymore but he got even more excited. He said, "Even better, you won't get pregnant if we do it now."

I was disgusted at the thought of having sex that way.

*****

"What are we going to do now?" Evil said. Fear spoke up and said, "I'll terrify her a little and make her do something stupid."

*****

On Thursday, two days before we had to go home, the four of us planned to go that night to the boardwalk to play games at the arcade. Of course, the two boys were high, but our parents couldn't tell. Mr. Riley agreed to let Peter drive his car, so we wouldn't have to walk so far at night. In the back seat, Charlie started grabbing me again in inappropriate places and trying to make me feel his privates.

He'd say, "If you don't want sex at least pleasure me, I need to have it and I'm tired of being teased by you all the time. I can't keep taking this rejection from you, Rachel. It's a win, win, you get to stay safe, and I'm relieved."

Immediately I refused, I was so shocked at his actions and insults. I felt like I was being verbally violated as well as physically at the same time. It really made me mad and a little frightened. When I pushed him off, I told him "Stop trying to make me feel you up. I'm not interested in doing anything with you out in the open where people can see."

He was livid and that's when he opened the car door and shoved me out in the street, calling me all kinds of names.

I heard Fay screaming at Peter, "Go back now and get her, her Daddy is going to kill you if he finds out! Look at where we are, don't you know that this is not a good place for her to be."

I didn't know what to do except walk back to our hotel. My mind was racing, and I didn't know if it would be safer to make it to the beach and walk the two miles back in the dark or to stay on the street. It was getting dark and I'd be alone either way I chose to go. So, I decided to stay in the light of the street lamps. I hoped Fay could convince Peter to come back for me.

I'd walked about two blocks when I saw the car coming up the street, Peter had gone around trying to find me. When Fay rolled her window down she could see that I had been crying so she said, "Get up front with us, you don't have to sit back there with that jackass. We'll take you back and you can tell your Mama you don't feel well, okay."

I knew she was afraid I was going to rat them out about the pot and tell them what Charlie had done. I wasn't mad at her and Peter, I was afraid of Charlie. From that point on, I didn't want him anywhere near me. As I was getting out of the car, Charlie said, "I'm sorry Rachel, I don't know what got over me. I need to think this out."

"Sober up Charlie, you're a different person when you are high. I'm not going to discuss anything until you're straight." I told him.

Mama noticed when I came in the hotel room alone, "Why are you back without the others? She asked.

"I got sick to my stomach," I told her "I just need to lie down and rest."

It wasn't but a few hours before Fay came in that night and she asked if I was all right.

"Sure," I told her. "I can't believe how all this has gone down. I thought we were going to have a great time with the guys at the beach. I really thought Charlie liked me."

"He does, that's the problem, don't you get it?" She told me. "He is attracted to you so much it hurts and that is why he can't control his actions when the two of you kiss so much. You're giving him mixed signals and he can't handle the stress well, especially when he is high."

"I don't want to hurt him, but I can't have sex. Not while I'm on my period. Charlie was attractive to me until this happened tonight, and I really think I might have had sex with him eventually. I just can't do it now, you know, bleeding. Maybe it was a good thing that I was. And I certainly wasn't going to give him a special thrill in front of you guys, that's disgusting." I told her.

"Fay, I don't think I want to be near him now. You didn't see his eyes when he pushed me out of the car. He doesn't care about my feelings at all nor does he understand my issue. All he cares about is himself, and I don't want to live in fear of getting hurt by my boyfriend when he doesn't get his way. Yes, my feelings were hurt, but he looked like he wanted to strike me also." I expressed.

The next two days, were miserable. Charlie and I hardly talked except around my parents. So, I kept our conversations casual. I didn't want all hell to break loose if Daddy suspected any hanky-panky had been going on.

I wasn't surprised after we got home that Charlie never called me again. I think I was glad. You would think I'd learn by now that sex was all boys thought about. They had no concept of romancing a girl. Just get in her pants.

Even the rest of the year, when Daniel could come to see his parents I'd keep things light between us. When we'd get together I was afraid that he'd be like the others and I'd get my feelings hurt all over again. I wanted to keep him special in my thoughts, I liked having a good-looking football jock liking me and

I didn't want to think about him becoming a jerk like the others. So, for the time being, we just stayed friends.

My twelfth-grade year was supposed to be one of the most special of my life, so everyone told me. Being love shy now, I wouldn't go out with anyone except Ed. He was my buddy, but even he needed a girlfriend who really liked him romantically. When he started dating Cindy our outings stopped and I got lonely on the weekends after that.

The kids at our school lived so far apart it made it very hard to date each other and it was not so much fun to just be together at school. We all needed other outlets.

I was still friends with Fay and Peter. It wasn't their fault Charlie and I didn't stay together. So, I became the third wheel a lot because my parents and hers always wanted to hang out with each other. Because I was with them so much I got to know kids from her school as well as Peter's. There was only one problem: their friends were a little on the wild side. But I didn't care, I just didn't want Daddy to find out. I needed places to go and people to see.

I made a couple of good friends from Belmont High and we'd hang out together on the weekends and ride up and down Silver Drive, '*The strip*' we called it. We'd ride up and down the strip, until we saw others parked in store parking lots talking so we'd stop and talk also; just a bunch of kids hanging out and talking not really pairing off at all.

101

I don't think I had a real date that whole year until I invited one of my cousin's friends to the prom. Gary, my cousin told me his friend, Frank, thought I was cute. He invited us over and we started hanging out at his house, so we could get to know each other. Frank was cool so when I needed a date to my prom I asked him if he was interested. I was shocked when he said okay.

Frank was a college guy that went to school at a college in Atlanta. He was a Georgia Tech guy and I just knew my Daddy was going to freak out because he was a few years older. He didn't when my Aunt Gloria told him Frank was a good boy and came from good people, so he was okay with us dating some.

When he showed up to take me to my prom, he was in a BMW that was so small I couldn't get in because of the type of dress I was wearing. Daddy thought it was funny and felt sorry for us so he let Frank drive our family car. We had fun at the dance and I enjoyed the special senior breakfast that was prepared for us by our parents afterward.

After our prom date, Frank and I dated a few times, but we didn't have much of a relationship, it just didn't make much sense when he went to school so far away and didn't come home often. So, we drifted apart. I will always think fondly of him because he took me to my senior prom. That night he was my prince charming. He bought me flowers and was dressed in a tuxedo, looking very handsome.

After graduation, I had two things on my mind, seeing Daniel more and getting to go to college!

My desire was to major in art. Eventually, I would use my talent to create illustrations or cartoon designs like the ones used at Disney. That was my dream, but Daddy had other ideas. He said, "I'm not spending my hard-earned money for you to draw and color. Ladies need to focus on learning a trade, so they can go anywhere to work."

We compromised. I took classes in Secretarial Science and he agreed I could take the courses I really wanted to study. I had been accepted at Belmont Junior College for the fall term, but I would have to wait almost three months before I could start.

*****

"What is our plan for Rachel now?" Evil asked the other demons. Abuse spoke up and said, "I know something about this Daniel that no one else does. He is fed up with being told what to do with his life. He hates the thought of playing ball just to get away from home. He wants to be his own man and do his own thing. So, let's use him. Give him the idea of using Rachel as an outlet. Then after he gets his way, we'll screw up things really good for both."

*****

Daniel was now home living with his parents. He had graduated and had received a full college scholarship at Mississippi State University playing football while he studied for a degree in Physical Education.

103

I had a football jock interested in me! All the girls at church were gaga over him and he wanted to be with me.

He was the greatest. He treated me like a princess and never tried to force me into a sexually charged position like Tommy or Charlie had. But by that time my hormones were raging, and I felt like I was ready. It seemed like every girlfriend I was hanging out with was having sex or already had sex. Their talking about their experiences made me curious.

My problem was I was just too shy to make any moves, and Daniel wasn't making any towards me. *What was the problem?* I thought. When he took me home after each date he left me a little frustrated. I was beginning to think something was wrong with me. He never tried anything.

So, on one of our dates, before he took me home, I was stunned when he asked unexpectedly. "Will you marry me?"

"What? Are you kidding?" I said. "What brought this on? I was beginning to think I wasn't attractive enough for you. You've never said you loved me or tried to seduce me, nothing."

"You are the prettiest girl I know," he said. "I'm very attracted to you; I always take you to your door fast so that I'm not tempted into molesting you. I fell in love with you last year but didn't know how to tell you."

After he said that, I was so flattered I said, "Yes, I will marry you." Then I asked a simple question because I was still confused. "When? Shouldn't we wait until after college?"

"I don't know, and right now I can't think about it. I know I'm happier than I've ever been and want to stay here with you." He replied.

We were caught up in the moment and very confused about what to do about our educations. We didn't tell our parents because we both knew they would be upset. They would only say we were too young and were throwing away our futures. So, we went on with our lives, happy and sad at the same time.

We'd stay up all hours of the night talking about being together. The Vietnam War was going strong and many men Daniel's age were being drafted. Even though he had a good job at the local tire plant that summer, he was afraid if he didn't get in school soon he would wind up on a battlefield overseas. That wasn't part of his plan. He didn't want to go to war and he didn't really want to go to school either.

"I'm going to apply at Struder Junior College and see what happens." He told me. "They have a P. E. Program there and I won't be so far from home," Daniel said.

"Your parents are going to freak when you tell them you're turning down your scholarship and they are going to blame me for ruining your future," I replied.

His comeback to me was, "I don't have to go. I just want another option if we decide to marry pretty soon."

Belmont Junior College didn't offer any Physical Education classes, so he didn't consider even going there with me.

I knew not to even ask Daddy if I could go to Struder Junior College. He wouldn't agree to me going away to school. He didn't really like the idea of me going to a college anyway. He wanted me to go to a trade school. Daddy was being very difficult about me going to school period. I couldn't figure out what his problem was.

When it came close to the time for school to start, Daniel told his parents, "I'm not going to Mississippi State University. I've been accepted at Struder Junior College. I have a part-time job lined up and will work myself through school." He lied and said, "I really don't want to live far from home and be away from you guys or Rachel."

His parents tried to understand, but they were worried he had ruined his future. They were afraid he would get tired of working as well as studying and probably drop out before he could finish. Little did they know; their fears were justified.

When school started, he had a part-time job at a hardware store chain working at night while he went to classes during the day. Because he was working to pay for his education, we never got to see each other. He had to work weekends to make the money needed to pay all his bills.

Before school started, Mama convinced Daddy to get me a car as my graduation present, so I'd have a way to go to school. I was allowed one tank of gas in it every week to go to school. Arrangements were made with a local gas station owner for me to sign a ticket each week for my tank of gas and he would pay the bill every month.

After school started, I missed Daniel so much I'd sneak to Struder to see him every day or so when I was supposed to be in school. Then I would be home that evening before dinner. I couldn't concentrate very well wondering what he was doing and who he may be seeing. My grades were not great the first quarter.

My accomplishments made Daddy very unhappy; not to mention that he wasn't pleased with my gas usage. These issues made our relationship very strained.

I came home from one of my visits to Struder to find Daddy waiting for me in the living room. He said to me, "Rachel I know you've been driving more than you're supposed to so why are lying to me? I wrote down your mileage the other day and compared it with last nights. You have driven too many miles just to be going to school. Where are, you going?"

I told him the truth, "I'm going to see Daniel. Daddy, I can't stand being so far away from him." Daddy exploded. He was so angry with me he grounded me for a month. I was to go to school and be back home by 3 o'clock p.m. every school day. It made me feel like a little kid all over again instead of a grown woman.

I wasn't allowed to call Daniel either. It was long distance and Daddy wouldn't hear of us talking up a large phone bill. If I didn't know better, I'd think there was a conspiracy against us being together.

The stress of this school arrangement finally got to both of us and Daniel and I started to fight. I'd get jealous, or he'd get jealous and we made each other miserable.

That Christmas he called our relationship off. It was at a church party Daniel told me, "I'm finally doing what I want. I'm out from under my family's thumb and I can be my own man."

"What about me? Did I ever truly fit in that plan?" I asked.

"Yes, at first, I was really into the marriage deal," he said. "The more I'm on my own, though, I don't think so anymore. I don't want to hurt you Rachel, but I think I need time to be by myself for a while."

After he told me that, I felt I'd fallen into a deep well. My eyes couldn't focus, my head started spinning, my hearing got fuzzy and I had to lay down quick before I fell. He just walked away leaving me alone as if I didn't matter in the least.

My life fell to an all-time low after that. *"Wasn't that a great Christmas present."* I thought. For weeks after the breakup, it seemed I had turned into a complete introvert. I didn't hang out with hardly any of my friends. Just going to class was a struggle.

*****

Preservation knew if he didn't do something Evil would win this round and he would have a hard time when love did show up for Rachel. So, he opened her eyes to a Bible written for young adults that she could read and find out about the truth. He would get her interested in reading it to escape from her problems.

✳✳✳✳✳

I found I could relax and quit thinking so much when I read. I had one outlet, a Bible that was given to me for a graduation present. It was designed for young adults and written in a language that I understood. I would read it every chance I got and learned so much.

Jesus was special to me and I prayed to Him often asking for His help to get me through my depression. He became my superman, someone that would take my devil on and could make my life happy again. I didn't want a friend, I wanted a warrior. I had been hurt so much I didn't want friends at that time. I wanted an avenger.

I'd get off into a pity party and think, why am I so unlovable, or just an object to get used? I was sick and tired of the whole issue of romance, why bother. Even when Daniel visited his family and came to church with them it was hard on me. He tried to be friends, but that is not what I needed from him. His rejection hurt me more than anything the other guys ever did to me.

✳✳✳✳✳

"She is playing right into our plan," Evil told the others. "She may even become a man-hater by the time we are through. Wouldn't it be fun seeing her become a tease to them for her enjoyment? Hard-hearted towards love and bitter towards anything men say to her. Let's work that in with the other problems we have set for her to increase her pain the better."

In a conversation, Jesus had with His Father, He said "Rachel is learning why I came and the truth about love, but she still hasn't received my peace. She doesn't call on me as her friend Sunny, any longer. She is only focused on justice."

"Only you can defeat her tormentor and do it in a way where she will be able to receive the peace she must have. Guide her mind to the words she needs through her new Bible. She still must go through so much. Prepare her for the journey; just know she will call on Sunny again when she truly needs you." God told him.

*****

I took communion often asking for forgiveness, but I really didn't know what I needed forgiving from. I prayed whatever I did that caused my torment would go away and leave me normal again. I had never felt so unloved or unwanted in my life. I was constantly dwelling on my past and even getting angry and hurt about how my Daddy had treated me over the years.

I became jealous over the loving and favorable treatment I saw my brother receiving from him and I worried I had developed a rebellious heart. I needed love so much, but I didn't know how to get it. I knew Mama loved me, but I couldn't express to her what was wrong either. As I read my new Bible, somehow it relieved some of the longings.

I was asked out on dates by several guys from my college classes, but the same old theme rang from their lips, "If you really like me, please don't send me off to war without having you. Let me know you care." Or they would say, "What's your problem? Are you a Jesus freak or something? Are you too good for sex with a real man?" All they wanted was to tag and bag me in their sexual conquests like some trophy.

THE BEAST UNLEASHED

Lust and Perversion wanted a chance, "Our turn, let us ruin her. Can't you see she feels like a freak of nature? Let us turn her own desires against her." They quibbled. "We'll use the oldest trick in the world. The lust of the eyes. Seeing something just out of reach. The facts about the actions she really wants to experience. Our plan for her eyes to see and want."

*****

"*Wait a minute!*" Preservation said to himself after overhearing two evil demons. "If she is going to lose control I have to make sure it is where she can't get hurt. Some things are inevitable but controllable. I'll lure a good boy to come around and desire her."

*****

It seemed most of the nicer guys I met were churchgoers, either from my church or some others our choir group visited on our revival outings. It was around mid-April of the next year after Daniel broke things off, my eyes were directed to a very tall boy during service. He was kind of cute, but he didn't quite seem to fit in with the crowd yet.

Something inside of me just knew we'd wind up together. I don't know why because he wasn't physically attractive to me. I guess I was still leery about getting involved with any guy; I just wanted to go with the flow. His name was Drake Newton, and his family had moved from a city up north to Wellington a few months prior. Mr. Newton had taken the job of manager of the dairy farm that was adjoined to Daddy's farm.

Daddy had gotten to know Mr. and Mrs. Newton before I even knew they had two sons. Drake started coming to young adult meetings at church and that is how we were introduced. He was very sweet and polite to me but at that time nothing special. I wasn't against having him as a friend, though. I remembered how it was having a boy as a friend. Ed was great, and I enjoyed hanging out. I really needed that kind of friendship again.

Drake was going to college at Struder to get his degree in Animal Husbandry, so I didn't see him during the week. But we would pair off together on the weekends when we needed partners for various events at church and it got to be a very natural thing hanging out with him. We could talk about anything, so I didn't feel like being on guard all the time. I was finally able to let my defenses down and relax some.

When summer arrived, and we were both out of school, we started doing things together away from the church crowd. We had a lot in common: we loved animals, we loved fishing, playing music, and going to movies and we loved to eat. His mother was a great cook and I loved it when they invited me over.

Even though our relationship had developed a little more romantically, his friendship was more special, and I needed a good friend.

I was constantly being bombarded with talks from my girlfriends about their sexual adventures and of course my interest in it was being peaked all the time. "How would my first time be?" I'd think. I was scared, and I knew it, but I wasn't scared of Drake.

One evening Mama and Daddy had gone off somewhere with the Rileys and I was left alone to wait on Drake to come get me. As was my habit, I would go to my parent's bedroom to set on their bed and watch for my date's arrival out of their bedroom window. That was when I noticed a magazine under their bed on Daddy's side. I picked it up to see what it was to bide the time while I waited. It was a magazine of hardcore porn; boy, was it explicit! The images I saw in it were making my body feel all kinds of sexual urge. My hormones were raging by the time Drake parked his car.

He didn't stand a chance. When I got in the car I told him what I had just seen. That's when I made the remark, "If I don't get laid soon, I'm going to explode just out of frustration."

Of course, he obliged. He asked, "When and where?"

It was the first time for both of us. My first time was with my friend and now he was my lover. We hadn't even said we loved each other yet. We were caught up in hormone mania. Thank God, he was prepared. He told me, "Dad always makes Eric and I carry protection. He's a firm believer that it's the man's responsibility to be safe. He told us, you'll never know when it will come in handy."

After that first time, we didn't care if we were going to a movie, going fishing, whatever, it was time again for hormone mania afterward. We'd have sex if we had to hang upside down like bats, we didn't care.

It was on a weekend visit to his grandparents Drake made the comment to me while we were going back home, "I'm tired of going to school. Mom and dad are thinking about moving back north because dad's job is not panning out for him in Wellington. You want to get married so I don't have to go with them?"

Being in love with the lust, I answered him, "Let's do it. I'm so ready to be on my own and I can't think of anyone in the world I'd rather be with."

So, from that day on, we were engaged. He bought me a pretty, little diamond ring, and I thought I was something showing it off. I was getting married!

That same year Daddy finally built Mama her dream house. It was up the driveway from our old place. JL and I got to pick out the furniture for our rooms and Mama is in heaven choosing her new stuff.

Daddy had the bright idea of offering Drake our old place to live in since his parents were planning to move to north Georgia. Drake had gotten a job at the local tire plant making good money and was saving for us to have a nice honeymoon. Mama and Daddy both really liked Drake and wanted us to live close to them when we did marry.

I hated the idea because I wouldn't be leaving anything. I told Drake, "I'm still going to be stuck in the same place I've lived most of my life. The only good thing about this is that I'll be married and able to do what I want with you."

"It won't be so bad," he said. "Someday, I'll build your dream house and it doesn't have to be right under your parent's noses."

Drake wasn't through with school, but he didn't want to continue. I had more to go. He was so sweet about it and told me, "I don't mind you finishing your education. Only six more months and you'll have your Secretarial Certificate. We can make do on my salary until you finish getting that."

He liked the idea of supporting me. It made him feel important. I agreed to finish so I'd have my certificate, but I really wanted to go longer and get my major in art. I don't know why I didn't say anything about it.

Our wedding was planned for that fall. Every time you turned around Mama and Daddy were arguing about how much it was costing. He constantly complained to her saying, "I refuse to buy Rachel an expensive dress to wear one time. I will not buy a lot of party goodies for people to say 'oh, look at her nice party'. And don't even suggest wearing a tuxedo."

Mama did the best she could. She told me every chance she got, "Don't worry honey; I'm saving part of my paychecks each week, so you can have a nice reception and a pretty wedding." I tried to compromise by reserving a dress we could rent from a local bridal shop and I didn't complain about what she was buying. She was doing the best she could. I didn't really care what was to be served at the reception if I at least got a wedding cake.

*****

The evil spirit Neglect was working on a plan; he and Confusion would work on Drake. "Let's cause his working conditions to make him tired all the time. We'll cause problems by combining it with his lack of interest in Rachel's desires." They agreed.

"We can cause him to focus on what he wants to do instead of trying to keep the flame in their relationship. We can make it impossible to charm her at all. Then when he has time to do something, all he'll want to do is focus on his own needs instead of hers. He is young enough to use his sex drive in our favor. He'll want her close for his release. Then we will make him crave his own wants over hers after he is finished with her." They thought this plan was hilarious.

*****

Ever vigilant, Preservation didn't know what to do. He asked the Father, "Sir, please show me how I can help her. This isn't part of the plan, is it?

"Everything is part of the plan," God told him. "She is going to have to be dependent on us eventually; even if things don't look good for her now."

Drake was working the night shift, 11 p.m. to 7 a.m. so he slept during the day while I was at school. This worked out well because he would join the family every evening for dinner and we'd get to spend some time with each other before he went to work.

We never dated anymore. We just watched TV with the family in the evening. When we needed to be alone we'd sneak off for intimacy. I started feeling a little neglected because he never wanted to go anywhere or do anything. I think it was during this time I started doubting myself in marriage, but I kept my feelings to myself.

On, October 20th we got married. It was a lovely ceremony. Everything was beautiful, and Daddy even wore a tuxedo. Drake's dad was his best man and his brother and JL were our ushers. I had three bridesmaids: my best friend, Leah: Daniel's little sister Joan; and Drake's cousin, Shelia.

After the reception, Drake and I went on our honeymoon. I didn't even know where we were going. He kept the designation a secret until the last minute. As we were driving off he told me, "I've got us reservations at the beach."

"What beach?" I asked. I was really hoping it was not Daytona. I wanted it to be somewhere I'd never been before.

He said, "Panama City Beach. It is one of my favorite places and I think you'll like it. The sand is so pretty, and we can walk the beach for miles if we want."

"Great, I've never been there," I said excitedly. "What's on your agenda when we get there?" I asked.

"Well, I want to take you to this fancy restaurant that is very romantic and then we can buy some wine and take it back to our room." He answered.

"Wine? I've never had but a few tastes of wine in my life. Are you planning to get me drunk so you can have your way with me?" I asked.

"That's the plan," he said playfully in a deep seductive voice.

I wasn't even nineteen yet, barely old enough to drink, and I'd never been drunk before. This was going to get interesting. We had a great meal and then went back to our room to party. We had a great time, and yes, we got very drunk and then very sick. Both of us did. We felt so bad the next day.

We were finally adults and could do what we wanted without answering to anyone. I think that was the thing I liked most about being married. I didn't know how bad I had wanted out from under my house rules until that night. Was that the real reason I wanted to get married? Or did I really love Drake? I asked myself.

*****

Satan himself was having fun watching his demons mess around with this union. But he had plans to make the whole thing explode with time. That's when he called in his champion. "Anger, here is your chance," He said, "Bait Rachel into hating Drake. Cause her to feel sorry for herself so she can let loose your tricks through her own mouth."

✳✳✳✳✳

We stayed at the beach for two nights and then Drake had another surprise for me. "Guess what we are going to do today?" He asked.

"I don't know. You've taken me off to this lonely place so I'm at your mercy," I said jokingly.

"I know how you love fishing." He said.

Excited I asked, "When, today?"

"Sure! We have to check out of the hotel and drive about an hour before we meet up with Grandpa and Grandma Todd." He told me.

I think every bit of air was let out of my balloon. My honeymoon was going to be spent fishing with his grandparents. Great! I was so disappointed I couldn't speak. I think he took my silence to be excitement so he kept on telling me how much I was going to love fishing in the flats for redfish. They had always had so much fun doing it as kids and he was sure that I'd love it.

Never once in the weeks of wedding planning did he ever ask me what I wanted to do on our honeymoon. I thought he knew me better and was planning something very romantic and special for us to be alone. He kept telling me he was saving all this money for something special.

I didn't know until later he was saving to rent fishing equipment with a boat and guide to take the four of us out fishing. We even stayed in the same two-bedroom condo with them. I was furious. If I could, I think I would have had my marriage annulled that day.

I was cordial to his grandparents and I went along for the fishing. I had fun, but it wasn't what I had envisioned as my honeymoon event.

After we got home, we went straight to the house that I grew up in. When we walked in the door, there was the same old furniture I had in the house growing up. The same bed Mama and Daddy slept on, the same dining room set; nothing was different. I was stuck in a rut or time warp with a man that had as much romance in him as a fly.

I should have been proud to have a place to stay with everything in it I needed, but I wasn't. I felt life had dealt me a severe blow. I was so angry with Drake and this whole mess.

That night in the shower I prayed to the good Lord. "Father, please help me change my attitude about the house. Also, Drake is a good person. Please show me how to let him know that he made me angry on our honeymoon. Teach me the right way to show him what pleases me. He won't know unless I have the courage to tell him without anger. I really don't like being mad and not being able to express myself truthfully. We were able to talk about anything before we got engaged, please help us get that way again."

*****

"We hear you, Little One, we hear you," Jesus replied. "Allow us to give you peace. Please; you must open your heart. That part is up to you."

*****

I went back to school the next week excited about being married. I didn't have a curfew or anything restricting. I was looking forward also to buying our first groceries. It was funny little things like shopping were making me happy.

I was a horrible cook. I was never allowed in Mama's kitchen other than to wash dishes, so I didn't know anything about cooking. The first dinner I tried to cook was a disaster. I took a whole fish, about twelve inches long, and tried to fry it in a shallow frying pan. I burned the thing so bad that the outside was black, but the inside was still raw. Drake was a good sport about it, though. He told me, "I'll filet the fish for you next time and I'll show you how to fry it." We wound up eating a bologna sandwich that evening.

I spent a lot of time on the telephone with Mama and Drake's mom while they'd tried to teach myself how to cook. My specialty was hamburger meat browned with about five different cans of beans and corn drenched with catsup. I thought it was great. I think Drake knew better than to comment.

Over time, I learned how to cook properly and started loving to experiment.

Cooking for our first Thanksgiving meal was fun. I baked cookies, brownies and even tried to make candy. Our grocery bills were high, though, and Drake started to complain about not having enough money to pay the bills. He was also worried about not having enough to buy Christmas gifts if I kept cooking so much. I guess I was trying to fill my boring afternoons with projects and cooking as my new one. Drake loved to eat, but the issue was how much it cost.

The week after Thanksgiving I went shopping with a friend and came home with a surprise for Drake. He was in the habit of sleeping every day from 9:00 a.m. to 7:00 or 8:00 p.m. so he could work all night. When he finally woke up I told him. "Honey, I have a job. Rhonda and I went shopping this afternoon. Roger's Department Store needed a secretary in the office, so I applied and was immediately hired. Rhonda got a job there, too. She will be a clerk in the lady's dress section. Just think, I'll be putting my education to use."

"What about school?" he asked. "And who is going to cook and clean?"

"You're not happy that I'll be helping out with the bills finally?" I said peeved.

"Yes, I'm happy, but we'll never see each other." He answered.

"I haven't even told you my working hours yet and you are worried about not seeing me. We don't get to see each other now so what's the difference." I said angrily.

"I'm sorry for ruining your surprise. Tell me about it," he said.

"You know that I don't have any classes after 1:00 p.m. I'll eat a quick sandwich for lunch and then go to work. I'll have to be there at 2:00 p.m. and work until 6:00 p.m. Just four hours a day during the week with eight hours on Saturday. My pay is $6.00 an hour so it should help out with all of our expenses." I told him.

"What about dinner, are you going to feel like cooking?" He asked.

"I haven't really thought that out yet, but we'll think of ways to eat. I'll do the laundry after dinner. We'll make it. Just think, I have my first job. I'm excited." I answered.

Two weeks into my new job, going to school, being a wife coming home to cook and do housework, I was exhausted. How did Mama do it? I thought. Oh yeah, she has a maid.

Winter Quarter registration was coming up soon and during Christmas lunch, Daddy said, "I don't think you need to waste time in art classes anymore. Don't you see I was right? Your Secretarial skills are what got you a job. If you insist on taking art classes from now on, you'll have to pay for them. I'm done paying for those courses."

"But Daddy, I don't want to be a secretary for the rest of my life. I'm really a good artist. You've seen the paintings I've done for you and Mama. It's going to take at least two more years for me to finish." I complained.

'I didn't say I wouldn't pay for college. I just have a problem with paying for something you'll never be able to use in this area," was his reply.

"Look," I begged, "I can go into advertising and probably get a job at the paper. Please, Daddy."

"No, I have to start thinking about sending JL to college he wants to go to Struder. It's time for you to do something constructive and finish your secretarial classes as soon as you can." He answered.

I was so mad I could not think. I excused myself and went home. My Christmas was ruined, and Drake didn't even try to soothe my feelings. I think he agreed with Daddy.

Angry! Angry! I was angry all the time. I needed a break. Who could I talk to? No one wanted to listen to a complainer. I couldn't go home to Mama, I was at home. I'd never left! I was still under Daddy's thumb. Only now, Drake was under it with me. Weren't married people supposed to leave their parents?

I felt like an angry beast was taking over my body, and eyes were glowing red all the time, I was even becoming short-tempered with Drake.

The first week of February I was given my layoff notice from the department store. The rush from the Christmas Holidays was over, plus, the end of inventory for the New Year. So, Roger's didn't need a part-time secretary any longer. I walked down the block from the store to the Newspaper Company to see if they had any jobs in advertising. They didn't. Now, what was I going to do?

That night Drake surprised me when he said, "I'm glad you don't have a job anymore."

"Why?" I asked

"You are always grumpy, and the house is always in a mess. Now you'll have time to do things around here again. Maybe you can start cooking goodies for me again. That seemed to make you happy." He replied.

I screamed, "It was because you were always complaining about me cooking and not having enough money that I got a job in the first place! Now I don't even have classes to fill my day and I'll be finished with my secretarial courses in March. Then what? You expect me to stay home to cook, clean and do your laundry after you go to work so I won't wake you up? Think again!"

He certainly didn't get a meal that night. If I didn't feel like eating, then he wasn't going to get anything unless he fixed it himself.

*****

Satan couldn't help but laugh. "It takes a master to make things happen," he thought. Anger was the correct choice for the implosion. Raw emotions always trapped the victims.

*****

No matter what I did or said, I couldn't get Drake to understand why I was unhappy. I couldn't even pinpoint the reason. Was I going crazy?

After graduation, I had nothing to do. Being at home during the day was horrible. I couldn't make any noise because Drake was sleeping. Cleaning was out. I couldn't watch TV because he said even that caused him to stay awake. The slightest noise bothered him. He had to rest, or he couldn't work.

I'd go shopping or go to friends' houses. I couldn't be at home without anything to do.

It was that spring my world would change forever.

LOSS

On one of Drake's nights off, Mama and Daddy invited us over for dinner. They had something to tell us and wanted to wait until we were all together-JL, Drake, and me.

Mama started the conversation by telling us "I haven't been feeling well for a long time. My pain has gotten so unbearable I can't work anymore. I've been on a few doctor visits to have my chest examined for the problem, and the news is not good."

I gritted my teeth and braced myself because I knew this was something we were not going to like hearing. I could tell by her anxious movements and her shaking voice.

She went on saying, "I have lung cancer. I will be having surgery on Thursday to have a tumor removed. Then I'll have to have chemo treatments for a while. The doctors don't know what my prognosis is yet, so I can't tell you much more than this."

Daddy said, "We are prepared to take your mother to Emory if the need be. Fighting this thing is our main priority. She will need one of us to stay with her around the clock, especially after surgery."

He asked me, "Rachel, will you stay with your mother during the day?"

I replied, "I'll have it no other way. I'd move heaven and earth to be with her if I could. You didn't have to ask."

That night my mind just raced. I couldn't sleep. I'd toss and turn then get up to watch TV. I was miserable. Drake had made it a point to stay awake most of the day so that we could sleep together in the same bed that night. Even though I couldn't sleep he passed out from exhaustion. My thoughts were running amuck. I was so scared. What was I going to do if something happened to my Mama?

The day of the surgery was awful. The wait for a doctor to come and tell us something seemed to be an eternity. Finally, after her surgery, her doctors assured us she would recover, but she was going to be weak due to only having one lung. They had to remove the whole right one because the tumor was so large. That week following her surgery was very hard on her and the hospital stay was most uncomfortable.

Over the next few weeks, her chemo treatments were making her very sick. Even though she couldn't eat much she gained so much weight from all her medications. Her hair fell out as well as her eyebrows, making her very sad. I caught her crying and worrying about her appearance. My Daddy was someone who always talked about pretty women and compared one to another so, of course, she was worried about being attractive to him.

One thing I can say about my Mama, though, she never blamed God for cancer. She talked with Him often about it. I know because I'd hear her while she was in the bathroom taking her bath. I was scared to leave her side for fear she may need me. I usually sat close by and I was privileged to hear her prayers without her knowing.

She would have some very sweet conversations with Him, saying things like, "Father God, you have given me such a wonderful life, if I can win this battle for you to help others, you are going to have to show me how. My kids may need to know how one day so let's show them, okay?"

Mama grew stronger each day, but she wasn't the same. I could tell by looking at her she was afraid. My suspicions of her fear were confirmed when I overheard her ask a favor of Pastor one day during one of his visits. She asked him, "Please keep me in your prayers, Brother Moree, I'm in trouble."

He asked, "Emily are you afraid of dying? Or are you afraid of cancer?"

"Both," she told him. "I don't know what I'm facing, and it scares me. I hate being this helpless and dependent on my family just to help me with some of my basic needs. I know they are scared, too, and I can't stand their concerned actions. All I see is pity on my friend's faces. I don't like being a burden physically, emotionally or financially and it frightens me."

He replied, "You're no burden, Emily, they all love you and don't want you to suffer needlessly; you just let God handle the rest. His shoulders are strong enough for everything you can hand Him. He'll listen to your prayers, but I promise I'll add mine to yours."

His visit seemed to help her some. I was glad I could hear her express herself. That way I knew how to help her better.

Instead of just doing things for her, I'd ask her if she needed assistance first. This way she could get some independence back.

Before JL started college in the fall, Mama and I had a wonderful conversation where she told me one of her desires. She said to me, "Rachel, honey, I want you to go back to school. I think your true calling is in patient care. You have a way with people that they really need."

I was shocked at this. I asked, "What brought this on suddenly?"

"You know how to help and when not to," she said. "I also wished sometimes I could have been a nurse, but things didn't work out that way for me. Would you be interested in nursing if I can get your Daddy to pay for you go back to school?" she asked.

At that point in my life, I would have done anything to make my Mama happy, so I said, Sure."

Daddy was a little leery, but he also wanted to make Mama happy. He asked me the next day, "Rachel, do you really want to be a nurse? Or are you trying to pacify your Mama?"

"Daddy, I think I'd like giving it a try. I really don't like being a secretary." I answered.

I could tell that he wanted to do just about anything at that point to make my Mama happy, so he agreed to send me to Belmont Technical School to get a Nurse's Aide Certificate. He thought if I did well there and liked the courses that when I finished he might send me back to Belmont Junior College to get my Registered Nurses Degree, so I could apply for a license.

With JL and I both in school, Mama was going to need someone to watch after her during the day. My aunt Gloria agreed to come over to their house and check on her every day until I could get out of school. My classes were from 9:00 a.m. to 12:00 noon each day so I could be with her in the afternoons until Daddy got home or until Drake woke up.

To my surprise, I loved the courses and made good grades. I even enjoyed my clinical days where I had to do hands-on training with patients at the hospital. You could never have convinced me before that I would want to do patient care as my profession. Usually, smells and certain human noises when people got sick would make me sick. I trained myself to focus on a problem and remove my mind from myself to get on with the task.

After each course, the school would refer students who excelled in the class to the hospital for possible hiring. To my delight, I was referred to Belmont Memorial Hospital as the Technical School's choice for the next Nurse's Aide position. In December, after I got my certificate, a lady in the human resource office of the hospital called and asked if I wanted a job.

The lady's call flattered me, but I told her I needed to discuss this offer with my husband and family. If they agreed, I would come by their office the next day.

I could hardly wait for Drake to wake up to tell him my news.

"Drake, I have something to run by you. I've been offered a job at Belmont Memorial. What do you think?" I asked excitedly.

The first thing he asked was, "What hours?"

"I don't know. We didn't get that far in the conversation. They only asked if I'd be interested in working for them. They told me I was the school's honorary candidate for their next position. Why?" I asked.

"I'd really like it if we could work the same shift, so we could be together more. I don't like sleeping without my wife every day." He replied.

"That's so sweet," I told him. "I'm planning to check it out more tomorrow so we'll see where it leads. I was just concerned you wouldn't want me to have a job since you were unhappy with me working before."

The next day, I couldn't get to the hospital fast enough. When I got there and met with the Human Resources Manager, I learned they usually had two or three opening for each shift. The one they needed the most help with was the third shift starting at 11:00 p.m. lasting until 7:00 a.m. the next day. I could get a position working the same hours Drake worked at the tire plant. I knew this was going to make him happy and we'd get to spend more time together. We also would have the added reward of riding to work together for a while. He could drop me off each evening and I'd wait in the break area until he came to pick me up each morning.

Mama was ecstatic that I was fulfilling her dream and Daddy was proud of me for once in my life. He even agreed to let me attend college and further my education if I really liked the work. The two of them even had Drake convinced this is what I needed to do if I liked my work. So, before spring quarter started everyone had convinced me that I needed to finish college and go further in this field. I had three people working on me to do this: Mama, Daddy and now Drake.

Because I had already been to college, I would have to take only those classes pertained to my nursing degree. I enrolled in three classes a day to start off my first quarter. There was one problem with this plan, one class was at 8:00 a.m. and the others were from 11:00 a.m. to 1:00 p.m. When would I sleep?

Daddy came through for me again. He asked his sister, my Aunt Ida if I could nap at her house between classes since she didn't live far from the school. She was glad to help make my new journey a little easier. I'd nap in my car from 7:30 a.m. to 8:00 a.m. before my first class started. After that class, I'd go to her house and nap until 10:45 a.m. I'd have to go to my next class at 11:00 a.m. I'd nap in my car again after that class until the last. After my school day was finished, I would go home, take a quick shower and pile into bed with Drake until we both woke up at 9:00 p.m. to get ready for work. My sleep schedule was really getting confused, but I managed.

Everything seemed to be working in my favor concerning my education. The hospital even allowed nursing students to study while on duty if their work didn't suffer. Each night I lugged my books to work and could keep up with my homework. At last, I thought, I was doing something that seemed to be making everybody happy with me.

Mama didn't like the fact I would be out driving so late at night. This was the only drawback and caused her unnecessary concern. I promised to call when I got in the building every night to let her know I was safely inside. She was always scared of attackers in dark parking areas and worried until I called.

One night I was distracted due to an emergency in the wing where I was stationed and didn't call her until about an hour later. She had been crying and worrying about me. Naturally, her actions changed my world. Guilt gripped my heart and I swore I'd never forget her ever again or I would have someone call her even if I couldn't. Her feelings had to be one of my priorities from then on.

"Let's hike up the pressure," Evil said to his buddies. "Infirmity, you work on the mother. Guilt, you, and Exhaustion work on Rachel. We're about to break what spirit she has left. We've certainly been able to keep her away from Him lately." He laughed.

Jesus, spoke to the Father, "Father, do you hear? What can we do?

"Operate in patience, my boy. This is just part of the process. She has what she needs. You've made sure of that already. Time is on our side. You know the outcome. Now, all we need to do is wait." God consoled.

Then God said, "Preservation is with her still and he has been ordered not to allow her spirit to break. He will place things or words in her path that will guide her when the time arises."

*****

About two months into my new position and school, Mama started to have symptoms that had all of us concerned. While cooking one night, instead of frying the chicken she put the rolls in the grease. She didn't even acknowledge the error until she took up a few and turned to see the chicken still in the sink. Daddy was shocked. He called and woke Drake and me telling us to come to their house, Mama needed us.

When we walked in, I heard my Mama while she was crying, as my Daddy, "Jason am I losing my mind? What is wrong with me? I do some of the strangest things lately and it seems to be when my head begins to hurt."

I butted in, "Mama you haven't said anything to us about your head hurting, how long has this been going on? Where is, it hurting? Did you hurt yourself?"

Daddy didn't let her reply. He spoke to her, "We'll call the doctor tomorrow and have him look at you. You've been a little off lately, I agree. I think both of us will feel better if we have you checked out."

Then he turned to me and said, "She didn't hurt herself. She told me her head started hurting about three weeks ago. I'll just have Doc look over her soon. Will you and Drake clean up her mess in the kitchen before you go to work while I get her ready for bed?"

The next day, Daddy called the doctor about her problems. This alarmed the doctor enough he wanted to see her immediately. He put her in the hospital. The tests he would have to run on Mama needed to be done under anesthesia in a sterile environment.

Drake knew I needed to be with Daddy while Mama was undergoing her tests, so he didn't have a problem with me taking a day off from work. When I finished my shift the next day, I went immediately to Mama's room to wait for the process. Daddy hadn't gotten there yet, so she and I had a little time together. She shared with me how afraid she was and wanted me to know Daddy was upset too, and she wanted me to be patient with him because he could say things that may offend without meaning it.

When he came in, I could see he hadn't slept very well, if at all. I understood what Mama meant, about the need to walk on eggshells.

It was while we were waiting for Mama to come out of the examining room he told me about all the things he'd caught her doing lately. "I'm afraid to leave her alone." He said. "She is doing the strangest things. I'm afraid she is going to hurt herself or burn the house down around her while I'm not at home. I've asked your Aunt Gloria to spend as much time with her as possible, but can you be with her after you get out of class?"

"I'll be asleep most of the time until you get home, but at least I'd be there if she needed me," I told him. "Just make her aware I need to be awake if she wants to cook something or tries to cut something up, okay."

I just answered Daddy right off the top of my head. I didn't even think to ask Drake if he minded. That night when we left the hospital it was late, and I hadn't had any sleep. When I got home, Drake was up and getting ready for work.

He asked, "How's your Mom? Did the doctor tell you and your Dad anything?"

"Not yet. It is going to be sometime after lunch tomorrow before he comes in with the results." I answered.

"Daddy needs me to stay with her after she gets home. She's been doing weird things lately and he is scared. I told him I would and that I'd get up to check on you after he gets home. Is that okay?" I asked

"I'd been sleeping without you for a long time before you started this job; I guess I can do it a little longer. Your family needs you and I'm just going to have to take a back seat." He replied.

I didn't go to any of my classes the next morning because I wanted to be with Mama. She was anxious to hear the outcome of her tests. I knew that even if she wasn't saying anything she needed one of us with her. That afternoon we would know the results of the tests and she would have the family with her. She needed someone to help her endure the wait for the news.

The tests came back but the news wasn't good. Dr. Ivory, Mom's oncologist, told us, "The spinal fluid I collected yesterday came back cloudy and the x-rays show you have a mass on your brain. Emily, I feel it is safe to say cancer has spread to your brain."

Daddy was the first to say anything, and he asked, "What are you suggesting we do, Dr. Ivory? Do you think we can beat this thing?"

"Jason, I don't know." He replied. "I feel we need to start her on radiation with chemo treatments again. I need to do several blood cultures to determine if she is strong enough to go through this extensive process. She'll need to stay in the hospital another day."

Mama lost it. She started crying and said, "I can't go through that again. Just let me go home and meet my Maker. My family can't keep patching me up and spending our life's savings on trying to win a losing battle."

It was like she just gave up. Right there before our eyes, she decided she was done. Her remarks upset JL so badly he left the hospital because he couldn't handle any more of the drama. If

I hadn't had Drake with me, I think I might have fallen apart, too. He took me outside the room and just held me while I cried into his shirt.

"Mama can't give up" I cried. "How can I convince her to fight, Drake?"

"She is not your responsibility, Rachel. Honey, your Mama is the only one who knows the limits she can take. I don't think she wants to give up. She is just scared right now." He consoled.

The next week, Mama was undergoing both kinds of treatment for brain cancer. Depression kicked in and she hardly talked. All she wanted to do was sit in their living room and play the same song over and over- 'One Day at a Time.' I bet I heard that song a thousand times over the next few months.

As hard as I tried, I couldn't keep my grades up. I was worn out. My clinical classes were especially taxing after a hard night's work. Plus, our house would have been condemned if the Health Department visited. Dirty dishes were not our problem because we were always eating fast food or going over to Mama's and Daddy's to eat their leftovers. Daddy seemed to welcome the company during those times.

Three months of treatments and Mama didn't get any better. In fact, she got worse. It got so bad she had to be hospitalized because she couldn't remember things well or function properly.

After class, every day I'd go back to the hospital to stay with Mama instead of going home to rest. I'd sleep in the chair as much as possible until Daddy could get there then I'd go home, visit with Drake, get us something to eat and get ready for work again. During that time, I'd try to wash a load of clothes every few days because we both needed clean clothes. They never got folded or put away, I just dumped them on our living room sofa and ironed what we needed as we needed to wear them.

I was a mess. Even Drake complained he didn't have a wife anymore, -he had a zombie. I didn't care what anyone thought about me. The only thing that mattered to me was keeping Mama happy by staying in school and keeping Daddy happy by watching over Mama until he could get to her. Drake knew he was in the back seat of my life and I didn't care. My job was just that now, a job.

One night during my shift I was stationed in the section next to Mama's room, when I heard a "code red" monitor go off. I looked up and saw it was Mama's room that had the emergency light blinking over the door.

I got the attention of the unit's charge nurse and begged, "I need to go down the hall. My mother is in code red. Please let me go see what is wrong."

"Go, but stay out of the way," she said. "You can't be liable for anything because you are family, understand."

"Yes Ma'am," I replied then took off running.

141

"What's going on?" I asked an orderly that was standing nearby.

"The lady in room 312, has fallen and is stuck between the bathroom door and the entrance. They are afraid she is hurt but can't get her out of the way without hurting her more." He replied not knowing she was my mother.

That's when I started screaming, "Mama, Mama, can you hear me." "Let, me talk to her, she is my Mama!" I pushed at a nurse.

I got down on my knees next to the door and started talking, "Mama can you hear me, it's Rachel?"

I heard her moan, but she did respond to me. Then she said, "Rachel, honey, I'm hurt and can't seem to stand up."

"Well, can you move closer to your bed, even if you have to roll?" I asked her.

"I'll try," she said.

And to our amazement, she moved out of the way enough for the nurses and the orderly to get to her. They refused to allow me in the room until they had her back in bed and examined. My charge nurse came down to check on me and was so kind. She just stayed there and patted my shoulder until I calmed down.

"You know they are taking care of her, don't you?" She asked. "She is well cared for."

"Yes Ma'am, I just can't stand seeing this happen. Please put yourself in my shoes and try to understand how you'd feel if it was your mother in there." I answered.

"Go, back to your station and I'll have them call you when they have her settled, okay. Try to get your mind focused on your job or I'll have to send you home." She told me.

When they called me, I tried to ask if I could have the rest of the night off. I needed to be with Mama not working. I was very fortunate to have a compassionate supervisor. She knew what I needed and told me to go before I even finished my question.

When I got to Mama's room the nurse told me she had a bad bruise on the back of her head. Somehow, she slipped as she stepped into the bathroom and fell backward hitting her head hard. The blow to her head stunned her and she couldn't move. That didn't keep her from calling out. Thank God, or no one would have known until much later that she had fallen. It was Mama's screaming she was hurt that caused the station nurse to pull the code alarm for help.

Evil was laughing so hard his side hurt but he wasn't finished with his prank just yet. He was going to cause Jason to show his temper and make Rachel a lunatic with his accusations. He would make this girl hate her Daddy so much she would never want to be around him again.

*****

I'd called Daddy right after I got back to my station. By the time, I got to her again, he was coming in the room also. Mad was not the word to describe Daddy. He was furious at everything and everybody.

"Am I spending thousands of dollars for you stupid nurses to let her hurt herself? Why didn't someone make sure her room was safe?" He yelled. "If she has repercussions from this, I'm going to sue every one of you and this hospital for negligence."

Then he turned his anger on me, "Why weren't you here until I came up? Your Mama is hurt! Does your job mean more to you than she does? Apparently, it does." He hollered.

*****

Preservation was ready; he knew that he had to somehow intervene. So, he prodded Emily just in time before verbal hurts could go any further.

*****

I stood there stunned until he finished. I wanted to punch him, but I held back. Why was he blaming me for her accident? It was Mama, who stopped his rant. "Jason, stop it!" She said. "Rachel has been here all along. She is the one who helped me through this by telling me what to do so they could get to me."

144

"I'm sorry, honey," He said. "Tell me what you know and then maybe I can stop this panic and anger raging in me."

Of course, classes were out of the question for me that day. I called Drake when he got home and asked him to bring me a change of clothes on his way to work. Nothing could make me leave Mama's side that day for anything. I'd just have to bathe in her bathroom and take care of my needs at the hospital. I made a pallet right there in the corner of her room by taking some of the hospital's towels and sheets then slept sitting up against the wall while Daddy stayed in the only chair in the room.

The next few days were a blur. I functioned as usual, but I can't recount what I did. I know I worked, went to school, studied, and functioned as a wife in body only, but not in mind or spirit. I didn't have a heart for much of anything. My life was pulled in so many ways I was about to become Humpty Dumpty.

To the family's surprise, the doctor told us Mama could go home. There wasn't much they could do for her that we weren't able to do for her at home. She was better and the bruise on her head was going away. The fear of damage had passed.

The school quarter was over, and I got a little rest from all the extra duties. I promised Mama I would enroll the next quarter and it seemed to make her happy. The two weeks before I'd have to enroll for the next term would go by in a hurry.

At least I could spend more time with Drake. He had been supportive and very understanding about me taking care of Mama, so I felt he needed more of my attention. We went out on a date

145

and had a lovely dinner. It felt good to change the routine. We weren't hurting financially so we splurged a little bit. We even used some of our savings to pay Mama's maid to come over and give our house a proper cleaning. It had been neglected and hiring the maid took some of the stress and guilt off me.

JL was also home from school so he stayed with Mama which gave me a little break. Drake and I would visit them in the evening just before we went to work to make sure everything was taken care of and everyone was happy.

Summer quarter enrollment was easy. I convinced myself this quarter was not going to be as rough, so I still took on three courses. I just made sure my classes were closer together to enable me to go home sooner. I scheduled clinical studies for my first class, so I didn't have to leave the hospital. This would allow me just enough time to go in a lady's room and change into my school clothes.

Nutrition and Biology II were my two other courses. I was supposed to be finished with all my classes by noon each day. This would make it possible for me to check on Mama and make sure she ate before I tried to sleep.

When Daddy came in from the fields around lunch we had time to eat and talk a bit. Then I'd make myself comfortable on their den sofa until his workday ended late in the afternoon. Like a robot, I'd get up and drive to my house, about a two-minute ride away, and crawl into my own bed alongside Drake- sometimes fully clothed. I didn't care. I just needed undisturbed sleep.

146

*****

Evil looked on and shared with his other companions that it was time to nail the plan shut. It was time to dislodge Rachel's faith. "Let's finally do it," he said. "Death, take the body away from Emily and destroy it. Make Rachel and everyone in the family doubt and say bad things about Him. We won't allow any praise to go His way, only heartache and disappointed complaints."

*****

Towards the end of the quarter, Mama's developed another symptom, she started having pain in her back. No matter what she did she could not get comfortable. Then one day she called out to me, scaring me so bad I sat straight up from a sound sleep. "Rachel!" she screamed.

I ran to the bathroom and found blood everywhere the floor, the toilet, and on her clothes. She was bleeding profusely. I called the doctor's office immediately and told them I was taking her to the emergency room. Then I called and woke Drake. "Drake, you've got to get Daddy out of the fields. Mama is in a bad way and I'm taking her to the hospital now." I informed him.

When we got there, Dr. Ivory was waiting for us. He made sure Mama was taken in immediately for treatment, but I wasn't allowed to follow.

Daddy came straight from the field. He told the emergency room's receptionist who he was, so they allowed him in the

147

treatment room with Mama. I was glad Drake wasn't far behind Daddy. They had taken separate cars because they didn't know what to expect and Drake hardly ever missed work.

The time seemed to drag in the emergency room's waiting area. "How do people stand this?" I said to Drake. To ease the stress, I got up and found a pay phone to call JL. I left word with his dorm master about Mama and asked that JL phone the hospital whenever he could. I was sure whatever Mama was going through would put her back in the hospital's care.

Daddy finally came out to speak with us, and he had been crying. "Your Mama's kidneys temporarily stopped functioning; they are doing x-rays on her to see if cancer has spread to them. Dr. Ivory thinks cancer has spread to her lymph nodes and if that is the case, she won't have much time left."

When Daddy told us the news, it finally hit me just how critical Mama's problem really was. The classes I had taken recently taught me about the seriousness of lymph node cancer and the fast track the nodes created for diseases to destroy the body.

All of us, even JL, were waiting in Mama's new hospital room for her to come back from tests. The doctor came in first to discuss her diagnosis. Dr. Ivory asked Daddy, "Is it all right for me to disclose the findings with all of your family?"

Daddy assured him, "Yes, we all need to know, Doc, so please just give it to us straight and don't sugar it up."

"Okay, Jason, Emily's cancer has spread to her kidneys, her bladder and possibly to her other lung. The tumor in her brain has shrunk, but it is still there. With her kidneys failing she may have two weeks left to live if that long."

"Doc, is she in very much pain?" Daddy asked.

"She is very good at not letting everyone know the extent, but even her strong threshold for pain will not help much now. But to answer your question, Jason, yes, her pain is severe. I've ordered the nurses to make sure she is well medicated and to make sure she has oxygen to help her breathe. I'm also pushing IV fluids to keep her kidneys operating." He responded.

Dr. Ivory also said he would have a nurse come in after Mama returned to the room. She had to ask us a few more questions we needed to be discussed among us before Mama's condition worsened. Dr. Ivory felt Mama needed to be involved with the answers as well.

Mama looked sad when they brought her in the room. When she saw JL, she couldn't help herself, her bottom lip started to tremble and then she started sobbing.

"I've tried so hard to get well for all of you. I ate right, I took my treatments I did everything I was told to do but to no avail. All I'm doing is stressing all of you and making your lives miserable." She cried.

It wasn't five minutes after she made the statement that the charge nurse arrived with her clipboard to ask us the hard questions Dr. Ivory told us about.

Nurse Andrews asked, "Have all of you been informed of Mrs. Parody's condition?"

We answered, "Yes."

"Okay, I have to ask the following questions for our official hospital records, so let me begin. First, is there a Living Will for Mrs. Parody? Second, what measures do you want us to take to sustain life?" She asked.

Mama spoke up immediately, "It is my life, or what is left of it, and I do not want any heroics or extra measures taken to keep me alive. I do not want to be kept on life support further burdening my family."

Daddy also answered, "I want her to be as comfortable as possible but nothing else. I want to honor her wishes."

Then he turned to face JL and me, "Kids, I ask you both to please comply with Mama's wishes. She needs to know we will not put her through something that will only keep her body working."

I looked at Mama and said, "Okay."

So, did JL.

After the nurse left, Drake, JL, and I went downstairs to get something to eat and to talk. Daddy wanted time alone with Mama. When we finished, Drake and I went home to get ready for another night's work. JL went home also, but Daddy was determined to stay all night with Mama.

*****

Preservation witnessed Evil's conversation, so he knew what those demons were up too and he had to do something quick to change things before they totally had their way. He decided to awaken a need in Rachel that was planted long ago, the need for peace she could only get from God.

*****

My plan was to return to the hospital before my shift, checked on the two of them and see how they were doing. I needed to Dad where I would be stationed and explain if they needed me to have one of their nurses get me.

I went to Mama's room and realized they both wanted to sleep. So, I decided to clock in early for work. On the way to my station, I had to walk by the hospital chapel. When I passed, I could have sworn I heard someone calling me. I went inside. It was dark and kind of spooky in the room. There wasn't anyone there, so I assumed I must be hearing things. I didn't leave right away because I felt a tug in my heart to pray. I hadn't talked to God in a long time and I truly needed His peace.

Shame washed over me as I started to speak, "Dear Jesus, I can't explain the pain in my heart right now or the fear of a future without my Mama. She has always been my confidant and provider. My Daddy has never been very supportive of me until Mama got sick. What am I going to do? I don't want her to die but I don't want her to suffer either." I told Him.

I sat there a few more minutes in the little room but I wasn't alone. I knew God had heard me because I received a sense of divine courage that night to release my Mama into His care no matter what happened in the next few days. I knew she would be better off with Him, and I thanked Him for this peace.

Her heartfelt prayer was like music to the Father's ears, Preservation was doing his job directing her. Of course, He would allow His peace to wash over her after she had tapped into His compassion.

Worked dragged that night, but I got through it. I was thankful there were no Saturday classes to attend. I was exhausted. When I went to check on Mama and Daddy they both insisted I go home and get some rest. I could come back that afternoon and trade places with Daddy, so he could go home and clean up.

When I got home, Drake was already there. I crawled into bed with him and just cried. I was so tired and emotionally drained.

He said sweetly, "I didn't know if you were coming home. I set the alarm to get up early, so I could bring you some clothes and something to eat." Then he asked, "How is she doing?"

"She is hooked up to all kinds of monitors and IV's plus she has a catheter bag to check her urine flow. Right now, she is lucid, but I'm afraid she won't be for long if they start giving her much pain medication." I answered.

"Get some rest. We'll go see her early this afternoon. You need to be rested and ready. JL called me before you got home. He is getting ready so he can go to the hospital and let your Daddy have a rest." He said.

When Drake and I got to the hospital that afternoon, he and JL went to the hospital café to get us something to eat. Mama said she wanted to talk with me while it was just the two of us.

"Rachel, I want you to promise me something. I want you to encourage your Daddy to remarry after I'm gone." She said.

"What?" I asked. I couldn't believe Daddy being alone would be on her mind right now. Then I asked, "Mama, why are you worried about that? I don't have a problem with it, but I don't think Daddy will be ready for a long time."

She said, "He has always been so dependent on me. And he has a very high sex drive. Do you understand what I mean? I

153

just can't worry you and JL will hinder him from finding someone good for him."

"No, Mama, like I said, I don't have a problem with it. I also want him to be happy." I assured her.

She didn't need to worry about us or anything else, but I had to let her vent. Removing her fears was part of her release. I was grateful for the inner peace while I understood she needed to talk.

Other family members arrived to see her. She was growing weaker while visiting with Grandmother and her brothers and sisters.

The following Saturday afternoon, after everybody left, she appeared to be sleeping. Daddy got scared and asked me to check her pulse. It looked like she was breathing but she wasn't responding to any of his questions.

When I started the countdown for her pulse, I realized she was gone. It was the oxygen pumping into her lungs that made it appear she was breathing.

My emotions went rampant and I instantly dove into a severe pity party. Why was I the one who would have to find out she was dead? Why couldn't another nurse or doctor have to tell everyone? Why had fate played me this sick joke?

"Daddy, she's gone." I cried.

He pulled the alarm immediately for a nurse to come in but she made the same call I did. Mama had left this world.

RESPONSIBILITY

Preservation planned to take advantage of the situation and infuse responsibility into Rachel. She hadn't needed much before, but now she needed to grow into her new role as caregiver in a different way. He knew that the Father was planning a blessing to come soon from all this pain, so the time was right to set the stage.

*****

We had people staying everywhere. Until Mama's funeral was over some stayed at Mama's and Daddy's house, some stayed with us and others with my Aunt Gloria. It was depressing after everyone left and JL went back to school. We were used to going, going, going that the quiet and lack of duties were almost unbearable.

A few days went by before the facts set in my Mama wasn't around anymore. I was alone when the panic set in. Who would comfort me when I needed comfort, who would assure me during hard times? I was scared. Drake didn't know me the way my Mama did, and both of my Grandmothers lived so far away. I really needed my Daddy, but I had never received comfort from him before, and I didn't know how to ask him for help.

To my surprise, Daddy showed up on my doorstep at the same time I was panicking. The sense of loss was getting to him and he needed me. I couldn't believe it-he, needed me. For the first time in my life, we could console each other.

The weekend after the funeral, Aunt Gloria and one of my cousins came to Daddy's house to help me with the thank you, cards. I was telling my aunt Daddy was attempting to have a better relationship with me when she asked me a question. "Rachel, your Daddy can't help wanting to be with you right now. Do you know why that is?"

"No, why, Aunt Gloria?" I asked in return.

"Look in the mirror, child. You are the perfect likeness to Emily. He sees your Mama in you. He's lonely and any reminder of her helps. Seeing you makes her live in his heart. He does love you, honey, don't get me wrong, he just never knew how to show you. He has always come across as being hard." She said.

She kept on, "Your Granddaddy was always hard on him and he doesn't know any other way but to be overbearing at times. Right now, he is a very needy person so be patient with him. It's what your Mama would want you to do. Use this time of adjustment to your advantage and find out for yourself just how much he has always loved you."

It was my last day of the summer quarter at college and I needed a break from school. I had passed all my classes but not with very high marks. It wasn't surprising with all that went on in my life those three months. Telling Daddy about my grades was going to be hard. I decided to face the situation and go straight to his house with my news hoping he wouldn't be there. He was so I went in with the determination to spill the news about my grades and ask him if I could take the next quarter off. It was his money that was sending me, and I didn't want him disappointed.

"Daddy," I started

"What's up? You seem anxious." He said.

I answered, "School is over for the quarter, and I didn't do too well this time. My grades were low C's and D's, but I know they are low due to all that went on. I really want to finish, but I'm tired and need a break from school. Would you be disappointed if I skipped the next quarter and started back winter quarter?

"Wouldn't that mess up your schedule?" He asked

"I don't think so. It will put me behind in clinical classes but that shouldn't be a problem. Many students stop and start for various reasons and the school is accommodating." I told him.

I was shocked when he told me he didn't mind me taking a break. He could see I needed the rest and time to regroup. During this conversation, he also had something to ask me.

He started, "Rachel, I would like for you and Drake to move in the house with me. I can't stand being alone in this big new house and I need someone to help me out. Do you think you and Drake would be up to it?

He went on, "I still have our maid to keep the place clean, you would do our wash and cook. I think it would be a win-win situation for all of us."

"Wow!" I said. "I'll have to get back with you on that Daddy. Drake may not have a problem with it, but I need to make sure."

I was so anxious that I couldn't sleep. I kept asking myself why my Daddy wanted us to move in with him. Before I knew it, the alarm was going off for us to get up and start another night's work. As I cooked for us, I told Drake, what Daddy had asked me.

"Drake, Daddy asked the strangest thing today. He wanted to know if you and I would move in his house and live with him. I didn't know what to say, so I used the excuse I needed your permission. What do you think?"

"I think that's a great idea. Think of all the money we could save and you'd have someone to clean up if he still uses your Mama's maid service. Yeah, I'm all for it." He replied with his mouth full.

"Why do you think he wants us to live with him? I could wash his clothes on my day off and we could go over there every night to cook. I just don't know his reason." I said pondering.

Drake replied, "Maybe he's lonely and doesn't like the feeling. I understood. When you were always over there taking care of your Mom, I felt like a bachelor having to fend for myself all the time. I didn't like it."

"Oh, I forgot to tell you, I'm not going back to school next quarter. I even had the nerve to face Daddy head-on about it and he agreed I needed a break. We can start riding to work together again like we use to. Would you like that?" I shared.

"Are you sure you want to do that? It is always so hard to get back in the mood to begin classes again. But, yes, I'm going to love having you all to myself every day and not having two cars on the road. Once again, more money in the wallet." He laughed while tickling me.

On, our next scheduled day off, Drake and I packed up our stuff and moved in with Daddy. We took the room they had prepared for me before Drake and I married. We stored our washer, dryer, dishes, and cookware in the storage shed because I wouldn't need them at his house. There wasn't any point bringing any furniture because it was Mama's and Daddy's old stuff they didn't want anymore, so we just left it in the old house.

Every morning when Drake and I came home, Daddy would be up eating his cereal and have coffee before he went to work in the field. So, we had the house to ourselves most of the day. Daddy only came home to eat a quick bite of lunch, but he never disturbed our sleep. We didn't even know when he came and went.

Our marriage relationship was improving because I wasn't always taking care of someone else. I didn't even mind taking care of Daddy's wash since I had to do ours anyway. He seemed to like my cooking and was even complimentary. I was happy for a change.

I had a problem when my brother would come home. You would think the boy had a year's worth of clothes for me to wash for him in a two-day span before he left for school again. He also had a ravenous appetite. One night I had to cook two whole chickens for us, one for JL and one for the three of us. It was ridiculous the amount of food he could eat and never gain weight.

We were in the second month of our new living arrangement when I started feeling strange. Everything that had the slightest odor made me sick. One night for dinner, Drake and Daddy wanted bacon and eggs with hash browns. As I was cooking, I started gagging, the smell was overwhelming.

Drake followed me to the bathroom asking, "What's going on, honey? You seem to be getting sick all the time. Is there something I can do?"

"Right now, go make sure the bacon doesn't burn. I'll be there in a minute." I answered back.

When I came out, Daddy was grinning from ear-to-ear.

"I know what's wrong with her," he said. "Her Mama did the very same thing when she was pregnant."

No way, I thought. Could I truly be pregnant? That sure wasn't in my plan. When had I had my last period? I couldn't remember.

Drake said with a stunned look, "A kid, good Lord, I'm going to be a dad. A son!"

"Don't go there yet, big boy." I said, "I need to be checked out by a doctor before you start thinking about names."

During work that night I worried. How could I be pregnant? I thought we took precautions. Many times, the charge nurse brought me back from my own imaginations. The last time she interrupted my dreams, she asked. "Rachel, why are you preoccupied tonight? I think I've had to wake you from a trance three or four times. You are sitting there with this blank stare on your face."

"I think I'm pregnant," I told her.

"That's great! Isn't it?" She asked.

"Oh, it's a good thing. I'm just in shock. I can't remember when I had my last period. I started feeling strange about two weeks ago, and tonight the smell of meat cooking made me vomit." I shared.

Then she turned from her work and said, "Rachel, why don't you go down to the lab and have them run a urine test? You will feel much better knowing for sure and it won't cost you anything. I'll call my friend Judy, who works in the lab and ask if she will do it since you are a hospital employee."

"That would be fantastic! Does it take long for the results?" I exclaimed.

"I don't think the test takes but a few minutes. I'll call Judy now." She offered.

When Drake arrived after work the next morning, I had proof positive on a piece of paper. My lab test proved Daddy's theory. Yes, I was pregnant.

When I got into the truck, I handed Drake the paper and said. "Happy early Christmas." When he looked at it, he said with tears in his eyes, "You're giving me a baby! What an awesome responsibility!"

"Well, you're going to have to wait awhile for the gift to show up. Judy, the lab nurse, said that I still needed to go to the doctor because she couldn't determine how far along I was." I shared.

Drake could hardly wait to get home and call his parents. "I'm going to be a dad!" He told them.

Just knowing I was pregnant seemed to keep me focused on being sick all the time. I threw up morning, noon, and night. I couldn't wait to see Dr. Smith and find out if there was anything I could do to stop this torture. He was Mama's Gynecologist and the one I used before getting married to discuss birth control, etc. so he was my logical choice for a doctor.

During my visit, he told me by his estimation, I was about two months along. He also informed me he was no longer in the baby delivery business. He was too old, so he referred me to a younger team of doctors who were very well thought of in town.

Before I left I asked him, "Is there anything I can do to stop nausea? I don't think I can stand being sick all the time."

"Nibble on saltine crackers and sip ginger ale. Most women swear by that." He told me. "It will go away in a few weeks."

My next doctor's appointment was scheduled in two weeks with Drs. Randolph and Sapp. We were going to get to know each other very well in the next eight months or so. Whoopee!

Trying to work while being pregnant was like living in a cartoon. If the patients threw up, I'd throw up; if I smelled gross scents, I'd gag. I was getting tired of explaining why I seemed sicker than some of the patients.

One evening, during an emergency, I was expected to lift a patient, so we could put monitors on his back. He was dead weight and gave me no help. It was then I got a burning pain in my side and dropped to my knees beside his bed. I managed to get out of the way and start focusing on his needs instead of mine. Thank God, he settled and stabilized, but I didn't.

Infirmity had been having such a good time keeping Rachel sick, and he couldn't believe his luck when she voluntarily tried to do something stupid. He kicked her right in her side to make her feel pain while he tried to take the baby.

Preservation saw what Infirmity had done so he had to make sure Rachel wouldn't be placed in another situation at work where she had to put someone else's health ahead of her own. He would need to influence Drake to make her leave her job.

*****

I was rushed to the ER because I had started bleeding. Drake was called in from work because they were afraid I might miscarry. When he came in the room with me, I had already been examined by Dr. Lotus, the ER doctor.

Dr. Lotus, told us, "Rachel has strained herself, but fortunately, she is not losing the baby. I've written her an excuse to be out of work for a week. She will need to see her gynecologist for his opinion. Take her home and make sure she stays in bed for at least two days."

Drake was so scared his color was ashen. He said a little hysterically! "She not going back to work! If they expect her to lift patients twice her size while pregnant then I won't have her working at all."

When we came home during the middle of the night, it Daddy woke up. "What happened?" He asked when he saw Drake carrying me inside.

Drake answered, "Those idiots at the hospital made her lift an old man twice her size almost causing her to miscarry. The ER doctor wants her on bed rest for two days."

"They didn't make me do anything, Daddy. I was doing my job. The man was in distress and needed help. I was there, that's all." I interjected.

Drake went on, "I'm not allowing her to go back. I can't worry about losing the baby or her. That so-called job can wait until the baby is here and all is well."

Daddy was in full agreement with Drake. It didn't matter what I said. They ganged up on me and refused to budge. That night was the end of my nurses' aid career. Drake made me promise I would call and give them my resignation. I complied like an obedient wife.

I spent all the Christmas Holidays in bed. Drake and Daddy wouldn't even let me out to go shopping.

We were hardly past Christmas when Daddy received a call from my uncle that Grandma wasn't doing well. The doctors didn't expect her to live much longer. So, he, my Aunt Ida and I went off to Louisiana to see her. She had moved in with my uncle and his family after my Aunt Jane retired and wanted to travel.

I was glad we made the trip. She passed away a few days after we returned from our visit. My Uncle Roy had a mortuary vehicle carry her body back to Belmont for burial next to my Granddaddy.

Daddy handled the loss of Grandma better than I thought. He never talked about her much, so it seemed he was okay.

I was bored after the holidays. After Grandma's funeral, I enrolled in school for the winter quarter. To pacify Drake, I took a few classes that didn't require me to work with patients. I was still not satisfied. Maybe it was hormonal. I didn't know.

Drake was sensing my unease and offered to change shifts at work. "Would working from 3:00 p.m. to 11:00 p.m. be better?" He asked. "We could be together more, especially when you come home from school."

"Sure, I'd like that. Maybe we could do things together and break up the doldrums." I told him.

Now he was awake during the day, but was he home, NO! He was either fishing or hunting with one of his buddies. Now I had to help clean fish or skin something which did not help matters when I was always trying not to gag. He was having fun, but I sure wasn't.

After winter quarter, I didn't go back to school. There weren't any classes I could take. All remaining classes involved clinical studies so school was out of the question. Now I was really bored. I was no longer sick to my stomach so consequently, I started experimenting in the kitchen again.

Drake and Daddy were my guinea pigs. If I craved it, they had to eat it or make do with something else. I bet I ate a hundred pounds of lasagna, thousands of peanut butter and jelly sandwiches, pounds of cashew nuts, and watermelon, especially, after it started getting hot outside.

One night before Drake went to work, Daddy came out of his room all dressed up. I asked him, "What's the occasion?"

"I'm going to our old club for a 35 and older singles dance." He informed us. "Think I look sporty enough?"

"You look great. All the ladies will be fighting over you." I remarked.

After he left, I told Drake about my promise to Mama. "One day when Mama and I were alone in her hospital room, she asked me to encourage Daddy to date and possibly remarry. At the time, I would have promised her just about anything to make her happy. Now I'm a little hesitant, maybe a little scared, I don't know."

He hugged me and made the comment, "He's your Dad. You can't see him with another person just yet. If it is meant for him to meet someone, keep your promise and encourage the process."

After Drake left for work, I was uneasy. I watched the clock like I was the parent instead of the child. Just how long was Daddy going to stay out? Finally, he came home around midnight.

He was shocked I wasn't in bed and asked, "Why are you up so late?"

I lied and said, "I had been waiting for Drake to come home and decided to wait for him to come in also."

He knew I was fibbing and asked, "Curious, aren't you? Yes, I had a very good time. I plan to go to the next dance they have scheduled in a few weeks."

"Well, tell me about your night," I said.

"I met with some old friends I hadn't seen in thirty or so years. We enjoyed the dance. Then some of us went out to a Waffle House for breakfast." He answered me.

"Meet anyone interesting?" I asked.

"I met a lady who is a friend of my old friend. I think we hit it off okay. She and Merle said they plan to attend the next dance, so I'm going to meet them there." That was all he'd say.

Drake just sat at the kitchen table stuffing his face while I talked with Dad. He was watching my reactions very carefully to see if I was going to adjust to this news.

I was cool with the news. I knew how it felt to be lonely. It was just strange hearing about my parent's date.

The next weekend JL was due home for laundry drop off. When I could get him alone I shared the news about Daddy's dance.

"JL, I need to talk with you," I started our conversation after Daddy went back to work from lunch.

"What the problem?" He asked.

169

"It depends on how you look at it. Daddy is starting to go out and he has met with some old friends who have a lady friend he's interested in." I told him. "Do you have a problem with this? I asked.

"Nah, I promised Mama I wouldn't keep him from finding someone else. Rachel, she made me swear." He shared.

"She made me promise too. I just didn't know she had talked with you. She was concerned about him being alone. I actually felt her relax after I promised." I told him.

"Sis, let's deal with this fear now, between the two of us, and just wish him the best. Mama did everything for him. He really needs that again. No matter how hard you try to take care of him, he needs something more,-get it?" He laughed.

Daddy and Joan started dating regularly after the second dance he attended. She was a nice lady; one I think Mama would have approved.

As my pregnancy got further along, my appetite increased as well. I gained so much weight I had to have help getting in and out of bed. It was a good thing Drake changed shifts just so he could help me out of bed in the middle of the night when I had to go the bathroom, (which was every few hours).

I didn't have anything to do but laundry and cooking. Most days were spent laying around reading romance novels, watching television dramas and snacking. Daddy started getting concerned about my lack of exercise. He took me to the new mall in Belmont a couple of nights each week, so we could walk around. He liked to people watch. This also gave us chances to talk and really get to know each other. We even laughed one time when I got stuck in a diner's booth. You would think that father and child would already know each other well, but we didn't.

It was during some of those evenings I shared how unhappy I was right after I got married and how I didn't like living in our old house. I even shared my doubts about whether Drake and I were going to make our marriage work. I told him I sometimes thought about Daniel and this bothered me. I wasn't sure if it was because of the way we broke up or if it was something else that kept him on my mind a lot. He explained the ones that got away would always make us wonder what might have been. We seemed to connect more during those few months than we had the whole previous 21 years of my life. He even asked me if I had been a good girl before I got married. I knew what he meant. I just smiled and told him Drake was my one and only. This seemed to make him happy. It wasn't a lie. Drake was my first and only, I just hadn't waited until we were married.

Early in the morning on Friday, August 27th, 1976 I went to the doctor for my regular checkup. I was hurting. Dr. Sapp told me I wasn't ready. The pain in my back didn't stop all day. I hurt so bad my tears were uncontrollable. How could I hurt this bad if I wasn't in labor?

I begged Drake to stay home, "Please don't go to work this afternoon. Call in and blame it on me. Please don't leave me alone. I'm scared."

"What do I need to do? Should I call the doctor or something? He asked.

"No, this morning the doctor told me I wasn't ready. I must be having false labor pains or something." I answered.

When Daddy and Joan came home from their dinner date, she took one look at me and was convinced I was in labor. "Drake put your hand on Rachel's stomach and feel. If it tightens followed by a pain, she'll let you know."

We found I was having bad pains about every ten minutes. This convinced everyone to get me to the hospital. Thirty-six minutes after midnight, Emily Darlene Newton was born. Our little butterball was blonde haired, ten and a half pounds, nineteen inches long. We had been expecting a boy most of my pregnancy due to my physical indicators and the baby's heartbeat. It was a surprise for us to have a girl.

Drake called his parents with the news, "We have a girl, and she is a little cutie. Not the little man they told us was coming, but I can't be happier." He told his Mama.

She asked, "Did you and Rachel have a girl's name picked out just in case?

"We decided to name her after Rachel's Mama. Her name is Emily Darlene." He replied.

"I think that name is lovely. The whole Newton family is going to be pleased you've had a little girl. There hasn't been a girl in the family for many, many years. Tell Rachel I'll be there

172

tomorrow to help. She'll need me especially after she and the baby are released. I can get things ready beforehand. Jason told me a while back I would be welcome to stay in the guest room when the baby was born. I can't wait to see her Drake." She babbled on excitedly.

The next few days for me were different indeed. I was either laughing or crying. My hormones were out of control. I was grateful for my training, so I knew what was happening. Otherwise, I might be asking for help from the psych ward.

I was glad when Drake's mom arrived; I needed my Mama during those days and Mrs. Newton's presence really helped. She was so kind and good-natured. The baby just lit up her life. As I watched her with Darlene I wished Mama could see my precious bundle of joy. I had to believe Mama was watching us and loving every second.

I had worked in the nursery many times during my nights at the hospital so holding and caring for a newborn wasn't strange to me. It was just nice watching all this care being given to my little one. This child was all mine. The feeling was mind-boggling and joyous. What would our future be?

After Mrs. Newton went home, I had a routine established for Darlene. She easily slept, only waking me once each night to eat. She was such a good baby. Drake was so scared to hold her. Changing her diaper was out of the question, but he loved watching me do things for her-especially at first.

Daddy stayed in awe of her. He thought it was the neatest thing when she started eating cereal from an Infa-Feeder at two months of age. He said it looked like I had a syringe stuck in her mouth and was pumping her full. At cereal time, she became a little piglet and it made her so full she slept all night.

Yes, we had a little piglet, but the Mama was a hog. I'd lost a few pounds when the baby was born but then I turned around and gained all of them back. I ate everything in front of me. If it wasn't in front of me I went and got it. I was huge and didn't care. Drake never mentioned that I was getting too big, so I didn't think it was a problem. Drake's Mama bought me several things to wear that accommodated my huge size. I was eating and loving bars of candy, bags of chips, cakes, pies, or ice cream. If I wanted sweets, I ate them, and I was addicted to coffee with lots of creamers.

OLD FRIENDS, NEW AQUAINTANCES

Things have been going just too good lately. We need to mess things up a bit. Let me visit the past to see what I can do to change the course of things, Evil said to himself.

*****

One night before Drake went to work, Daddy and Joan told us they had news to share.

Daddy started out saying, "We are going to get married soon and want you to know."

"When's the date? I asked.

"Probably in the next week or two. We will be moving her things here soon. That leads me to something else I have been thinking about but I need your opinion." He said.

"I think I know what you are going to ask Daddy. Were you hoping we wouldn't mind moving back into the old house so you two could have privacy?" I asked.

"Yes and no,-we need our privacy, but I don't want you to move back into that old house. I was considering buying a trailer and drilling a well farther down the road. I remember you hated living there after you got married. I don't want you to live there again." He said. "What you say to that?"

"You're going to buy us a trailer?" Drake and I asked in unison.

"I'm planning to find a nice used one. If the prices are right when we look, then we'll go from there." He told us.

That's when Drake spoke up, "We've saved up a good amount of money since we moved in here with you, so we can help. What do you think, Rachel? I like the idea."

"Can we go looking tomorrow?" I asked Daddy. "Or do you want to go with us?

"I want the two of you to do the footwork then come back and report to me when you think you've found something reasonable. Keep in mind, I'll have the well and pump put in so my budget will be limited." He informed.

I was so excited! I was finally going to have a place of my own. Somewhere I'd never lived before. I could hardly sleep that night thinking about our adventure tomorrow.

We got up early the next morning, dressed Darlene, packed her gear and took off on our hunt. We went to several mobile home dealerships but found nothing we could afford. Next, we checked the newspaper advertisements. The first one we came across was in a mobile home park. It was about ten years old and in good condition. It had two bedrooms and one bath. It was just the ticket, so we called Daddy and told him about it.

Being the wheeler and dealer that he was before he started farming, he could talk the owner down several hundred more dollars from his asking price. Drake and I could buy it with our savings. This really made Daddy happy since he was paying for the rest of the set up and moving fees. He covered the well, the septic system, the electric pole and the gas lines needed for cooking and heating. We were responsible for the telephone line and the electrical company hookups.

We were in our new/used trailer just days before Daddy and Joan got married.

I hadn't been to church in a long time. It felt strange being there for Daddy's wedding, and I felt guilty for not being a more faithful member. With all that had been going on in my life, I hadn't even thought about attending church. I talked to God and prayed every now and then. It was my justification for a lack of commitment.

I told Drake after the service, "We need to start going to church again as a family. We need a church home."

"Okay, let's plan to come back here tomorrow and feel things out." He agreed. "I'll take us out for lunch afterward."

"We've had too much success and made progress keeping her away from Him. Something must stop them. They can't be allowed access into His presence again." Evil expressed to his friends. "Do something that will keep them up all night, so they won't feel like doing anything but sleep the next day."

*****

That night, Darlene kept us both up by screaming. I hate it when she cries, and I can't tell what her problems are. Usually, she is such a good baby, so when she does cry, I know something is wrong. Drake came up with the idea about driving around.

"Honey, you know every time we go for a ride, Darlene falls asleep right off the bat. I will try anything to get her to sleep." He said.

"Let me get my shoes and a coat to put over my bed clothes. I can't take this crying. She is not feverish, or I'd be worried. I don't know what to think." I agreed.

Twenty minutes into the drive, Darlene was asleep. When we pulled up at the trailer to get out, we were almost too scared to touch her for fear she would wake up. We were exhausted. It was two in the morning and we hadn't had a moment's peace since before she ate dinner. I can honestly say, when it came time to get up for church, we both knew we'd be the ones asleep during service instead of Darlene.

Daddy and Joan came home the following week. We loved our new home. I liked being responsible for Drake and Darlene only.

We were free to live our own lives and enjoy friendships again. We started inviting some of our old church friends over and they invited us in turn. During, our nights out with friends, we'd pack Darlene's food and clothes, so we could put her down on a pallet to sleep after she ate. She was such a good baby we could

178

feed her and put her down anywhere during those days and nothing we did would disturb her.

*****

"It's time to throw another wrench into their little mix. Greed, Lust, and wrong associations should do it. We'll get them focused on their own desires and ruin the family unit from the inside out. Happiness is in not the plan. Jealousy and Loneliness will also play into my plan. I just love it when we aren't being watched so closely." Evil exclaimed in joy.

Jesus can't watch when someone sins, so we'll keep the pot stirred up. We will keep the little family very involved in their own wants and needs He will never be thought of again. So, much fun! I can't wait." Evil laughed,

*****

Jesus heard Evil's conversation and was very angry. "Father, help me watch patiently, I know there has to be a time of separation between Rachel and me. I'll rest in your promise to her that says, 'where sin abounds so will grace'. I have the victory already." He professed.

"Yes, Son we do have the victory already with Rachel, but Satan thinks he has been set loose to destroy her. Once he has tried to do this, she will bow and crave the truth once again. Our patience will have its perfect work." God explained.

*****

Daddy called a family meeting one night when all of us were available. "I don't like the sound of this meeting," I told Drake. "What could it possibly mean? He's so serious."

"It's probably nothing so don't get your panties in a wad yet." He snipped.

When we got to their house, Daddy started out by saying, "I'm considering a life-changing decision. Before I go through with my plans, I want to know what you think. I'm getting too old to continue farming by myself. If one of you wants to farm I need to know. JL, do you plan to take over the farm one day? Or do you plan to move on?

"No Daddy, I've never wanted to farm. I don't mean to hurt your feelings, but I hated it every summer when you made me help. I want no part of farming." JL spoke up.

Then Daddy asked Drake, "How about you, son? You come from a dairy farm background. Would you be interested in doing something here for you and Rachel?"

"No sir, I like what I'm doing right now. I thought I'd like to be a rancher, but I don't think so anymore." Drake answered.

"Rachel, honey, do you like living here on the farm?" Daddy asked me.

"Daddy, I've always wanted to be a city girl. I'm like JL. I hated working in the garden every summer too." I don't think I'd like to farm," was my reply. Then I asked him. "What are you trying to tell us, Daddy?"

"Well, if none of you want to farm, or hire someone to farm for you, then we are going to sell out and move back into Belmont. I plan to give you and JL some of your inheritance by building each of you a house. Of course, I'd wait to build JL's after he got married. His money would be saved until then. What do you think?" He asked.

"You'd build us a new house?" I asked

"That's my plan. To provide an investment and give you a place of your own." He said.

I was so shocked I couldn't think. Happy, confused, and very excited about having my own new house.

"I think I like the idea," I finally replied.

"What do you think, Drake?" I asked my husband

"It's your call." He answered me.

Daddy just sat in his chair and listened to the three of us discuss his plan, but his mind was set. He had felt in his heart all along that we didn't want to farm.

Weeks later he put the farm on the market for sale, got a bid and took the offer. He was very excited! He called me to talk about it one night at dinner.

"I did it, Rachel. I actually sold the place." He shared with me.

"I got enough money for it Joan and I can live comfortably for a long time off the interest it will accrue. Then we can make arrangements for the final balance of the proceeds to be split between the three of you at my death." He told me.

He continued, "If everything goes along with my plan, the payment installments will pay the taxes and I'll bank the rest-of-the money for emergencies. I feel so much better now about our futures. Now we can find land and start planning what kind of houses we want to build."

When Drake got home that night from work, I could not wait to share what Daddy had told me.

"Drake, I have good news," I told him when he came in the door.

"I bet the farm sold," he said.

"Yep, and we can start looking for a lot to build our house on now. I'm so excited," I said.

Then Drake spoke up, "Rachel, I don't want to live in town. I don't like living in congested areas or on busy streets." "We need to find a place just out of town but close to things, so you won't feel like you are still in the country?"

"We won't know what we'll find until we start to look, so let's don't worry about areas yet. I agree with you to look for property outside of the city limits." I answered.

One day, Drake asked me, "Would you care if I invite this guy I've met at work and his family over for dinner soon? We haven't had any good friends our whole marriage. It seems from the start we've had all this drama with school, work and your Mama getting sick. I think it's time we made some friends to pal around with."

"I miss having a girlfriend to talk with. It's different from having work-related friends. I think I'd love having someone over for dinner." I told him.

"Who is this person? Do I know him?" I asked.

"I don't think you know him. His name is JT Fables and his wife's name is Dana. They have a son about one and a half or two." He informed.

"Are they from here?" I asked.

"I don't think so. I haven't asked." He said.

"When you see him at work tonight ask if they can come over Saturday for a fish fry. Let's plan a feast." I said excitedly.

On Saturday, I fussed with getting the placed cleaned for that night. I took some fish out of our freezer to thaw. I went to the store while Drake watched over Darlene, so I could buy everything else we needed. I was really having fun. This was my first time entertaining and I was very excited.

When they arrived, Drake let them in and to my surprise, JT's wife was a girl I knew from junior high. She was the friend I did basketball drills with me when I got hurt.

"Oh, my God!" I screamed as I ran over to grab her in a hug. "It is such a small world! How have you been?" I asked her.

"Great!" She said.

That night we had so much fun sharing our experiences since school. Drake and JT enjoyed comparing fishing and hunting stories. It was a good night for all.

It seemed Daddy and I did more searching for property than Drake and I did. Finally, we found land he and I both really liked. It was about three miles from town and the subdivision wasn't fully developed yet. When we showed it to Drake, he loved our choice. Our next step was to find a house plan we liked and that fit into Daddy's budget. That was fun.

As we watched our house being built, Drake and I selected carpets, paint colors, tiles, and fixtures. I don't think I've ever had so much fun. We'd also been saving for a new living room and dining set for the new place. We decided to use some of the old furniture that had been in storage since we moved from the old home to Daddy's house.

Dana and I would pack up our kids and go looking for things to put in my new house. We could shop for hours. I think she was having as much fun as I was. We were becoming close friends. It seemed my life was peaceful and happy for a change. After Drake and I moved into our new place, I seemed to be with Dana more and with Drake less. He and JT would spend time together hunting and fishing while she and I would do things with our kids.

When Drake bought a fishing boat, he and I didn't spend any time together. We didn't even see much of each other on the weekends because he and his buddies were always gone.

It was during those times, Dana told me how unhappy she was in her marriage. She and JT were talking about divorce. It saddens me because I couldn't talk to Drake about it. She had confided in me and didn't want others to know.

It wasn't long before they split up and everyone knew. I felt I had been dishonest somehow with my husband by not discussing this with him. He was extremely fond of JT and I was loyal to Dana, so their separation divided us. We weren't fighting. We just couldn't talk about them without fussing about who was at fault when their problems weren't ours at all.

We were still friendly with both even after their divorce but not as a couple. I was either with Dana or Drake was with JT.

Dana and I were so much alike people often thought we were related. We liked the same music, books, food, and clothes. Our favorite thing to do was read romance novels. We were always sharing our books and talking about the characters in the books. Why couldn't we find a prince charming like our books talked about and have romantic experiences like those we were reading about?

I was happy when she met Robert Miller and I was happy for her when she married him a few months later. I was even happier when Ginger came along nine months later. My friend Dana was finally going to be happy, so we thought.

Drake didn't like Dana's new husband at all which caused problems for me and Dana to have a friendship. Drake didn't even like me visiting in their house because of Robert. He said the guy creeped him out and he didn't want Darlene and me over there. Dana and the kids were welcomed at our house, but Drake didn't want us going over there. I developed an attitude and got a little rebellious. How could he expect me to stay at home when he didn't want to be with us? He only wanted to do boy stuff with his friends.

To please Drake, I made it a point not to go over when Robert was around. But I wasn't going to let these two ruin Dana's and my friendship. We had become too close, and I loved having a girlfriend in my life again. However, Robert seemed to always be at home! It limited our time together except to talk on the telephone and we'd do that for hours.

Most of my time was spent reading romance novels, watching daytime dramas, talking on the telephone, and taking care of the house and Darlene. During those days, I gained even more weight because I was lonely. All my friends were happily married to partners who wanted to do things with them and be with them. My partner found reasons to be with anyone else. I cooked for kicks and ate what I cooked.

PLAYING INTO THE DEVIL'S HANDS

It wasn't long after Dana's baby girl, Ginger, was born that she and I decided to do something about our weight. We were about the same size and needed the challenge to keep us on track. We began by counting calories, comparing notes, and helping each other when we were tempted to eat wrong. It took us almost a year to get back to our high school weights again.

When Dana started really looking good and getting her figure back, Robert became abusive to her. She finally had to leave that marriage for her safety. Having nowhere to go, she and her kids moved in with her parents.

Drake's feelings about Robert were justified. He turned out to be a real creep and caused my friend a lot of stress. After she got out from under his control, she started sharing with me what had really happened in their relationship and how happy she was it was over. The only thing she got out of the relationship that mattered was her precious baby.

After her divorce from Robert, she and I felt the need to firm our bodies, so we started exercising. She did her workouts at the house, but I joined the YMCA. I couldn't commit to exercise if I had to stay at home. My home was my prison during those days and I needed an outlet.

The YMCA had a babysitting service. I took Darlene with me to let her play with other kids while I enjoyed the aerobics class and the spa. I was really feeling good about myself and could buy clothes that flattered my body.

188

Dana was interested again in dating and I started feeling jilted somehow when she was getting asked out for dates. Was I jealous of not having male attention? I didn't know what I was feeling. I wanted to be noticed, loved, and appreciated. I didn't want to watch my friend get what I wanted. So, secretly I started desiring what I shouldn't.

"We got her now," Evil said. "All we have to do is push her just a little bit more into infidelity and then her marriage is toast."

*****

When I was alone at home, I would fantasize about a different life. I'd picture myself like one of the characters on my daytime drama or in my romance novels: loved, desired, fought and sought after. I didn't feel very likable or desirable. I sure wasn't getting the attention at home, I needed. Drake and I had sex, of course, but there was never any romance. I felt like an object for his pleasure, a maid, and caregiver instead of wife. We weren't even friends anymore.

One day I got a compliment that caused my self-esteem to soar. An instructor at the YMCA told me I was beautiful and had really changed my appearance since I began. He was flirting with me and caused me to crave more of the attention. So, not only did I go to the YMCA in the mornings, I went back in the afternoons after Drake went to work. I was obsessed with becoming fit and attractive.

In the evenings, after my workouts at the YMCA, Darlene and I would go over to Daddy's and Joan's new house. They had built theirs just two streets over from the YMCA which made it very convenient. I knew Daddy must be wondering what was going on. I'd never been one to exercise or do physical things so why now. On his front porch one night, I told him how unhappy I was, and I needed a change to make me feel better about myself.

"Be careful, honey. Marriage is a job that needs constant work. If you don't share your feelings with Drake, he will never know how to make it right then you'll never know if he wants to." He shared seriously.

"Daddy, I've tried with little hints here and there. It's like talking to with a brick wall. I'll ask him how I look, and he'll say something stupid that does nothing for my ego. I'll ask to go on a date and he'll just laugh. I'm tired and lonely." I told him.

"I just want your happiness, honey. Try a little harder, for me, okay?" He asked.

Even Daddy didn't understand the deep void in my heart.

On my birthday that November, Dana, and another girlfriend wanted to take me out to a supper club in town that had a live band with dancing. I innocently agreed to go, planning to let Darlene stay with Dana's parents and play with her kids. My only stipulation was to leave at eleven to get us home before Drake got home from work. I knew he would freak out if I came in a few hours after he did, dragging our baby in that late.

190

I bought myself a couple of new outfits since I'd lost weight. On our girl's night out, I picked my favorite and drove over to Dana's parents.

When I walked in the door, Dana's brother gave me a cat call then said. "You look good enough to eat! Boy, you're pretty in that getup. It's a shame you're taken." He said.

That made my ego soar. When I got to Dana's room she also whistled then said, "You look great. I don't think I've ever seen you look so sexy. Are you trying to turn every guy's eye tonight?" She asked.

"Maybe I need to feel desirable even if it is for one night," I said it jokingly even though I truly meant it sincerely.

When our friend, Anne Pierce, arrived we went directly to the nightclub. I was very excited. I'd never been to such a place. I'd been to dances before but never where alcohol was served. The music was uplifting and made me feel great. I even ordered myself a glass of wine, promising myself I would only have two at the most. I was the one driving and I wasn't used to drinking.

The slow burn of the wine gave me confidence and a sense of empowerment I didn't have before. The beat of the music made me feel sexy. As the night progressed, I noticed that indeed I had power over men in that place. I hadn't danced so much with different guys at a dance in my whole life, not even when I was younger going to the fundraisers for school. I just didn't attract guys well. But tonight, I was a guy magnet and it felt wonderful. The time flew by before I knew it we had to go. I had to get home

191

before Drake. Even though he knew I was going out with the girls, I didn't want to give him any reasons to fuss or complain.

When Darlene and I got home, I put her to bed and then took a shower. I washed my hair and removed all my makeup. I knew I must smell like a large cigarette from all the smoke in the club. When Drake did come home, I was fresh and wide awake. He asked if we had a good time and I said of course we did, that we had a few drinks and let our hair down.

I was sure this night was the beginning of more nights of fun to come. This lonely worm had turned into a sexy butterfly and wanted to have more fun filled nights.

Each night after that was torture until I could return to the club and let out the person I was keeping so concealed during the day. I loved being desired even if it was just to be a dance partner. Every other night or so, Dana and I would plan for the kids to stay with her parents. We became two vixens ready to see how many conquests we could have each night out.

"**Perfect**," Evil said "We've got her now. Let's introduce her to someone she can't resist. We know from comments she's made what type of guys turn her on, so let's nail the plan shut, giving her desires free reign. Her resistance to temptation will be futile."

*****

After about the third week of this. Adonis walked into the club. This man was gorgeous and had eyes to die for. This man was something fantasies were made of. He was interested only in me out of dozens of women in that place. His advances kept getting a little more intense with each slow dance. I couldn't resist the seductive words that rang in my ears or the strength his body was exuding that overpowered my mind.

Then towards the end of one of the slow dances, he kissed me and told me he liked me very much. I was done. My heart swelled as if it had been filled with the sweetest news I'd ever heard. Drake didn't exist to me anymore after those words. My heart immediately hardened against my marriage commitments. A dreamboat desired me. A man any woman would give everything she had to be with.

The curiosity of being with another man was tremendously thrilling. I could no longer resist after the third night of the same emotional rollercoaster. The forbidden happened.

"Now we have her! We have her mind, will, and emotions to play with for as long as we want. He has lost! He has lost!" Was the cheer of Evil.

Preservation was so weak at this point. Everything he tried to do for Rachel was an effort. She didn't have any words for him to act on lately, so his power was limited.

*****

This happened repeatedly for weeks. Every night I'd find an excuse to go out, leaving Darlene with Dana or her parents so I could be with this man who wanted me, who found me sexy and irresistible.

With the forbidden acts came the inevitable. One morning after about a month and a half of indulging in immorality, I woke up trying to vomit up my toenails. The unthinkable and the unwanted were a reality. I was pregnant. Now what?

I thought I had taken precautions. Maybe during my wine indulgence, I'd forgotten to use the preparation correctly. I couldn't remember. All I knew was this baby was not my husband's. Drake and I hadn't had sex in weeks. Being intimate with Drake would make me feel guilty and a little sick, so I always came up with an excuse to say no.

Drake wasn't stupid. He knew something was up with me. I had shut him completely out of my life and nothing he said or did could get my attention. When I told him the truth,-that I was pregnant with another man's baby, he was not surprised. He was extremely hurt becoming very pitiful and needy which made my respect for him hit rock bottom.

I truly don't know how Drake dealt with me or my problem during this time. He'd do anything to try and win me back. My lover didn't want the baby. I couldn't stand the thought of living with Drake after having another man's child. The decision was made to terminate the pregnancy leaving Drake with the financial burden.

Unbelievably, you don't have to go to a weird place to have this procedure. I went to my Gynecologist (the doctor who delivered Darlene) who offered to do this awful thing for me. He even made the procedure sound like it was necessary, so Drake's insurance would cover most of the cost.

I thought I was okay with this. I did not allow my mind to dwell on it I rationalized it was necessary for all concerned. Drake stayed with me during the whole experience. After he left to go to work, my lover/baby Daddy came to see me.

He told me he still wanted to be with me. Then he dropped the bomb! He needed to divorce his wife first. That was it, I was crazy. Had I heard him correctly? Did he just say to me he was also married? We both were guilty of adultery. His wife found out about us a few days earlier. She moved, taking his son and all their belongings to her Mama's in another state. He was now available. That was funny. We both were literally unavailable but had no regard for the feelings and concerns of our marriage partners. At that point, his appeal to me changed drastically.

"Change of plan. Now we are going to convince her she is hell bound. She has broken three of the Ten Commandments: not to lie, not to commit adultery and not to kill. She will believe she's doomed. We will make her hate herself and fall into complete despair. Depression has a turn to make her self-destruct."

*****

When I was released from the hospital, I hated myself. I was disgusted with Drake and I was suspicious of this other man. I knew I was going to hell. Everything I believed and deemed horrible, I had done. I knew my mind, as well as my heart, were ruined beyond repair. When my Daddy found out, he was so disappointed and confounded he didn't want to talk to me for weeks.

The only ones I had on my side for sure were my precious Darlene and Dana. My emotions were completely unstable at that time. When I filed for divorce, no one was surprised. Since I wasn't good company or exciting, my admirer lost interest and went off to find his wife.

I was alone. Drake moved into an apartment in town. I didn't have a job and bills were screaming to be paid. What was I going to do? Night after night I couldn't sleep. If I did, my dreams were tormented. The only thing that kept me moving forward was Darlene's needs. I still had her to take care of and nothing or no one was going to keep me from doing that.

I read the newspaper each morning to see what jobs were available. I found a receptionist job at a large local church. The religion wasn't what I'd been raised to believe but I didn't care. I needed a job. I was granted an interview because of my education. When the Pastor asked if I smoked or had been divorced, I couldn't lie. I was in church and I knew he probably smelled the smoke on me so I told him the truth. I was promptly told I wasn't what they needed. They had judged me by what I did instead of my degree in secretarial science.

I applied for job after job with no success. I finally went to an employment agency that found jobs for people for a fee. When they learned, I had artistic ability, they sent me to a local interior design shop that specialized in picture framing and home décor. The owner of the shop, Mr. Alston and I hit it off immediately. I was hired for the job. Now, I had to come up with the funds to pay the employment agency. How was I going to do that?

A light switch went on in my head. I'd use Daddy's acquaintances at the bank and apply for a loan. I marched right into our bank, asked for Daddy's friend who was an officer there and told him what I needed. After a few minutes, he excused himself. He returned with a check payable to me for $400. He told me that he called my Daddy. I was shocked to learn Daddy agreed to co-sign the loan for me. I was overwhelmed. Daddy hadn't wanted anything to do with me but here he was supporting me in this action. I was very grateful.

I called Daddy that afternoon and told him how much I loved him. I explained that he was making it possible for me to support Darlene and myself doing something I loved, dealing with art.

"Honey, I know you are a good person. You're my kid and I'll always love you. I just couldn't deal with what was going on at the time. I had to let the chips fall where they would and stay out of your life. Your well being is my main concern and I won't let you or Darlene ever go without your basic needs. I'm proud you wanted to take out a loan by yourself, but you needed credit, so I was called," He told me.

"Thanks again, Daddy. I was scared you had deserted me because of Drake." I shared.

Because Dana didn't work outside of the house, she agreed to take care of Darlene for me in the afternoons. Earlier, Drake and I had enrolled Darlene in a church pre-school and she was almost finished with her first year. We decided she would continue with Drake making the payments for her classes. Everything else concerning our married life was to be determined by the court system later. We agreed Darlene's needs were both of our concerns, so we put our issues aside for her.

My first day on my new job was awesome. The owners were wonderful people and my co-workers were great. Arrangements were made with them for me to take my lunch break at noon, so I could get Darlene take her to Dana and then get right back to work.

After my first week and my first paycheck, Dana convinced me to party that night. We made plans to go to the club and have fun. Even though my divorce was not final yet, I was considered a single woman. I was legally able to do and be with whom I wanted so my conscience wasn't so conflicted about this anymore. I was still dealing with nightmares, self-loathing, and guilt but I knew I had to move on for me as well as Darlene.

To save money, Dana and I would buy a bottle of our favorite wine. We'd have a drink before we even went in the club. Then we'd go outside together later to drink another glass. This way we didn't have to buy so much from the bar. We always hoped we'd get lucky enough to have a guy buy us a few drinks thus saving our wine for another night. We had so much fun during those times just flirting and dancing.

I knew I couldn't get totally wasted on booze or I wouldn't be able to drive. To be safe I promised myself I'd stop after three glasses every time. I liked to dance so I never wanted to sit still long enough to get drunk. I went out to have fun not booze it up. If we didn't find action at one club we'd go to another. There were about six places in town we could visit so I had to stay sober to drive us around.

About two months after my adulterous ordeal, my divorce was finalized. I decided to seriously date again. Men were a dime a dozen but very few I met were interesting enough to do something with outside of clubbing. My heart was still too raw for anything more than flirtations. After about two dates, most of them never called again because I wasn't easy.

199

Work was great. I'd become good friends with Mr. Alston and his daughter. They made me feel like part of a family. The place was really homey and laid back. If we got our work done and kept things clean, we could associate and cut up. Mr. Alston had several friends that would visit the shop and drink with him in the afternoons. They became my friends as well. Every afternoon we would have discussions about our latest nights out on the town, talking about who we were with, what we had done, but always keeping the conversations friendly.

Preservation knew he still had a command from the Lord to protect Rachel, but his power was limited because of her actions, beliefs, and no words to help him at the time. He decided to put some good people in her path to keep her focused on caring instead of getting lost in her own shame. He worked on it immediately.

I met a nice guy one night at the club. His name was Slade and from the first moment I laid eyes on him I knew there was going to be a connection. I wasn't wrong. He was drawn to me too. He was funny and very good looking. The more time we spent together the more I wanted to have a romantic relationship again. Before I fell into a trap like the last time, I had to make my life secure.

I made an appointment with my doctor as soon as possible to have a uterine device inserted to prevent pregnancies. I didn't want to go through that hell again. I still wasn't over the guilt and the pain I caused a good person. That would always haunt me. I had to take every precaution to guarantee I would never have to live through that again.

My boss, Mr. Alston, teased me about my plans. He didn't know the reason I was so stressed about having it done. The procedure was quick and easy. It was done in the doctor's office. I even went back to work soon after. Now I could relax mentally because I knew I had done the right thing.

Slade was great, but he kindly let me know right away he wasn't ready for a serious relationship. Slade's ex-wife hurt his feelings badly and he couldn't commit to anything serious yet. Friends with benefits were all he wanted. I agreed even though in my heart I felt it was wrong. Intimacy with Slade was comfortable and easy. We pleased each other, but the most important part of our relationship was the friendship.

We really did become great friends during our times together. We'd talk for hours at night on the phone, we'd play cards, go to movies, or just hang out. We would be each other's dates when events arose for either of us requiring an escort. My Daddy even liked Slade and so did Darlene.

His roommate, Jay, kept us apart. Jay was a party person and wanted a partner in crime to hang with. He would always make Slade feel guilty when he preferred to be with me and Darlene to just relax. Slade would go to please Jay and many times we'd even see each other at the clubs where we'd get together anyway.

Knowing how he felt about becoming serious, made it easier for me to go off with Dana other nights. I really did enjoy dancing and fellowshipping even if I did it without Slade. But sex I just couldn't do so freely. I wasn't made that way. I was raised believing in love and fidelity. Slade would be the only one for me until love arrived.

The friends with benefits lasted until I met John. This man swept me off my feet making me feel wonderful. Our relationship took off like a rocket. Had love finally showed up for me? Was this the man who would take me away from Slade? I was beginning to feel he was.

I thought John was the most romantic and caring person I'd ever met. He made me fall in love with him. He provided a type of relationship that was only written about in romance novels. He wasn't afraid to tell me he loved me while making every moment we had special. He'd treat me to expensive dinners, buy me jewelry and flowers and even buy Darlene some lovely presents. He wanted to spend time playing with her as well.

Summertime was here, and Mrs. Newton called wanting to know if I would allow Darlene to spend summer vacation with her and Mr. Newton. I assured her I wanted Darlene to always be close with them and I was delighted they wanted her. A few days later they planned to pick her up. It wasn't until after they were out of sight I felt my baby was leaving me and a void filled my heart.

Slade didn't like John at all, but he wouldn't tell me why. Many afternoons when Slade would visit before going home from work, he'd make comments I could do better, and I deserved to be happy. I dismissed the comments as resentments for not being intimate with him anymore. I think I really wanted him to be jealous.

I'll never forget one night when John was out of town on business and Slade called me around midnight. He was upset and said he needed to see me. I told him to come over. He arrived at my house more than slightly intoxicated and acted like he was mad at the world.

Because he was drunk, I insisted he stay the night and go home in the morning. Nothing happened between us but the next day he kept apologizing saying over and over, "If you only knew." "What in the daylights was he talking about?" I asked myself. Another mystery he wouldn't share.

"More fun guys." Evil told his companions. "She truly is a fertile cow. She just keeps giving us tools to make her life miserable. I love it that she is her own worst enemy. Don't you?"

Several days later, I awoke in a panic. The unthinkable was happening again. Same awful symptoms but this time with pain. I thought this can't be! Not again! I can't be pregnant! I'd made sure it couldn't happen!!!

I knew I had to tell John. I was hoping he would want to get married so we could provide this baby a good home. I asked him to take me to lunch so I could share the news and we could start making plans.

When he picked me up from work, I could tell he was in a bad mood. After we ordered our food, I looked up and saw some of Mr. Alston's friends come in the restaurant. I waved at them letting them know I saw them come in. John made a snide remark, "Those your new boyfriends?" I assured him they were just friends I knew from work.

After our food was served, I told him the news. My heart sank when he called me a lying whore and said I could go to hell before he'd take responsibility for the brat. He told me immediately that he'd pay for an abortion, but we would be through after that. I was so upset I had to excuse myself from the table to go to the lady's room. When I returned to the table, the waitress came over and told me the gentleman had left. Furthermore, the bill was ready when I wanted to leave.

I was shocked. The jerk not only left me stranded, he didn't pay for our meals either. I sat in my chair and started crying. I must have really been a pitiful sight. One of my friends, Al Winters, came over to check on me. I told him what happened. He paid for the food, even though I asked him not to. When he took me back to work he told the others what had happened.

Mr. Alston and Lena were very concerned. I told them how John had treated me and what he said. They were shocked. They also thought John was a great person. When I told, them, I was pregnant, I had their deepest sympathy and support. Mr. Alston said he'd work with me to keep minimal effect on my job. This meant a lot to me.

Dana was in a new relationship with a wonderful guy. They both wanted to take care of me. John sure didn't! All he wanted to do was pay me off and get rid of the problem.

When I told Slade the news, he apologized for not sharing some truths. He explained the mystery he kept from me the night he came over drunk and angry. That night he had seen John with another woman wining, dancing and treating her special. He knew John had fooled me into thinking we were going to eventually get married. When he saw John with someone else it made him see red.

I think out of guilt that same night, Slade offered to marry me. I almost took him up on it, but I couldn't do that to an innocent man. He was my good friend even in these awkward times. I needed good friends. I was really in a pickle. I was determined to keep the baby this time, even if I had to raise it alone.

When my doctor examined me, he found that the uterine device had severely slipped out of position and would have to come out. It would cause me serious problems the longer I waited. There was no hope in saving the baby. He explained removing it would destroy the sack the baby was living in causing the pregnancy to terminate.

This time I didn't have an insurance plan to fall back on, my doctor could only make an appointment at a clinic that specialized in abortions. He assured me this was the only way for me to get healthy again. The baby didn't have a chance for survival. The very thing that was supposed to prevent pregnancy failed and was now harming me and was going to kill my baby. I was finally a basket case, ready for the mental ward.

I was glad Darlene was still with her grandparents, so she didn't have to see me go through any of this. I contacted John, took the money he agreed to pay and asked Dana and her new friend to take me to the clinic early the next day. My appointment was at 9:00 a.m. After the procedure, we would need to stay over one night in a hotel close by the clinic to make sure I was physically okay before their physicians would agree to let me go home.

Physically I survived, but mentally I was destroyed. I cried all the way home. How could I ever live with myself knowing what I had allowed because I was such a scared and needy person?

When I got into Belmont, Dana called Slade, so he could come over. He just held me because he didn't know how to ease my pain. I was heartsick and physically drained. He was my rock staying with me that night making sure I ate and was comfortable. Hour after hour he would remain quiet never mentioning what had happened. He was just available. He was really a good friend.

ANNIHILATION

Evil spoke up in their latest meeting. "Her mind and emotions are putties in our hands. The guilt we've caused her to feel is irreversible and she is punishable by death. She has nothing left but judgment we've won!"

I went back to work the Monday after I'd had my baby killed. There wasn't any reason not to. Why should I care what happened to me? Darlene needed to be taken care of and child support alone couldn't do that. I needed to work to provide other needs.

All day long, Dana or Slade would call to check on me. I'd assure them I was fine, and I wasn't doing anything stupid. Mr. Alston watched me like a hawk too. He was proud I came into work. He said I needed the distraction. That afternoon, Al came by to visit with everyone. He was very sweet to me. I didn't have to ask him whether he knew. I could tell by his actions and remarks someone had told him my business. I didn't care.

After a few days, my exhaustion demanded sleep. My rest remained fitful and disturbed by nightmares. I really was not well.

Summer was ending, and I was getting concerned Darlene wouldn't return before her school started. I was panicking due to the guilt I had in my heart. I was so scared she had been taken from me that I called and asked if I could come and pick her up. I needed to hold her in my arms. The Newtons agreed to meet halfway so I could get my baby.

207

One afternoon, Darlene was in a hyperactive mood refusing to mind anybody. When we left Dana's parents to go home, I had to repeatedly tell her to sit down and not stand up in the car seat. Seatbelts were not mandatory then, so she was all over the car while I was trying to drive. Reaching over to force her to sit down, I took my eyes off the road for a second. When I looked up I was already on another car's bumper going about 30 miles an hour. When the impact occurred I only saw one vital thing, my little daughter's head breaking the windshield then her falling back and hitting the dash of the car. She was hurt, and my heart almost stopped. "What had I done? Had I killed another child?" My heart screamed. "No! No! No!"

"Good job Fear, you've made her so scared she's about to have a heart attack. Keep applying the pressure." Satan said.

It was a bad accident involving three cars. Mine was the one at fault. A policeman was there almost instantly wanting to discuss the accident. I wouldn't talk with him because a store owner who saw the wreck came out of his shop and took my child inside. I knew the store owner meant well, but at the time, I was panic-stricken. I threw my purse at the policeman telling him to find whatever he needed. I had to go. My child was hurt, and a stranger was taking her away.

I was very fortunate that the policeman was sympathetic. He followed me into the store carrying my purse to check things out. Once inside he asked an attending EMT to check Darlene while we talked. I asked him to please call her father and gave him the information. Then I asked him to please call my Daddy to be with me.

After the policeman retrieved all the information he needed from me, EMT's took Darlene, and me to the hospital in an ambulance. They were afraid Darlene had a bad concussion. When we got there, we were escorted to an examining area for tests and x-rays.

When Drake arrived, he was furious. He screamed, "Were you drunk or something? The way you live lately I wouldn't be surprised if you weren't high on something!"

"No, I'm not drunk! She was acting out in the car and when I looked up it was too late. I was already in the back of the other car." I informed him.

Daddy walked in with Joan. He asked if I was all right. I told him I only had a few bruises and bumps, but Darlene had a head injury. They stayed with me until the doctors said Darlene was well enough to leave.

The doctors assured Drake and me that Darlene was going to be fine. She would need to rest for a few days. I was so grateful for those words. We all left after Drake gave the hospital his insurance information for Darlene and I gave them my name and address, so they could bill me for my expenses. Daddy and Joan drove Darlene and me home because my car had been impounded.

That night the telephone rang constantly. Darlene's other grandparents called, Dana called, Slade called, Al called, and Drake called about every hour to check on Darlene. Calls kept coming and coming preventing us from resting until late. I appreciated the concern but all I wanted to do was cuddle with my little girl and thank the good Lord for sparing her.

The next morning Daddy came over to check on us. He offered to call my insurance company. He was a great help. I didn't know what to say but he arranged for a rental car, so I'd have a way to travel. He informed me since the wreck was my fault my premiums were going up. There might also be other expenses I'd have to take care of soon per my insurance agent.

I had a ticket from the police officer at the scene I needed to pay quickly. I wasn't prepared for just how much the fee would be. When I stood at the window to pay, I was told I needed $500.00 up front. I had to sit down it shocked me so much. I asked the lady if I could use her phone, so I could call Daddy. One more time, he bailed me out. He came to my rescue and paid my fine without batting an eye. I was grateful, and I promised I would pay him back.

Over the next few weeks, my paycheck couldn't stretch to cover my expenses plus the issues involved in the accident. Dana suggested I take in a border. I could use someone to rent my extra bedroom and help with some of my financial needs. Splitting costs of electricity and telephone would make life easier. I placed an ad in the paper stating what I was offering to a female renter.

To my surprise, I got a call the very first day the ad appeared. The lady that called turned out to be the sister of one of my friends from college. When Sandra arrived to inspect my house and extra bedroom, we knew the rental arrangement was going to work for both of us. Things were looking up.

I had to go back to my doctor for a checkup after my procedure. I was told I needed birth control pills. "Why?" I asked.

The doctor grinned and said "That should be obvious. If you plan to be sexually active the pill is the only sure course for you to take. Also, we need to get your hormones normalized so you'll feel better."

Being sexually active was a joke to me at that time. I didn't even want to think about it. I knew the nature of things and needs of the human body would kick in eventually, so I agreed to take the pill.

Dana and her new boyfriend, Mac, were getting very involved. They were so into each other I didn't have anyone to go out and have fun with. Sandra also had a boyfriend and spent most of her time with him. If I wanted to go out, I had to go alone which made me feel desperate for attention. Most nights I stayed home alone with Darlene.

I was still friends with Slade. He came around from time to time and we would just hang out, but our relationship seemed strained. I don't think he knew how to deal with my moods. I wasn't as carefree as I had been. The issue of benefits at the time was out of the question. One night during one of his visits he outright asked me "Why not?"

"Slade, I'm what doctors call a fertile Myrtle and I've only been on the pill for a few weeks. Give me a break! It's nothing personal. I'm scared and very nervous about sex right now."

Thank goodness, he understood. Slade was one of the most caring and compassionate people I'd ever met.

He said, "No, biggie, I was just curious. I was afraid to even hug you because you acted like you hated me at times."

"No, dear, I don't hate you. I hate myself. You, I adore." I assured him.

Al Winters was making his presence known. He was a nice person. He showed up after his day's work at the shop where I worked and just talked with all of us. He even asked if I'd meet him for lunch a couple of times before I took Darlene to Dana's. We'd meet at a buffet down the street from Dana's parent's house, so it wouldn't take long to eat. Darlene would get a good meal and our lunch would be paid for which was a good plan in my book.

A few times, Slade and Al unexpectedly crossed paths. I liked Al, but I really wanted Slade's company more. When both showed up at the house, Slade usually left. I never understood why Slade felt he had to be the one to back away. It puzzled me greatly.

Being without a girlfriend to go out with made me anxious. I needed to let my hair down some. Being cooped up at home all the time was getting to me. One afternoon I called to ask Slade his plans for the night. He told me he and his roommate, Jay, had planned to play poker. I really needed some time out. After my conversation with Slade, I called Al asking if he wanted to go to the club. I didn't care who I was with I just wanted to go out.

That was the start of more nights with Al. We danced, had fun, and I didn't feel committed. I wasn't aware his feelings were different. He started claiming me.

One time we were together, a waitress I'd come to know followed me in the lady's room to give me a warning. "Be careful with that one," she said. "Why?" I asked.

"He's a handful," she stated then walked away.

Darlene was fond of Al. He was attentive, liked to play, and cooked her favorite foods. She loved it. He was making his presence known more at my house but my feelings for him were strictly friendly.

One day, Slade called me at work asking if he could come over that afternoon to cook steaks. He also offered to mow my lawn. I didn't care how he knew my place was beginning to resemble a jungle. I was excited he wanted to come over. I hadn't been with him in weeks and I really missed him. I planned for Darlene to stay at Daddy's and asked Sandra if she would stay at her boyfriend's so Slade and I could be alone for a change. When she agreed, and Daddy was glad Darlene was coming over, I knew I was going to have a special evening.

While Slade was driving up, Al called inviting me out. I only wanted to be with Slade that night. I told Al I already had plans with Slade and I'd see him later. I didn't want Al to consider me his property or start being possessive. I enjoyed his friendship but that was all.

When Slade finished mowing the grass, I asked him, "How did you know that my grass needed cutting so bad?"

"I've been driving by and noticed." He said.

"Why didn't you stop?" I asked curiously.

"Al's truck was here, and I didn't want to interfere." He shared.

"Oh, good grief Slade! Al is just a friend. He's just good company. I can assure you nothing is going on between us. Dana and Mac are doing their own thing these days, so I get lonely. By the way, where have you been?" I quipped.

"Let me take a shower to get this grass off me. I'll come back and we'll discuss everything while we cook dinner." He said.

After his shower, we started to eat our meal and enjoy each other's company. I asked him to finish the conversation we stopped earlier. "Where have you been lately?" I asked again.

He started by saying, "I've been around." Then he asked me a question, "You know my daughter means everything to me, don't you? Well, I've been planning to move back to Columbus to be close to her. I need to be in her life and I can't if I'm living this far away."

My heart sank. I fully understood the love you can have for a child. I'd be miserable without Darlene. Sadly, I would be losing him.

I swallowed hard then asked, "When?"

"My job has made the arrangements to transfer me back within the next few days." He informed.

By this time tears started rolling down my cheeks. He grabbed me and hugged me tightly while talking very close to my ear.

"This is why I never wanted a serious relationship, Rachel. I knew once I got my head on straight I would move back home. Then I could deal with my ex-wife better and I could be closer to Sherry."

"I knew there had to be an issue that kept you from commitment. I could never put my finger on the reason." I said crying.

"Rachel, I did fall in love with you. I just couldn't commit to anything serious. My heart was severely damaged by my ex-wife's affair. I don't know if I can fully trust another woman again. I was afraid to try. I need to totally commit to Sherry. You are very special to me. I want you to be happy. That is why I'd back off when other guys came around. I can't give you what you really need." He said.

"So, you think you know what that is?" I asked him outright.

"It's my whole heart. You have your roots here in Belmont. You have this lovely home, with your Daddy close by and all your friends. My only true commitment is to Sherry. I want to be a good father to her while I can." He said.

"Then why did you volunteer to marry me when I was pregnant if you were so afraid and knew you couldn't stay?" I asked hurt.

"I don't know. I wanted to fix the problem. I really thought at the time that I could. I just confused the issue even more for you, didn't I? He asked.

"Slade, I love you. I've been too scared to come right out and say it because I didn't want to run you off. I knew even before I met John that I had deeper feelings for you than I should. I'll give up this place. I'll move away with you if you'll have me." I told him sobbing.

"No, Rachel, I need to move away without any attachments, so I can show my daughter that I'm there for her. I need to win back her love for me without anyone else involved. I must do this. Please understand." He begged.

The food we'd managed to prepare stuck in my throat. I couldn't enjoy it. We didn't talk much after we ate but we did hold each other and make love one last time. I'd get over Slade just like every other man I've had in my life. I knew getting over him would take longer making it hard to move forward.

The next morning Slade hugged me so hard I thought my ribs were going to break. "I'm sorry." He said.

I just nodded my head. I knew if I spoke the first word I'd start crying and make him feel bad. He was doing a good thing. He wanted to take care of his daughter. He wasn't like so many men who turned their backs on their kids after divorces. I knew Slade was really a good person. It made me hate myself, even more, when I thought that I did the same thing to Drake Slade's ex-did to him. That was probably the reason Slade couldn't fully commit to me knowing what I had done to Drake.

During one of their demonic meetings, Evil said. "It's time we put one of our puppets in her life. One we can manipulate into torturing her mentally and physically at her own agreement. We'll make her feel inadequate enough to want to do anything for her child's welfare even to the point of giving up her own personal happiness."

*****

217

The Saturday Slade left was the same day I drank myself into oblivion. I drank so much Sandra had to take care of Darlene for me. I didn't want to think about anything. At the time, everything going through my mind was negative or pitiful. I took a couple of bottles of wine and my cigarettes to numb my mind. Before the night was over, I was holding onto the porcelain throne heaving up all that I had drunk.

I was glad the next day was Sunday. My head weighed about a hundred pounds and wanted to explode. The pain in my head equaled the pain in my heart so crying came easy. Sandra and Dana both took authority over me later that day. They tried to reason with me telling me I was healthy, I had a healthy and happy daughter, a place to live, a good job and friends who cared about me.

As much as they tried, the only thing that got my attention was threatening to call my Daddy. "Heaven forbid," I begged. "Don't do that! He'll make me feel even worse by giving me a guilt treatment. I'll get up and try to eat. Please don't get him involved."

The next few days were a blur. I'd get up, feed Darlene, dress her, take her to school then go to work. At noon, I'd get Darlene from school, take her to Dana's then go back to work. After work, I'd get Darlene and go home because I just didn't want to visit. At night, I talked with Sandra before she went with her boyfriend. Some nights I'd take my telephone off the hook, go to my room and play with Darlene after we ate dinner. I wasn't good company and felt no need to make the effort.

At work, Lena and Mr. Alston were so nice to me. They didn't pry but waited for me to tell them why I was so sad. They told Al what was going on with me, I didn't. He had backed off some but had not given up.

Preservation knew what was being set in motion, but he could only watch. This perplexed him enough to visit the Father and ask for help. "Father, I know who the demons are going to use against her and there isn't a thing that I can do to stop it. What do you want me to do? "

"Watch over her, at all costs don't let Death overtake her. Her heart is very fragile and must go through this process to search for us again. I know this is difficult without her agreement, but good seeds from scripture have been planted in her heart. They will be there when needed in the bad times allowing you to act in her favor." He said.

Late one evening after dinner Al came over to my house unannounced explaining he just wanted to see if I was okay. He said he missed our having fun and his play time with Darlene. That was when I decided I was in full agreement with a song that was popular then: "What's Love Got to Do With It," by Tina Turner. Love wasn't real for me anymore. I invited him in and we watched television until I asked him to go so I could get some rest.

After that night, Al became a regular visitor, staying until I'd have to make him go home. We'd cook, drink a lot, and just watch TV. Darlene loved it. She started calling him Daddy "O". They were getting close.

Before Thanksgiving that year, Sandra informed me she and her boyfriend were moving into a place closer to her work. I'd need to find another renter. I was going to miss her because she had become a good helpful friend. Fortunately, I knew another friend from the club, who needed a place to stay. When I called Linda, she agreed to move in as soon as Sandra moved out.

Al didn't like it that I wanted another renter. When he got drunk he loudly expressed that fact. "Why can't we have this place to ourselves? It seems there is always someone watching our every move." I ignored him because I needed the money.

Dana and Mac would come over occasionally. Al didn't seem to like their presence but never said anything. I spent more time with Al because Linda went out to the clubs while Dana and Mac wanted to be alone. Even though I couldn't understand his moods, he was comfortable, like an old shoe, so having him around kept the blues away.

Each night ended with getting drunk after I put Darlene to bed. It wasn't surprising when intimacy entered the picture. Hey, a girl has needs too. He was there and liked me.

That Christmas he asked me to marry him. My first response was NO! Then I thought about how much Darlene liked him. She deserved a stable life and mine would be easier if I had help to depend on for our living. Child support from Drake always came on time, but it wasn't much. During our divorce, I felt so guilty about what I'd done to him I just couldn't burden him with a large sum for child support. I agreed to marry Al and have a loveless life. I'd put Darlene's welfare first. Surely in time, I could learn to truly love Al. He seemed to be everything a girl needed.

It had been a year and a half since divorcing Drake. I had met Slade to fall for John to knowing later that I really loved Slade. Now I was settling for a loveless marriage to Al. Where had, the time gone?

Our wedding was a simple ceremony at a local church. I was no longer a member of a church, so I decided to call the Pastor I knew as a child. Pastor Moree was preaching in Belmont and agreed to do our wedding.

Dana couldn't attend because she had an urgent matter out of town. I asked Linda if she would be my witness. She agreed and decided to disappear that night, so Al and I could be alone later. Al asked Mr. Alston to stand in as his best man. We had a minister perform the ceremony with just our parents and our two friends present. Drake's visitation rights prevented Darlene from being with me.

That night was the beginning of my time in hell.

PAYING THE PIPER

After the wedding, as soon as we returned to the house verbal abuse started. Then he wanted me to perform perverted acts for his sexual pleasures.

"You're my wife now. I want you to act like the whore you were with Slade and John. You were always saying how good they were to you. Now show me how good you were to them, slut." He said drunkenly.

When I didn't comply, he threw his drink glass at me hitting me square in the chest with it. I was terrified. Who was this person I thought loved me? Where was the man who had been so kind and considerate? That night sex with him was rough and demoralizing.

Night after night he'd get drunk and I'd get scared. He was never mean to Darlene. He would wait until after she went to bed to make crude remarks and push me around. He was careful never to strike me where it would show. He usually just shoved me into a wall or table when he didn't get his way quick enough.

Linda couldn't accept what was happening to me. One night she confronted Al about it. A few days later Al insisted she look for another place to live. He was adamant that she vacated the house stating firmly, "Newlyweds didn't need company." After she left I never saw or heard from her ever again.

He hated my relationship with Dana, he'd forbid me to invite her over. My relationship with her became strained as well.

222

She and Mac finally got married. When they moved into their own place I wasn't allowed to visit. Thank God there were telephones, so we could keep in touch if I had the opportunity.

Things got even worse when Mr. Alston had to fire me due to the economy. He thought since I was married, I'd be okay. He knew Al had a good job, so it was easier for him to let me go than another girl. Unemployment wasn't enough money for Al. He often hurled my inadequacies at me. I couldn't find work anywhere, not even at the hospital.

During a drunken fight one night, he shouted he needed money and it was my fault he was always short on cash. He demanded that I call Daddy. He said, "Your old man is rich. Tell him his precious daughter needs a loan, or she and his granddaughter will be doing without."

"No! I will not get Daddy involved in this. If the money is gone, it is your fault, not mine." I refused.

He slapped me so hard my teeth rattled. "Bitch! You do what I say, or I'll lock you out of this house. Do you hear me?" He threatened after pushing me towards the telephone.

He was so drunk he couldn't tell I was talking into space and not to Daddy. I was going through the motions to stop him from hitting me again. That seemed to pacify him. I'd done what he ordered so it wasn't long after my fake call to Daddy that he passed out.

The next day, after an argument, he'd always be apologetic promising me he'd never do it again. Most of the time he wouldn't even remember what he had done or said.

Every night was torture never knowing what to expect. If he wasn't mad at me about something or someone, he wanted to do crude and perverted things with me. I felt disgusted, dirty, and gross. I felt everyone, I encountered, could tell I was a tramp.

Al was always buying me disgusting clothes. No way could these items be labeled nightwear because they were so revolting. Then he'd make me put them on, so he could tear them off me. He'd be so drunk each time, if I didn't do what he said, he would hurt me. He'd make me dance while wearing these items declaring, "You'd dance for anybody at the club. Now dance for me." He would command things he wanted me to do during those times. They were so humiliating I can't even say what they were. I hated myself for being scared of him and complying with his treatment of me. Was I now paying for all the hurt and murder that I'd done? My guilt could find no other reason. Satan had me where he wanted. I was his plaything. Most of the time to stay sane, I'd play along numbing my senses by getting drunk along with Al.

Al was always sweet to Darlene, and she adored him. It was always when she was away that he got really perverted with me. After she went to bed other nights he'd get mean saying nasty things and pushing me around. I had a brief respite from all the abuse after his son moved in with us. Jim was older and didn't go to bed as early as Darlene, so Al would behave himself a little better. He still drank a lot, but he was more careful about what he said and did.

I finally got another job at an engineering firm. I could get my secretarial skills back up to par. I learned a lot from the owners and they were very patient with me while I caught on to the business. But the pay there wasn't so great. The next year Al forced me to look for work elsewhere.

After applying for job after job, I finally got a job at a local law firm as a receptionist for an attorney who was just hired. I really liked this job. It made me feel important and I could be at home shortly after the kids got off the school bus each afternoon. Since Jim was older, he had to stay with Darlene at the house until I got home. He resented that arrangement. He was mean to her and she would always be crying about something when I did get in.

Al had the bright idea that the attorney I worked for should help me sue Drake for more child support. He was always complaining, "I have to support both kids. Stop being such a coward. You were too lenient on Drake. Your guilt trip is over."

He hounded me night after night until finally, I couldn't take anymore. I succumbed by asking my boss if he could help me. When it was all done, we got a bill for services and Al had a fit.

Then I had to listen to him complain, "Those jerks charged you as if you were just a client off the streets. You are their employee! You shouldn't have to pay anything."

225

I just couldn't expect that and said, "No we are going to pay this. Not paying would be insulting to them. They did give me a good break."

My comment made the anger erupt and resulted in another glass being thrown at me hitting me in the back.

Around the same time that we were going through this issue with my boss and the lawsuit, Drake remarried. He wanted Darlene to visit more often. This gave Al the excuse to plan an outing for us. He planned also for Jim to go to his mom's. We were to go fishing in the Gulf of Mexico with some of his friends. Little did I know, one of our arguments on this trip would change me forever.

After we had eaten at a nice restaurant, we went to the attached bar. I knew I needed to be mindful and watch what I drank because Al had no restraints when he was with his friends. He always wanted to be the biggest and badest cat around. After he was totally wasted on booze he threatened to take his boat out during the night. It was too late for anyone but professionals to be on the water.

Nobody could convince him not to go. I tried again while we were standing on the top deck of a pier looking out over the ocean. I made him so angry, he shoved me backward causing me to fall two flights down. I fell six feet landing on my back striking a hard object that caused me to go numb from the waist down. I started screaming for help. I knew I was in trouble. Al was oblivious to what he had done to me. All he wanted to do was go boat riding in the dark.

The dock attendant finally stopped him from leaving by threatening to call the cops. He witnessed what Al had done to me and wanted him to take responsibility. An ambulance was called, and I was transported to a local hospital bound to a backboard with a neck brace. The EMT's made Al come along even in his drunken state. He complained the whole trip that I was ruining his vacation. I heard the EMT say, "Fellow you need to stop your moaning. Your wife could possibly be badly injured."

I had to stay in the hospital a few days because I had bruised my spine. It was very painful, but I wasn't injured badly enough to prevent me from walking. In fact, the doctor encouraged me to walk with assistance.

Once again after Al sobered up he told me he was sorry for what had happened. At least he acted sorry in front of his friends. That was the problem; he'd do crazy things, then say he was sorry, but never sorry enough to stop. It was insane trying to live on this emotional roller coaster.

I had a doctor's order to have a checkup with my own doctor when I got home to make sure things were okay. I thought I was okay, but while I was in Florida I had started bleeding heavily on my cycle. I assumed it was from the stress I endured from the fall. I wasn't worried. I was wrong again. My doctor found a problem with my uterus and said I may need surgery if the bleeding didn't stop.

Telling Al that evening was rough. He blamed all my past actions for my malfunctioning uterus. He couldn't accept that a fall had anything to do with my bleeding.

Stress built inside me and the more I worried, the more I bled. Dr. Little had no choice but to do a hysterectomy. I was bleeding too much to remain healthy. The only positive result from having the procedure was the guarantee I'd never get pregnant with Al's baby. I constantly had this vision of being like Rosemary in the movie "Rosemary's Baby" giving birth to Satan.

Normal people might think things would be better after a while. The consequences of my surgery were making my body more accessible for punishment. The abuse got so bad at times I'd go to work dressed in clothes too warm for the weather conditions, so I could cover up bruises. The attorney I worked for noticed my slow motion one day. He called me into his office and asked why I was limping. I told him the truth.

He was shocked I was putting up with the abuse but also understood my fear. I was scared to leave Al. He asked if he could take a few pictures for evidence in case I ever needed to prove I was being hurt. I agreed and revealed the heavier bruises on my back and thigh resulting from being pushed down the night before. He took the pictures then showed me where he stored the film if I ever needed to have it developed.

I started to gain weight due to all the stress. Eating was the only way I could cope. I'd sneak off to have a box of pastries just to relax. As my weight increased, I'd hear comments on how I

228

turned him off and my fat caused me to smell. I thought it would keep his filthy hands off me. That didn't stop him. I was a toy to him.

I noticed even his friends didn't want to go out with us because he would be so rude and hateful to people when he was drunk. The poor waitresses who tried to serve us hated to come around him. If his order wasn't exactly what he had in mind he threw it back at them. One night at IHOP we were escorted out by management because he was being rude and throwing food.

Al loved company. Since they wouldn't go out with us, he invited them to our house for parties. We'd plan for several couples. Drinks were plentiful, and I indulged myself. With tequila, I'd dance with friends and try to have fun. If we had company, Al behaved somewhat towards me. Our parties were such a hit with everybody. We tried to have one every month or so when the kids were gone for a weekend.

I started being friendly with some of the wives of Al's friend's and was introduced to another job opportunity. I hated to leave my current employer, especially since he had taken such interest in my welfare, but we needed more money coming into the household. I was offered a government job at the local mental health office.

Our finances improved. We could do a lot of new things. Al even started his own fishing business in the Gulf of Mexico. He bought a larger boat and fishing gear to take people fishing on the weekends for extra money. I thought it was going to be a lot of fun. I was wrong. Deep sea fishing was not for me. Every time I'd go out on the boat I'd get sick which would cause me more problems that evening after Al got drunk. Verbal abuse was guaranteed. I would have to endure his complaints about how worthless I was.

I hated going on that boat. Why did going for rides on that boat make me sick? I enjoyed the one we had at home when we took it out on the lake or when we'd take it to the ocean flats fishing for redfish in Florida. I couldn't win trying to make my family happy. I'd buy every kind of medication for nausea that was available, but it still didn't help. I finally realized the fear of getting sick on Al's boat is what caused my motion sickness.

Not all of Al's fishing associates were nice people. Some looked at me strangely as if I were something to eat. It was during one of our planned parties I these friends were trying to touch me inappropriately. I just brushed the thought off and went about mingling as a hostess. One night the tequila I drank kicked my butt and I had to lay down.

During my fogged state, I became aware of hands fondling me. So, I sat up and realized my husband along with two other men were touching me. "What are you doing?" I screamed at Al.

"Never you mind Rachel. My friends here want to show you a good time and I've agreed as long I can watch." He drunkenly slurred.

"No!" I screamed but to no avail. No one was in our house. All our other visitors were gone but these two men.

Even Al helped hold me down while those perverts had their way with me.

I was sore and bruised when I finally was set free that night. I was so ashamed I wanted to die. When Darlene and Jim came home the next day, I didn't even come out of my room to take care of them. Al acted like nothing had happened, but I was in a mental state beyond my control.

*****

Evil was excited. "Yeah, Rachel, do something foolish. Hurry up!"

*****

Preservation was in high gear and on the move to prevent the destruction of this innocent life. He'd focus on causing a distraction to divert the plan. He had to work fast."

*****

I could not go through another night of hell. As I lay in the bed that evening after Al had passed out drunk, again. I pondered ending my life. I took his gun and started to pull the trigger but then decided Al was the one who needed to die.

If I hadn't heard Darlene talk in her sleep I would have killed him. I knew I hated him that much. I dressed then got Darlene and ran out the door. It was late, but I didn't care. I had to go somewhere where Al couldn't find me. I escaped to Dana and Mac's house.

Since Al didn't want to associate with them, he didn't know where they lived. My friend didn't disappoint. She welcomed us with open arms. I knew if I had gone to Daddy's he would have done something stupid like kill the man himself.

I finally told Al I wanted him out of my house. My attorney friend was delighted to help get him out, so I could file for divorce. Daddy was also glad I was divorcing Al. He never liked Al and hated I settled for living with a drunk.

I changed the locks on all my doors at home. I asked my neighbors to watch my house. If they saw Al they were instructed to call the police for me. The man was insane and very dangerous.

MY AWAKENING

I celebrated by buying a new car. I chose a little red Chevy Sprint which was a sassy little car that made me feel good and gave me a new outlook on life. It proclaimed to me, "Free at Last" when I drove it around.

Preservation had an appointment with the Father and was told Rachel would place her life back in her Daddy's care soon even though she'd feel like she still was on her own. When that happened, her spiritual authority would revert to Jason covering Rachel's life for a while. This would give Preservation more help to direct Rachel's attention back to Jesus and the Father.

*****

I was happier but heavier than I been in a long time. Two co-workers had gone through gastric bypass surgery to lose weight and were looking great. I decided to have the surgery. I didn't ever want to be obese again, so I made an appointment and went for it. Since I had a state job I also had good insurance benefits. The surgery was considered an insurable operation at that time.

My appointment for the surgery was scheduled early in June. I planned for Darlene to go to summer camp with the girl scouts, so Daddy and Joan could take me upstate for the surgery. The surgery went as planned and I could return home the day before camp was over.

The only difference in my new life was the accumulation of bills from this surgery plus I couldn't eat. If I tried, I'd throw up because my stomach was now very small. I couldn't drink certain things especially anything carbonated. I hated not eating, but I loved the results. The weight just melted off me.

The bills started coming in and I was unable to take care of all my obligations. I asked Daddy to please show me how to manage my finances. He came to the house and I showed him my bills as well as my household responsibilities. He assured me he could consolidate the bills allowing me to handle the payments and even have a little extra cash to save for emergencies.

During our visit, I felt the need to explain why I divorced Al. Daddy was horrified and mad. I thought he was going to explode right there in front of my eyes. He swore he would never allow another human being to ever hurt or abuse me or Darlene again. I saw him cry. He thought he should have noticed things weren't as they seemed. During those years, he assumed Al was a drunk but never dreamed he was an abuser as well.

While I watched through the kitchen doors as my Daddy drove off that afternoon, my heart lurched. I had never seen him cry except when Mama died. I knew then he still loved me even if another man never did, and he would always take care of me no matter what.

"Do you hear that?" Jesus asked the Father, "Jason is praying for Rachel. He is asking us to restore her innocence, to save her soul and heal her heart."

"Yes, Son, his simple request is our cue to take over, I knew it was coming when she placed herself back under his authority as her father. It has given us permission to act." God replied.

*****

"No! No! No!" Evil screamed. "We had her for so long. What just happened to cause HIM to start caring for her again? She was one of ours. Now we have to battle for her all over again."

*****

Daddy helped me with a loan from his bank a few days later. I now have funds to do things occasionally with my daughter. I even allowed Darlene to get a kitten. We'd never had a pet and I thought the kitten would remove her focus from me and how I was acting.

I was also financially able to join a health club where I could begin getting my body back in shape. Dana liked the idea of exercising and Mac agreed she should join the club with me.

We enjoyed the summer going places with Mac, Dana, and her kids. It had been a long time since Darlene and I had fun with them. I wanted all of us to go to the beach before summer was over. When Dana and Mac couldn't go, I decided Darlene and I would go anyway. I allowed Darlene to invite her best friend, Kay, from our neighborhood to go with us.

I felt so free! Not only was I divorced, I was feeling independent. I could go to places when I got the notion and I loved the experience. On our vacation, we swam, went to a theme park in another town, and just had fun.

Jesus knew how to lure Rachel's attention. He'd remind her of the warmth of being hugged by the sun. He'd take small steps to get her attention because she was so frail emotionally.

It was during my time in the sun one day, that I had a strange sensation come over me. I felt like I was being hugged. Hadn't I felt that way before? What was the word? It was, De Je Vu. The warmth overtaking me was soothing. It made me feel secure and peaceful until a song on the radio interrupted the experience and reminded me of my predicament. The song was "Here I Go Again" by Whitesnake and it made me think about what was ahead of me.

"Ha! We stopped His advances this time, but we need to be on guard. We have a new bunch of angels following and listening to our every word. He is stepping in. We can't risk being annihilated. His very stare can destroy us." Evil told his friends.

Listening to the giggles and whispers of the girls made me realize how happy Darlene and Kay were during our trip. It made me promise myself I'd avoid the same road I'd traveled earlier. I'd start going to church and establish a stable life for us.

Daddy and Joan were very happy when Darlene and I started going regularly to their church. I was impressed Joan got Daddy to go at all. He hardly ever went with us when I was little. It was after Mama got sick that he went with us more to church. I remember how happy I was when I saw him walk to the front during an altar call to rededicate his life.

After church services, Darlene and I would have lunch with Daddy and Joan. It felt good to be family oriented again. We would even visit my Mama's sister sometimes to give her the opportunity to bond with Mama's granddaughter. I felt Darlene needed the connection because Mama was an important part of our lives. My aunt would be able to bring Mama to life for Darlene by telling her about her grandmother.

Dana and Mac didn't go to church much so conversations about religion were difficult. Dana understood the importance and sent her kids to a Catholic school near their home. Dana needed structure. She was more comfortable with rituals and regulations during a church service. When she did go to church she chose the Catholic church where her children attended school. They didn't go often enough to have any church friends to enjoy fellowship. All their friends were the same old bar buddies we had during our clubbing days.

*****

"**We**'ve got to get her interested in going clubbing again. She couldn't resist flirting and getting attention. We'll make them flock to her, again." Evil said.

*****

A new batch of angels had been dispatched to guard and protect Rachel since her Daddy's prayer. When they overheard Evil's plans, they sprang into action. They wouldn't allow Rachel to forget the crude and annoying actions of drunken men. The war was on and they were ready.

*****

I went out with them a few times to a new place in town. There was a buffet in the club. I couldn't eat but I felt weird ordering only water. Since my stomach surgery cola made me sick because of the carbonation. Alcohol made me drunk in minutes. I felt completely out of place. The thought of being with a man during those days frightened me. I didn't easily trust so when a man started flirting or acting interested, I'd be mean and tell him to get lost.

I only felt comfortable around the men at work or church. I was sure my experience with Al had caused me mental issues. I was fortunate that working at a mental health facility allowed me to talk about my phobias with one of my counselor friends. Kathleen was wonderful. She helped me deal with insecurities and

238

understand other fears. During those discussions, we became friends and discovered we could enjoy each other's company outside the office.

When their current plans failed, Evil planned another attack. "We need to ruin her church experiences, so she will refuse to return. The more we keep her away from Him, the better."

Darlene told me she wanted to accept Christ and be baptized. I agreed the next time we attended church we'd go to the altar at the invitation and join the church together. That's when we realized Daddy's church was not very accommodating. We tried to join the congregation but were told Darlene would have to take classes before she would be accepted for baptism. I had never heard of such rules. When I wanted to be baptized, I only told my Pastor that I knew Jesus and why I wanted to be baptized. I didn't have to take classes beforehand. I was a little offended. I thought they were being judgmental. I felt my past was the reason they didn't want Darlene and me as members of their congregation.

When we didn't return to Daddy's church he became suspicious and asked me why. I told him the truth. I had been offended and couldn't go back yet.

The new angels had to enforce their influence with patience by working overtime. She would be led to another place where she could find friends. They used her Daddy to encourage her to find another church. Kathleen's understanding of Rachel's need to change would also be used.

*****

"Honey, you can't keep Darlene away from the Lord. She needs to know she has Him in her heart no matter what you feel." He said.

"I know, Daddy, give me some time and I promise I'll keep us in church." Was all I could say.

The next workday I told Kathleen about what happened at church. She agreed with Daddy-I shouldn't let offense ruin Darlene's experience. She recommended we visit her church and invited us to be her guest Wednesday night. I promised I'd think about it and let her know soon. By the end of the day, I felt compelled to try Kathleen's church.

The First United Methodist Church located downtown Belmont was one of the largest churches in town. The sanctuary was beautiful and serene. I felt the presence of God by just being there. Everyone was so nice while Kathleen introduced me to some of her friends. She even made Darlene feel comfortable by showing her the building and introducing her to some girls her age. After the service, Darlene and I went home excited about our experience.

After about a month, I had gotten involved with the singles group Kathleen introduced me to at the church. Darlene was comfortable with the Sunday School group that was her age. That Sunday she and I looked at each other and decided with a nod that we would go to the altar during the invitation to join the church. We both felt like we'd found a church home.

She loved going. She joined the youth choir and girls club there. When it was time for her to be sprinkled, we were excited. Sprinkling was a different experience for me. I was raised Baptist and we were dunked. All that really mattered was she knew her heart belonged now to God through Jesus.

Our singles group was always getting together to do various things. To my surprise, I felt accepted and cared for. My only issue was drinking being permissible when we met for our functions. No one ever made a scene or ever got drunk, but the wine and beer were available to be enjoyed outside of the church where ever we gathered. I knew a Baptist would have an issue with that.

Time to reinstate a memory, Jesus thought. I'm going to make her remember me.

Christmas that year was one of the best I'd ever had. I was free from torture. I could spend what I wanted on who I wanted, and my family and friends were wonderful.

When we went to Daddy's on Christmas Day, Darlene and I started looking at old pictures of me and JL when we were kids. That was when I came across a photo of me sitting on a swing in the backyard of our old place when I was about 4 years old. I didn't know they had taken a picture of me. Looking at that picture, I knew immediately, as if struck by lightning-what I was doing at that very moment and Who was with me even though there wasn't anyone else in the picture.

Mama and Daddy had just told me my puppy, Sugar, had to go home to be with her Mama and I was so sad. I didn't have anybody. Then I met Sunny. I'd forgotten all about Him. He was my rock then. A friend whenever I needed one. I wanted Him in my life now. I realized I wouldn't have become such a mess if I'd kept Him close.

"Hurry, throw doubt into her mind, hurry," Evil told some demons close by. "She can't focus on Him, Hurry! Hurry!"

*****

Just a childish fantasy I thought. Children had to play make believe, didn't they? I pondered on Sunny for many days after that wondering if He had been real.

242

New Year's Eve that year was a great experience. Dana, Mac, and I decided to leave the kids with Dana's parents, so we could celebrate. I had lost a lot of weight by then and was feeling good about myself. I had purchased a nice outfit for the occasion. Even though I was going unescorted, I felt great. At the stroke of midnight, the bartender ran and grabbed me planting a kiss right on my mouth. He said to me sweetly, "I knew when you walked in the door you were going to be the one I kissed to start off my new year."

Even though I got a kiss, I never saw the man again. We didn't hang around long after and kiss, and he had to go back to attend the bar. I knew from that moment I was going to have a good year. I also knew in my heart I didn't want to be alone forever.

Other friends (Nick and Sue) invited the three of us (Dana, Mac, and me) to join them for dinner on New Year's Day. We had to ask Dana's parents again, to watch the kids. To my surprise, I was being set up with a blind date. When we arrived, we were paired off as couples. It dawned on me then what was going on. Kurt Singleton was nine years my junior, but his mannerisms made him appear to be much older. We hit it off and tried to make our relationship work, but he lived in Florida and it became too difficult for us to continue. I had fun during our times together. I realized I had much to offer someone. Finding the right person was the key. I had to be very, very careful this time.

I loved being with Dana and Mac but enjoyed my outings more with my new friends at church. Clubbing made me feel dirty.

The guys I'd met were always so demanding and treated me like a piece of meat. I loved to dance but every time I was asked it seemed my partner had a one-track mind which was to seduce me. It had the same effect every time, turned me off, and made me a mean person. When I turned mean-minded, I decide to have some perverted fun in the clubs. I would think like a man. I'd treat them like they treated me. I started using my dance partners as tools to have fun but never wanting to know the real people. They became objects for me to dance with then tormented in other ways by my indifference. I didn't really want a personal relationship with any of them, but I also had needs. I focused on my needs even though in the back of my mind I knew I was wrong.

"We can't use clubbing anymore to try to woo her back to our side. She wants no part of the men we have wanting her there. Plus, the new young plaything we threw in the mix didn't last long. She's gotten too picky. The only thing we know for sure is that she is lonely. We'll ask the master what he recommends." Evil and his friends discussed.

Jesus ordered Preservation into His chamber for a conversation. "Rachel needs to hear the truth. She must be directed to a church service where someone is preaching about me. Direct her to a minister who will grab her attention. Use him to make her remember how we were. It is time we are reacquainted."

*****

I was thrilled when a new family moved into the vacant house across the street from me. After I'd welcomed them to the neighborhood we quickly became friends. Betty was great fun and I loved how easily we discussed faith. I was Methodist, and she and her family were Pentecostal. They belonged to the church where I had been rejected many years ago, after applying for a secretarial position.

I had never attended a Pentecostal service so when Betty invited me to a revival service I was curious enough to say I'd go. She was so much fun, and I really wanted another friend who enjoyed church. Dana had no interest in church or religion making strained conversations sometimes.

REUNION

A meeting began with a question. "Fear, are you doing your job?" Evil asked. "He is planning something tonight., I feel it. If we can stop her from going to this service, we are going to have to move quickly."

*****

Preservation overheard Evil's plan and started putting a hedge of protection in place to prevent Fear from finding a way into Rachel's mind.

*****

It must have been ordained for me to go to the revival service. Darlene's best friend asked me that afternoon, "May Darlene sleepover at my house tonight?" This would free me to go alone.

When I took Darlene to Kay's house, I had a chance to talk with her mother, Diane. "This revival sounds like fun. I'm really excited about going tonight." I shared. "Would you like to join us?" I asked.

"No," she said. "But if you want to go tomorrow night, Darlene can stay over again. She is always welcome to come stay with Kay."

God had truly blessed me with a good friend in Diane. She stepped in to help after my divorce and was willing to watch Darlene after school every afternoon until I got home from work.

The girls loved to play together, and it was hard sometimes to get them to do homework, eat and then get ready for bed.

After leaving Diane's house, a wave of apprehension came over me as I was walking over to Betty's. What was I getting myself into? I had heard weird things about that round church. Then I saw Betty. Her excitement relaxed me. What harm would it do?

The moment I walked in the building I was greeted warmly and felt accepted. But it was the visiting minister who had me enthralled. From the moment, he opened his mouth I was hooked. I listened intently as he described a God who never slept, who constantly watched over me and could be my rock. He was the light of the world, loved me and wanted me to be happy. This God was my protector; counselor and friend who exuded love. Everything loved Him and followed after Him.

"I know this person," I thought. But it couldn't be! I made Him up as a childhood fantasy. NO! This couldn't be Sunny the minister was talking about. Or could it? This precious friend I had as a small child, and later when I started school, was real. Was He Jesus? "Don't tell me this," I thought. I had turned my back on Jesus, totally forgetting Him.

The revelation frightened me. Then I heard the minister say, Jesus was always waiting for us to come back to Him. That He was merciful and extremely patient. I broke. Tears were streaming down my face and I had to get away.

I excused myself and went into the lobby to find a lady's room. I needed a tissue and to collect myself. I'd never fallen apart in church before and I needed to get a grip on my tears. As I paced back and forth, I said to myself, "If Jesus really is forgiving, then He will understand. I need to go back in there and listen." I returned and sat next to Betty. She looked concerned but said nothing.

I heard one last thing that totally grabbed my attention. The minister said, "You can find this loving Lord in the pages of His Word."

I had to get home. I knew if I was going to see Sunny again, I needed to be alone to talk with Him. Boy, did I need to talk with Him! The ride home seemed to take forever. When Betty stopped at my house she asked, "Do you want to go with me tomorrow night?"

I answered, "Sure, I can't wait. Thanks for inviting me. I really had a wake-up call."

My heart pounded hard in my chest. I knew I was not alone, but I was scared and embarrassed. I had failed my Lord, and I didn't know how to apologize. I went to the bedroom, crawled up in the middle of the bed and turned on my lamp so I could read my Bible. Didn't the minister say we could find Jesus there? I had to try.

Nothing seemed to help. The scriptures confused more than sustained me. I tried to remember how He came to me when I was little. I closed my eyes and said, "Sunny please come to me."

Nothing happened. I tried again. "Sunny, please, I'm so sorry." Still nothing. I thought, "I'm crazy, just looney toons," and I started to cry. That's when I said, "Lord God, I'm so sorry! I really need you. I can't believe I never realized you were my Lord."

I heard the sweetest word's I've heard in a long time. He said, *"What did you call me?"*

I sniffed and answered, "My Lord God" Then I asked, "Is it really you?"

"Yes, Little One, it is me." He said.

I asked, "Why didn't you answer when I called you Sunny?"

"Because I am not just your childhood friend. Now, I am your Lord Jesus and I wanted you to acknowledge me that way. I'll always be the light of your world, but now you need to call me by my name. You needed to acknowledge aloud who I really am." He said.

"Can I see you?" I asked

"Let it be enough to hear me for now. Your heart is full of darkness. It will take time for you to focus properly. For the time being, I want you to get to know me again through my words." He replied.

All night we talked as I read passages of scripture. I'd ask questions then wait. As if I was instructed I would find a verse or chapter that answered the question. Yes, Jesus was making Himself known to me through the Word.

I was taken to the Word that answered why I couldn't see Jesus. It showed me why. My troubles were without number and surrounded me, and my sins had overtaken me, and I couldn't see. From those words, I learned my sins were preventing me from seeing with a childlike view.

I looked up trying to see Jesus. I still couldn't so, I just asked, "My sins are keeping me blinded, aren't they?"

"*Yes, for now, you haven't received grace,*" Jesus said.

"What is grace?" I asked.

It is total forgiveness of your sins and unmerited favor from the Father." He said.

My heart sank, as I thought of the things I'd done. How could He not be mad? Then I asked, "You know what I've done, don't you? How can you even want to be with me? I don't even want to be with me at times."

"*Little One, we know everything you've thought, said and done all the years we were together and the ones when we were apart. You don't believe that you have already been forgiven for everything. You haven't received God's loving forgiveness in your heart. You are blameless in His sight because you've come back to me.*" He assured me.

Then I was led to scriptures explaining how King David and Paul were forgiven of murder and how God still used them.

"How can you forgive me?" I asked.

"We saw the guilt in your heart and the shame the acts caused. We knew your conscience was grieved and it grieved us. We knew you really didn't want to do any of it so, by your thoughts, we determined your justification. If you had not felt shame or remorse, then forgiveness would not have been available. But you did and you still do." He answered.

"Why wasn't I prevented from my actions?" I needed to know.

"You chose the ways of the world; and was carried away by your lusts and desires so much any Word or knowledge of me faded. We had to sit back and wait. The Father knew in time you'd be back." He explained.

My next question was, "What changed in my life for me to lose my need for you?"

"The Kingdom of Heaven is ruled by order and permission. We were only given permission to save and protect your physical body until now." He answered.

Confused, I said, "What? I do not comprehend. Who gave you permission to do that for me?"

"Little One, when you were a baby, Satan tried to kill you and your mother prayed for us to save your life. We did, and we

251

have been doing that to this very moment. But, because your soul wasn't asked for, we needed to wait. Someone in authority, whether through your own permission or someone you've given authority over your life, could ask for it to be spared." He said.

I was still confused so I asked, "Who asked for my soul? Didn't I do that when I wanted to be baptized?

"As a young girl, you gave your head to me but not your heart completely. No one ever taught you about me as a person, just that I was the one to keep you from hell. You only thought that to keep from going to hell you needed to be baptized. You couldn't come to me as a person about your soul because you didn't know the difference between physical life and spiritual." He said.

"Well, who did ask for me?" I couldn't fathom.

"Your Daddy did the day you told him about your abusive marriage." He shared.

Instantly I remembered how I felt when I saw Daddy leaving me that day. My heart was being turned around even then, but I was unaware. "Oh, thank you, Daddy," I said to myself.

When dawn came the next day, I wasn't even tired, and I didn't want to lose my time with Jesus either. I picked up my telephone and called the office and asked if I could have a personal day to take care of business. To my surprise, my supervisor told me I could.

I spent hours in the Word that day. I must have drifted off to sleep at some point because Darlene telephoned, woke me up

252

and I remembered what was going on. She called me from Diane's house asking why I was home. She didn't know what to do because she was told to get off the bus and stay with Kay until I got off work. I was home, and she didn't understand.

I assured her I was fine and if she wanted to play for a while it was okay with me. Really, I was hoping she wouldn't come home right then. I needed to make sure my connection with Jesus wasn't severed.

"Where are you?" I screamed.

"*I'm still here, I've never left. You needed rest so we quieted down.*" He said.

"What do you want me to do?" I asked.

"*Go back to the revival. There is more to learn.*" He instructed.

I walked over to Diane's house to see my child and talk with her. When I got there, she asked, "How was the revival?"

I answered truthfully, "It was enlightening and caused me to do some serious soul-searching." I plan to go back. Are you sure Darlene can stay here with you?"

"Sure," she said, "You don't even have to ask."

I ran back to the house, got Darlene a change of clothes and told her mommy would be with Betty again that night.

She asked me, "Mama, am I going to go to my church tomorrow night or am I going to have to stay here again?"

I looked into her green eyes and said, "Darlene sweetie, you are more than welcome to go with me tomorrow night if you want. I don't plan to go to our church this Wednesday night. I haven't asked you to go with us because I didn't think you would want to attend a church where you didn't know anyone. Would you like to go with me tonight?"

"Nah. I'd rather stay here and play with Kay. We can do our homework and watch TV afterward. Tell me about it tomorrow, okay." She said.

So, with her permission to go alone, I went back to the house to get ready.

Betty was glad when I showed up on her doorsteps eager to go back. She told me on the ride over, "I knew you were upset last night and I wasn't sure what was going on. I'm glad you still want to go.

I shared with her about my rededication, "I hadn't planned on such a conversion, but I've had time to deal with myself. I need to try committing my mind to learning all I can."

Armed with my Bible we entered another service where the minister opened my eyes to a loving and merciful God. How He was willing to show pity and mercy to anyone who cried out. The minister showed us in the Word where God promises to give us a new opportunity to seek forgiveness and understanding from Him each morning. Every word amazed me. All I had heard my entire life was the threat of hellfire and brimstone if we didn't repent and change our ways. I don't remember hearing of a forgiving and merciful Father.

Boy, did I need mercy and forgiveness from God. Right there in the service, I spoke to Jesus, "Does God really forgive me of all my sins, even the deaths of my two children?" I asked Him from my heart.

"Yes, if I forgive you He does as well. Little One, don't you understand yet that He and I are one and when you talk to me He is with us also." He asked.

I sucked in a deep breath at that revelation. God, Himself was right there with us. I'd never understood until that very minute. At my new revelation, I hesitated for a split second before I spoke to God Himself from my heart. "Precious Father, thank you so much for loving me and forgiving me. Help me to be a better person so I can continue from this night forward to make the two of you happy with me."

The words, *"You're welcome and it will be my pleasure,"* sang in my heart clear. I knew without a doubt I'd heard from God Himself.

My heart flooded with love. God loved me plus, His son Jesus was my best friend as well as my Lord. I was in heaven I thought, but no, I was still on earth. I was having heaven on earth.

When I got home that night, I was physically exhausted, but my heart and mind were flying. I knew I needed to get some sleep. When I lay down I told Jesus how much I loved Him and asked Him to meet me in the morning. I rested well that night. It was one of the first nights in a long time I didn't have a nightmare of some kind.

The next morning, I waved to Darlene before she got on the school bus as I was leaving to go to work. I felt wonderful. I had awakened early, got some coffee, and went straight to be with Jesus. Now I was ready for the day's events.

At the office, Kathleen came and asked, "Are you ready for the evening?"

I didn't know what she was talking about, so I replied, "No, what?"

"It's our class' turn to serve and assist in the Fellowship Hall for Wednesday night's dinner before the service." She reminded me.

I'd forgotten all about it. I'd promised and couldn't decline. I was going to miss the revival service that evening but it couldn't be helped. So, I told Kathleen to count me in. I'd be there at 6:00 p.m. to set up for the meal.

Darlene got to go to her class, but I was not looking forward to my service. I really wanted to be at the Pentecostal church's revival service. Just as expected, the Pastor only talked about judgment that evening. I heard nothing about a God of

256

compassion. I left there feeling weary instead of uplifted. Darlene, on the other hand, had a great time and I was glad she was getting what her heart needed.

Later when I was alone again with the Lord, I remembered what he told me about Mama and Daddy praying for me. I wanted Darlene to be completely influenced by Him. So, I asked Him to take care of my baby and to make sure Darlene's spirit, soul, and body were in His care.

Drake and his new wife moved out of town a few years earlier. He didn't even call Darlene or want to see her anymore, so I wasn't sure whether he prayed for her or not. She was under my total care so I needed to put her in Jesus' hands while she was still young.

His reply was a little confusing because it was like a riddle, but I trusted in Him and could relax. He said, *"From this moment on, Darlene's spiritual life and soul are not yours to worry over. Just like you, she will need time to find me for herself. You've done right by giving us permission to watch over her. Don't worry and fret by what you see."*

Again, that night I rested like a little child. I knew if God wanted to rescue a super-sinner like me He wouldn't have a problem taking care of my Darlene.

"Yuk! Yuk!" Evil said to himself while sticking his finger down his throat to make a sign of being sick. "This romance of theirs is making me ill. It's so sappy." He said.

The Father just laughed, little did Satan and his bunch knows that they were in for a war.

COMPANIONSHIP

Thursday night was different. When I got home from work, Darlene and I ate a quick dinner and went to Dana's. I really wanted her to come with me to revival service. When I asked her, she informed me, "I don't believe we should be mixing different beliefs. We'll end up warped. I am confused enough as it is."

Discouraged again I couldn't get my best friend to share my love for Jesus, I decided to leave, but Darlene wanted to stay and play with the kids. Dana didn't have a problem with that and told me to go on. I wanted Darlene to come with me, but also didn't want any distractions to keep me from learning. I went with the intentions of enjoying myself. I would not feel guilty about leaving her behind.

Betty was at the church already and happy to see me. I asked if we could sit closer to the front. I wanted no distractions. I was excited and wanted to hear everything this minister had to say. Again, this man of God had a way with words that made Jesus desirable and very much needed. There was no way anyone wouldn't want Him as their Lord because of His willingness to forgive and help you change.

Right before the service ended, I heard the minister say Jesus wanted to give us the desires of our hearts, and then it was over. "Wait," I thought, "I want to know more about this new insight and desires he mentioned."

Darlene was asleep when I got to Dana's so Mac put her in my car to ride home. I hated to wake her up when we arrived, but

I had no choice. My baby girl had gotten too heavy for me to carry. She sleep-walked into the house and stood still while I undressed her then put her gown on. Before I could get to the door, she was asleep again.

I was glad Darlene went to sleep. I needed to be alone with Jesus.

"Jesus, I need to know more about the last thing said tonight in service. Will you direct me please to those verses?" I asked.

I looked in the index of my Bible for the word desire. It led me straight to the verse I heard the minister speak about. It said, 'Delight yourself also in the Lord, and He will give you the desires and secret petitions of your heart.'

After finding this verse, I asked, "Jesus do you know what I desire most right now?"

"Yes, Little One, I've known what you've wanted for a long time." He informed me.

That was news to me because I didn't know what my secret desire was. But one thing I did know was that I was delighting myself in the Lord. Having Him back in my life made me happier than I had ever been.

I was a little curious about my secret self but afraid to ask Jesus to explain. I read a little more in my Bible until I got too sleepy to comprehend any longer.

One more night of revival. I felt I had exhausted all my options for a babysitter. I just couldn't ask Diane if Darlene could spend another night over. I called and asked Joan if she and Daddy would watch Darlene while I went to a revival service with a friend. Again, I was blessed with a happy "Yes" as a reply. I took Darlene over to their house and had dinner with them before I went to the last service.

The service picked up right where the minister left off the night before. As he spoke a heaviness came over my heart. I realized my secret desire. I wanted another chance with love but this time with the person Jesus chose for me. I wanted someone to love me for who I was instead of what I had or could do for him. I didn't want to feel used or taken for granted ever again.

When the altar call was made at the end of the service, I was impelled to go down and make my petition to the minister. When I knelt at the altar stair, I was met by the very man who taught me about a loving Lord. When he asked me what I needed, I whispered I wanted to be loved and it was my heart's desire. The words that came out of his mouth were, "Jesus hears you. Now, wait and see. You'll know when the time comes because He wants you to be happy."

I rested in those words. I didn't share them with anyone but Jesus. Those words were for me alone. I had one warning from my Lord, He informed me I could not do anything to make things happen. I needed to trust Him by waiting and seeing. Jesus did give me one clue to look for, "*You'll know him by a sweet and gentle spirit.*"

It seemed several of my friends from that night forward were trying to set me up with dates. Kathleen introduced me to a Marine named Sid who she had met at a party. He was nice and very attentive. He even liked Darlene and invited her to go with us to a movie. The next day he invited her to go to the park on a picnic with us. She liked him because he spent money on her.

Dana had a guy she wanted me to meet also. We arranged to go out to a movie, but when the time came he stood me up and never called to apologize.

While laughing about my no date experience with friends at work the next day, I was introduced to a new girl starting work at the center. Her name was Katie. She was also newly single, and we found we had a lot of things in common.

One day while discussing men with Katie, she told me about her older brother who had moved in with her after her divorce. She thought he and I would get along great. I thought to myself, "Why not." So, I gave her my telephone number and told her to have him call me.

That night while I was watching TV with Darlene, Katie's brother Ralph called me. He was funny and easy to talk with. We talked on the phone several hours before I needed to go to bed. The next night was a repeat, again Thursday night. We enjoyed our conversations so much we just had to meet. We made plans to meet at the new supper club in town. Before we ended our conversation, Katie got on the phone with us and said she and her ex-sister-in-law wanted to join us also. Our first meeting wouldn't be awkward. She just needed an excuse to go out and used our date.

"This one is my pick," Jesus told the Father. "Ralph needs her as much as she needs him. She must overcome barriers put in place by her past experiences and he should learn to trust women again. She'll show him how to be more responsible."

Listening in to Jesus' plans, Evil asked the other demons their opinions, "What can we do to ruin this meeting? Don't you remember what she said she would never be with again? Also, we need to make her worry about physically being attracted to him and put doubts in the mix, so she will wonder if she's made a mistake."

I walked in the place alone looking for Katie because I'd never laid eyes on Ralph before. I felt he had to be cute because his sister was a doll. She reminded me of Princess Diana. But the fact was I knew I liked Ralph from the beginning. It didn't matter what he looked like. I was going to have fun this night regardless.

When Katie called Ralph over to our table I held my breath as I sized him up. No, he wasn't the type of man I usually was attracted to, but he was cute. I thought so until he opened his mouth. His teeth were in bad shape. Most of his front teeth were somewhat decayed. I never could deal with that. It was gross. I'd been brought up to take care of my teeth. Mama was a dental hygienist and made sure that JL and I knew how to prevent decay. I'd always considered bad dental hygiene somewhat of a character flaw in people. When I'd meet some guy with bad teeth it would turn me off instantly. I got a grip over my thoughts immediately before I bolted out the door. I focused on his good traits instead and how nice he was.

Darlene was at Dana's and I had not made prior arrangements for her to spend the night I needed to leave before it got too late. When Ralph walked me to my car I knew I really liked him even with bad teeth. When he wanted to kiss me goodnight I didn't refuse. He promised to call me the next night. When I left, him I felt okay. I'd made it through a very nice evening.

We talked on the phone again the next night and I made plans to have him over for Sunday night dinner with Darlene and me. My plan was to cook spaghetti with garlic bread on the side.

When Ralph showed up he was a little high on something and had been drinking beer. My mind went into protective mode immediately. I had promised myself never to get involved with a drunk again and here was one I liked. What was I going to do?

He gorged himself on three plates of spaghetti and Darlene was not impressed. She got my attention in the kitchen where he couldn't hear and told me very plainly, "I don't like him. He is

264

gross, Mama. Why can't you date Sid? He was nice and isn't a pig."

I thought she was funny being so protective. I told her, "Don't worry honey, I'm not going to get involved with any guy just yet."

After Ralph left and Darlene went to bed, I had to be alone with Jesus. He said I would know his pick for me by a sweet, gentle spirit. Well, Ralph had that, but he was not what I expected. I was very, very confused and unsure of myself. I was not going to encourage someone until I was sure. Didn't Jesus say not to make things happen? I needed some reassurance from Him.

Since our reunion, Jesus was right there when I called Him. I had many questions. First was, "How can I trust myself to know when to relax with a man when I am so scared?"

Led to the scriptures again, I read we are supposed to look at the good and pure in everything and not focus on the bad and to trust in the Lord to take care of us. I knew Ralph was a good person, but he was showing signs of behaviors that I swore I'd never allow around me ever again.

My second question was, "Should I listen to Darlene's concerns and focus on what she wants for us?"

"*You are the parent, she is the child. You need to influence her, not the other way around,*" I heard Him say.

During the next few weeks, Ralph would show up at the house high and slightly drunk. I made him tell me what he was high on and wasn't surprised when he said the drug was marijuana. As much I hated his drinking, he was happy and mellow when drunk. He was a very kind and affectionate person. I knew deep in my spirit he would not hurt me or Darlene.

Darlene came up to me one day furious with Ralph. He had let her kitten outside and the little thing was chased up a tree by the neighbor's dog. Rascal spent most of the day in that tree until he fell out trying to get down. Darlene was so mad with Ralph I thought she would never forgive him. She was rude to him a lot. I had to sit her down and tell her to get over it. Ralph was upset about the cat also. We hadn't ever told him not to let the cat outside. He didn't know Rascal had never been outdoors before, so it was an innocent mistake.

Dana and Mac both liked Ralph and Ralph like them as well. I was experiencing harmony in my life even with a marijuana smoking, beer drinking man hanging around.

Each morning during my quiet time with Jesus I would question whether Ralph was the one or not. Jesus answered my questions with other questions. *"Are you happy?* Yes. *"Was Ralph abusive?* No. *"Can you depend on Ralph?* So far. *"Was Ralph a sweet spirited person?* Yes.

With more questions being answered positively, my doubts about his drinking and pot smoking started to go away. Didn't about everyone I knew smoke some pot? Yes. I had even done it myself occasionally. Didn't just about everyone I knew drink a little? Yes. It was how they treated you while drinking that mattered didn't it? Yes. So, I settled my fears and started letting Ralph's advances towards me get stronger. It had been so long since I felt passion with someone. Most of the sex I had with Al was rough and scary, not passionate.

My moral meter was still set in the wrong mode. I couldn't hear the '*wait not yet*' voice that used to go off in my head. Before I knew it, I had jumped ahead not asking Jesus' permission or even wanting permission before entering a physical relationship. I still wasn't asking Him first if what I wanted was all right. Had I done something wrong?

"Finally, guys, we have a break here. Let's make her doubt His love for her and make her afraid of Him. If we can keep that fear alive in her then the doubts alone will cause her great problems. She can't be allowed to know His compassion and patience." Evil said to his companions.

Jesus, thought to himself, "Oh, Little One, I wish you could come to me like you did when you were small. I really hate that doubt separates us so much."

After it happened, I worried that I may have broken His one command not to rush things. I was afraid to ask Him. Even though I knew I couldn't hide anything from Him, not even my thoughts.

When Easter week came that spring, I was happily beside myself. I was going to celebrate the resurrection of my Lord properly. I could thank Him in person and with honor. It was all I could do to not weep uncontrollably during the Holy week's services. Ralph went to church with us on Maundy Thursday for the communion service. I was happy. He cared about my beliefs enough to want to share them with me. He even went to Darlene's youth choir concert the next night. That was the night Darlene's feelings about him changed. He had made a big deal out of wanting to hear her solo. After Sunday's service, we were invited to go to Ralph's parents, so Darlene could go on an Easter egg hunt with the rest of grandkids. We had a good time. Everyone made us feel like part of their family.

On Darlene's spring break that year Drake wanted to have her visit. While she was away, Dana and I made plans to go to the beach with a couple of our friends. We were going on a girls' getaway. Only one thing was trying to stop me from going and it was our cat. I needed someone to feed him while I was away. Ralph volunteered to stay at the house, take care of Rascal and remove a dead tree limb that was hanging too close to the roof.

When I got home from the beach, I was surprised by a pizza dinner, the place was cleaned, the dead tree limb hanging over the roof was gone, and the cat was fine. Ralph didn't go back to live with Katie again after that. I don't remember asking him to stay, we just slipped into that arrangement slick as grease.

Having him live with me felt natural and easy. I had one more hurdle to jump over and that was introducing Ralph to Daddy.

Daddy had suspicions and every right after my experience with Al. When Ralph met Daddy, of course, he had been drinking. Daddy's first impression was tainted a bit.

I had the wrath of Jason come down on me hard. "How could you get involved with another drunk after the last fiasco?" Daddy asked. "He will not take advantage of you or Darlene because of this house. I will not allow you or anything you have be a reason for a man to use you ever again. We'll see just how long he stays with you when you don't have a nice place to live in anymore." He told me emphatically.

Daddy had always suspected Al married me because he thought I was going to inherit a lot of money. He was not taking any chances with my next boyfriend.

The next week, my house was up for sale. I couldn't do anything about it nor did I want to I had placed myself in Daddy's care so long I trusted him to know what was best for me even when I couldn't see it. The house was in Daddy's name. I was just to inherit it after he was gone. He told me to start packing because he was selling it as soon as he got a good offer which didn't take long to our surprise.

I think Daddy felt bad about his actions after he saw that Ralph didn't care one way or the other where we lived. He cared about me and Darlene, not our house or what Daddy had. Daddy started looking for us an apartment to live in after he sold the house, so I wouldn't have to do it after work. He didn't work so he had more time plus, he knew more about rent and agreements than I did. It just made sense. Before I knew it, Daddy had found us a two-bedroom apartment on the ground floor in a very nice place.

The money he got each month from the sale of my house came to me for the rent on our apartment. I was very happy at my new place. It didn't bother me at all not to have the house. One morning during my quiet time with Jesus I asked Him this question, "Why am I not sad about losing the house?"

He said, *"The house was your personal den of iniquity where bad experiences happened to you and sin went rampant. You needed a clean start where good memories could form."*

That summer was great. I loved having a swimming pool close by where I could invite my friends over for fun. Dana came over often. She and her kids loved swimming and so did Darlene. Darlene and I would go to Ralph's softball games to watch him play and we enjoyed his friends as well.

Darlene met a few new friends at the apartment, so she was always on the go. We were always having visitors over. Ralph's friends, his younger brother Rodney and his family were frequent visitors. I was in my element because I loved to entertain.

I only had one issue the whole time, Ralph's contributions to our finances weren't steady and consistent. One week he'd give me thirty dollars another week it would be fifty. Every now and then, he would give me a hundred. When I asked him about it, he'd say, "Gene's Oyster Bar took it." That meant his tab came due and the owner demanded payment.

Nevertheless, I was content. I didn't eat much so all I needed to worry about was Darlene. Daddy had made sure the payment from the house sale was coming in regularly. It was enough to pay the rent and utilities. My paycheck took care of my food bill and gas and Drake's child support helped with Darlene's extra needs.

"This happiness just keeps making me sick," Evil said. It's time to see just how much this boyfriend can take. I'm going to make Rachel sick and put pressure on him to take care of Darlene. He won't be able to do his thing in the afternoons and it will cause him to tuck his tail and run. He's not one for responsibility and Rachel needs to see that fault in him."

*****

Preservation knew his orders were still to be enforced, so Evil's plans were going to have problems. Not only did Rachel have him, but the presence of the Lord was with her continually and Satan's plans would be frustrated.

271

*****

After a night of entertainment with a lot of smoking, I went to work not feeling well. I had coughed all night and was having a difficult time breathing. After lunch, a nurse at the center said, "Rachel you look blue around your mouth. You need to let Dr. Evans look at you." Before I knew it, I was being driven to the hospital and admitted.

I had the office where I worked call Daddy. I knew he would make sure everything was taken care of. I couldn't call Ralph because he wasn't family and was not considered my caregiver. Joan went to take care of Darlene, and Daddy came to the hospital to be with me. It was when I was taken to a room after all kinds of tests and x-rays that I could call Ralph to let him know what was going on.

Of course, Ralph came to the hospital high and smelling of beer. Thank goodness it was after Daddy had left. I told him something had ruptured in my lung and would have to be in the hospital a few days. Concerned for me he volunteered to take over. He took responsibility for Darlene and made sure she did her homework each night and she had dinner. Those days were good because they were getting along well and worked together as a team when it came to eating and laundry. By then Ralph won over Daddy after he saw how much Ralph cared for us.

Before I would be released to go home, I had to abide a warning from my Doctor, "Not to smoke another cigarette because I could die." He meant that literally. When I had been rushed to

272

the hospital that afternoon from work my x-rays showed smoke in my body cavity around my heart it was causing heart problems as well as breathing issues. The smoke came from a tiny rupture in my lung. Being addicted to cigarettes, I had been smoking even though I could hardly breathe that day. Now I had to quit cold turkey. Ralph wasn't even allowed to smoke near me.

I prayed a lot while I was in the hospital knowing Jesus was there with me every minute. I asked Him to help me overcome my addiction, so I could heal. He answered me because I never smoked another cigarette after that.

Because it was close to Christmas after my stint in the hospital I started cooking cookies, cakes, and candies to keep my mind busy. I had so much fun doing that for a family again. I was cooking this year in honor of Jesus' birthday and loving every minute of it. When Ralph's girls came over I'd have all kinds of treats.

We made a nice little Christmas for Darlene and Ralph's two daughters plus a half-sister to his two that he had claimed many years as his own. It was also my first Christmas that I could claim Jesus for real in my life. It was special to me to know His spirit was close by, just a breath away. It was so nice that our family group could go and celebrate His birth at the midnight candle lighting ceremony.

It started bothering me during the week of Christmas that I wasn't married to Ralph. It was hard not to complain to him about it. I knew in my spirit I was being convicted because I hadn't bothered to even ask Jesus about it before we started living together.

But after Christmas, my flesh got in the way and my guilt overtook my mouth. We had never fought about anything.

When our fussing started making waves in our relationship some of my old fears started to kick in.

One morning I had to talk with Jesus after a night of arguments. Ralph and I decided to split up. I asked the Lord what to do finally. I loved Ralph and I didn't want him to leave. But, I knew I was living in sin and couldn't deal with it anymore.

The Lord said within my spirit. *"I told you from the beginning not to influence your circumstances and you disobeyed. Now that you have repented, ask Ralph to forgive you and tell him you'll be patient. Then do as I said. Wait and see. Always give me your worries and fears and let's deal with them together. You have met the sweet gentle spirit I told you about. Learn to relax and things will change."*

Comforted by His words to my heart, I did what I was told. When Ralph got home that evening I didn't hesitate I told him. "I'm sorry I got so angry the other night. I don't want us to break up. I love you. I'll stop pressuring you about it."

He replied, "I love you. I'm just not ready yet. I haven't been divorced long and I don't want to be tied down just now. Let's get off the subject and start again."

It was hard to accept those words. I felt like he had punched me, but I had strict orders not to complain or fuss about it anymore.

Our relationship did start over. My attitude had changed because I had a stronger force helping me through my discouragements. My self-worth wasn't in Ralph, it was in what the Lord had said to me. And just as Jesus had said, on Valentine's Day, Ralph asked me to marry him.

We decided to get married one year from the date of our first meeting which didn't allow a lot of time to plan. We had one month and four days to work with, so we had to move fast on a few things. I knew Ralph had creditors snapping at his heels, so I suggested he file bankruptcy. I didn't need my credit ruined with his. I had learned how that worked from working with a bankruptcy attorney. We called my friend the bankruptcy attorney to get the process started.

When we told Daddy, we were getting married, he gave me Mama's wedding rings as a token of his blessing. He was happy we weren't going to be shacking up anymore. Now that I had my wedding rings we needed to get a band for Ralph.

Everything fell into place extremely fast. Even the bankruptcy was filed quickly. We confirmed the date with my church and secured a minister to perform our service. I found dresses for me and Darlene. I played with artificial flowers, so we could have bouquets and headpieces to wear.

Ralph and I asked his ex-wife to get dresses for their girls because we wanted them to stand up with us when the ceremony was taking place. I also asked Dana to be my matron of honor.

I bought the food. I found tablecloths, plates, and cups in a spring design that matched perfectly with the color scheme I was using. I had everything I needed.

I cooked for days before the date, so we would have a nice reception at our apartment's clubhouse after the wedding. Dana even blessed me by ordering a three-tiered cake and Mac offered to provide us with champagne and beer.

I thought everything was ready until Dana and I saw the décor in the clubhouse. The day before the service, we ran around town hunting decorations I could afford. My money was almost gone, and the clubhouse looked blah. At Wal-Mart, we found some paper bells and ribbon, so we did what we could with those. When Dana went to get my cake, she saw a flower arrangement at her friend's house that would look great as a centerpiece on the reception table. She asked if she could borrow it for the wedding. I was very pleased with the outcome.

My wedding day, March 18th, 1989 at 4:00 pm I was at the church with the kids and Dana waiting on Ralph. Everyone was there except Ralph and his best man, Doug. We were beginning to worry. Even his parents were worried about a possible no-show. Thinking it was hilarious, Ralph walked down the aisle instead of me, followed by Doug. Doug was the reason they were late so he tried to make a suspenseful situation appear funny.

276

Because of my new-found relationship with Jesus, as I stood to say my vows to Ralph, I was also saying them to my Lord. He had shown me just days earlier a threefold cord was not easily broken so I included Him with every word I professed. He had to be our glue.

I can honestly say our sweet little ceremony went off great. The vows were exchanged, the rings were placed on each other's fingers and then we were officially married. Now everyone was ready for our reception and fun.

When we arrived, Dana took over. She made sure people were served, pictures were taken, Ralph and I could cut the beautiful cake and make our toast with champagne.

We had so many gifts to open and lovely surprises one after another. It truly was one of the best days of my life. Our friends were so kind. They apparently knew we were low on cash. By that afternoon, we were rolling in the dough.

After our parents left the party started. Ralph proceeded to get really wasted. I can say one thing about him, though, he was a happy drunk. During one of his antics, he tried to shoot my blue garter to his friends with his mouth. When he did, one of his front caps popped off causing him to be snaggle-toothed. We have pictures to prove it.

When our party slowed down, and people were leaving, we were rushed off to our honeymoon suite located at the Downtowner, a nice hotel in town. It was a gift from my friends and co-workers. When we arrived at the hotel, Ralph wasn't finished partying. He wanted to go to Gene's, of all places to show off. So, we dressed in casual clothes and went to the oyster bar. Since Ralph was well known at the bar, people were buying him one beer after another to congratulate us. I couldn't drink because someone had to be the designated driver.

When I finally convinced my new husband to leave he was beyond stable. I had to help him in into the room. As I was getting dressed for bed, I heard a moan, and then him begging me, "bring me a trash can, I'm going to be sick." Yes, he was sick, vomiting two or three times before he rolled over and passed out. I knew I couldn't let him stay in his clothes all night, so I proceeded to undress him. That's when I noticed marks on his arms, legs, and places on his sides. "What in the world?" I thought. It looked like he had been whipped. I asked myself, why would his friends do this to him last night at his bachelor party? I became so angry when I saw some of the marks on his sides seeping fluid. His skin was raw.

Because I didn't have an alert husband right then to talk with, I spoke to the Lord, "Sweet Jesus, what have I gotten myself into this time? Only you know. At least I have you to talk with tonight because Ralph is out cold."

At that point, I poured myself a glass of champagne and sat there looking at my new husband asking the Lord to protect him and not allow anything or anyone to ever hurt him again. Something came over me that night and I did something I never did for Drake or Al - I gave Ralph over to the Lord. I officially had the right to pray for him because I was his and he was mine so, I gave him to my God for protection and help.

After giving my husband to the Lord, I rested in knowing He does what we ask Him. I relaxed and forgave Ralph for his overindulgence. I just couldn't be mad at him. It was sort of funny when I thought about it.

That night I also knew Jesus was making me face certain issues I had with Drake. This time I was going to learn to depend on Him and not Ralph. I had tried to make Drake my protector and companion, but he failed. Ralph would fail as well because he is human, but Jesus never will. He will never leave me or forsake me, and I was happy with that knowledge. It freed Ralph from the responsibility.

I felt so alone during my first honeymoon. Even though I was alone in this honeymoon suite, I had my Jesus and didn't feel neglected. We didn't need a honeymoon night. We'd already done that part. So, after I had my champagne I got into bed beside Ralph, dressed in my honeymoon nightgown and thanked the Lord for a good day then went to sleep.

My poor husband was in no shape the next morning for the breakfast buffet that was provided in our honeymoon package. I ate my share while he tried to drink his coffee. He was pitiful, and his eyes showed me just how bad he felt. I had to ask the question, "Ralph why do you have stripes all over your body? What happened and who did that to you?"

"The guys thought I needed to know what it was like to be bound so they tied me up with duct tape and stuck me to a tree. The marks are from struggling against the tape not because they beat me or anything like that. It was all done in fun and when they cut the tape away it left marks." He said to appease me.

"Well, I don't like it. They were too rough. You have places that need attention and an antibiotic cream." I said.

"I'll let you do that when we get home. All I want to do is find something for my head and stomach and rest awhile until softball practice." He said.

"You don't mean that you are going to practice ball this afternoon feeling as bad as you do and on the very next day after our wedding, do you? I asked.

My spirit said, *Stop it! Take him for what he is and let it go.*

His reply was, "I'd like to go practice with the guys. Why don't you and Darlene come with me."

I could complain or make it fun, the choice was up to me, so I decided to go with the flow and do what he wanted. Believe it, or not, we had a lot of fun that day. Our first outing as a family was watching a game and getting a burger afterward.

MAKING THINGS BETTER

A few days after we were married we decided to combine our money into one bank account. Ralph trusted me enough at that point to do right by him and not totally strip him of everything. He and I met at my bank, so we could do the transactions but were surprised when the bank officer refused to do what we wanted. Her reason was that Ralph was a high risk due to his filing bankruptcy and his bad credit. Offended, we left my bank and went to the bank his mother and father used. They accepted us right away. I wasn't going to do business with a bank that didn't accept my family and Ralph was my family whether he had a history or not.

The next plan of attack was to get a loan where we could get Ralph's teeth properly taken care of. He had the estimate for how much it was going to cost. We knew what we were facing but we didn't have that kind of money saved between us.

I prayed about it and asked for guidance and was led to ask Ralph's father for help. I knew better than to ask mine. I explained to Ralph's Dad why we needed a loan and what the dentist had told us. We explained his teeth would cause other health issues if not seen about soon. Ralph's Dad told me to start the necessary arrangements for the loan at the bank and he would co-sign on the note for us. In one day's time, we had the money.

Over the next couple of weeks, Ralph went through dental torture, but his teeth turned out beautiful. He was happy with his new smile. It made him a new person. He had confidence once more and smiled a lot.

We were still going to church but not as regular as we had been. Each message at my church did nothing for my spirit and it did not edify my sweet Lord. Why do Pastors want to make people feel so bad about their lives? Don't they know it only causes them to feel unloved even more? Jesus doesn't go about helping people that way. He certainly didn't get my attention again like that. One thing for sure I was really excited about worshipping Him on Easter Sunday. I wanted to love all over Jesus for what He was for me. I was only to be disappointed again when the message didn't express His love for us. I left there feeling empty.

We tried attending our new Sunday school class as a married couple, but we were not encouraged. All they wanted to do in class was to eat and socialize. Where was the interest in Jesus? Nothing was ever being said about Him. Most of the messages were on how to keep your marriages together or raising kids. There wasn't anything about Him being the actual glue for marriage and the building block for having and raising children.

Several months after our wedding, Daddy's mind was set on getting us back into a house. I think he was satisfied knowing Ralph was nothing like he first thought.

Day after day Daddy dragged Ralph and me to place after place so he could show us what he had found. I didn't care for hardly any of the houses he showed us. Finally, he took us to this cute little house that was almost brand new and was owned by a sweet little family. Walking around I felt a sense of calm come over me. When we were shown the master bedroom I knew why. Over the bed hung a brass cross and on the night-table was a worn-out Bible. These people knew my Lord. I knew instantly, and I think Ralph did also this was going to be our new home.

Every legal need to obtain that house went smoothly and we moved into it quickly. Because the house was located only a few miles from our apartment it didn't take long to set up the house. Darlene didn't have to change buses to get to school. Every motion was blessed. Daddy even gave us new living furniture as a belated wedding present. Ralph's best friend gave us a large living room rug and entertainment center for a gift. Now our new house was beautiful.

✳✳✳✳✳

"It's time that we cause attitudes to change and hearts to be mended," Jesus said to the Father. "Ralph needs to feel better about himself and Rachel needs to face her fear of confrontations. Let's set up the scenario for this to happen."

✳✳✳✳✳

When Evil tried to stop the progress of Jesus' plans he was always met with opposition. Angels were everywhere protecting and defending Rachel's new family.

✳✳✳✳✳

For Father's Day, the girls and I decided to spruce up Ralph's softball gear. His tennis shoes were worn out and his shorts were horrible. We bought new cleats, socks, and shorts. He looked sporty the first time he wore them to a game. I thought he was very cute and I was proud he didn't look thrown away anymore.

After the game, one of his so-called friends started making fun of his new shoes. He said they blinded him on the field because they were so white. He went over to Ralph and kicked dirt on them and stepped all over them to make them dirty. I went livid, furious was not the word. My flesh rose, in indignation. Mama bear was wide awake! I was holding a cup of cola in my hand, so I marched right up to his friend, poured my drink on his shoes and kicked dirt on them. My words were, "You need to respect the fact that these girls spent their savings on their Daddy, so he could look good for the team. You ruined their gift and insulted him right in their faces." Ralph didn't say a thing.

What had come over me? I've never been one to confront someone like that. I wanted to fight, and this bully was my focus. I was tired of these so-called friends treating my husband like a worthless piece of trash. He couldn't see it, why? Ralph's fun-loving and happy nature caused these people to mistreat and take advantage of him and I was tired of it. When he would get high or drunk around them he would become their object of jokes or their go fetch guy; just a dog to kick around for amusement. My heart ached for him because his girls and I wanted to make him look like one of the team and they were making fun of him.

After that incident, I didn't see much disrespect for Ralph when I was around. I knew I didn't fit in with his crowd of friends. We had nothing in common and I always felt out of place. Jesus showed me in the Word why I wasn't comfortable around them.

After that, I didn't fret anymore about it. Our spirits were at odds with each other, so I chose not to hang around with them long.

That summer Ralph and I wanted to go to the beach as a family, so he asked his best friend to contact his father who lived at the beach. It was a blessing because his friend's father was going out of town that weekend and said we could use his place. Getting there was another issue. All we had as transportation was my little two-door Sprint. Being determined, though, we managed to get luggage, three kids, Ralph and I to Panama City Beach for a two-night, three-day trip. We made the most of our accommodations and had a very good time.

When we got home and told Daddy about our trip, he laughed. He said, "That had to have been a sight, five people squished into a matchbox of a car with no air conditioning at the beach. I wish you had taken a picture." So, what did he do next? He proceeded to find me a car. He didn't let up on the issue until I agreed to something larger with better features. One week later, I had a new car with a larger car payment, but Daddy was happy.

I knew Daddy always felt he was doing what was best for me. At times, I wished I could stand up to him a little better. I didn't always want what he wanted and even though the car was nice it wasn't something that I would have really picked out for me. I could say for sure, though, it was roomier and had air. Along with the larger payment, the insurance also went up and it seemed during those days our money wasn't stretching very far.

I was a stickler for Ralph to make his child support payments regularly. Sometimes due to his bad habits, it caused me to have to dip into household funds to make it happen. He was still running a tab at Gene's for his beer drinking with the guys, so money got tight some weeks. I was becoming a little stressed over the bills.

STRESS

"**D**o you guys see what I see?" said Evil. "I've found another weak spot in her mind. She is worried about finances. If finances cause her stress let's turn the pressure up higher and take away some of their money."

*****

One afternoon after work Ralph came home early. I knew something was up because he looked miffed. So, I asked, "What's up? Why are you home early?"

His reply was, "I got canned today. I asked for a raise and when Bob said no, I threatened to leave and he fired me."

"Go apologize," I said immediately "We need your job."

"It won't do any good, he's too stubborn. Plus, I can find something better I need a new scene anyway." He said.

While Ralph searched for work he was allowed unemployment but that didn't go very far. My stress level hit an all-time high. How were we going to make payments and eat? I was embarrassed about our predicament and was intimated by bill collectors.

Finally, Ralph got a job working with his younger brother, Rodney as a house framer. They built houses all around town for a good establishment. The only problem was when it rained. They couldn't work and when they didn't work both brothers proceeded to play by getting high on anything and everything they could find and get as drunk as they could. They were a pair.

I liked Rodney a lot but, he was always leading Ralph into things that weren't safe or legal for that matter. I came to find out if a drug made them feel good they'd take it no matter what it was. I was scared and the only assurance I had was trying to rest in my prayers. I asked Jesus to keep Ralph safe and out of trouble, but my faith was so weak. I must admit I complained a lot.

"Trust me," Jesus would say.

I was still a baby Christian in many ways. Faith had not been instilled in me yet and I found myself begging Jesus for help a lot.

Ralph confessed one night after a heated discussion that he and Rodney would take LSD, uppers, downers, marijuana, acid as well as legal prescriptions for pain or nervous disorders when they could get them and some time snort cocaine. They enjoyed being high. It made their lives interesting and a lot more fun. So, I was told politely to butt out. He knew what he was doing, he was grown.

*****

"**We**'ve got her mind in our control again guys," Evil said. "We'll cause her to have sleepless nights and stomach issues due to stress. We'll make her doubt her marriage, now that she isn't going to a church anymore."

288

*****

For two and a half years Ralph and Rodney worked together, I would thank God when the rainy days didn't come. Not only did they both not make any money when it rained they both went stupid trying to see who could outdo the other getting wasted.

Rodney's wife was always fussing and causing an uproar in the family. Ralph begged me not to do that. He hated a moaner and complainer and vowed he wouldn't live with one. His warning was taken and stored.

My stress got the best of me and my stomach was always in knots. Plus, the weight loss surgery, I had gone through years earlier hadn't help matters. It was causing me so many problems that I had to be hospitalized at times. I even had to undergo another surgery because I wasn't digesting my food properly and this caused me to develop gallstones.

I was grateful Darlene was older and could take care of herself pretty much. Ralph was hardly ever sober in those days. I was scared and worried all the time. He was still the sweet-spirited person I fell in love with but, he was under such horrible influences and I had no control over it. The bad influence was a family member; go figure.

During those years, my only solace was Jesus. I had him to talk with and I tried to give him my worries. Dana and I couldn't agree completely anymore. She was in the process of leaving Mac and wanting to party all the time. I was not in agreement. Mac was a good person and I didn't like the way she was treating him. Whenever I asked her to seek Jesus, she would brush me off and say I was living in a fairy tale and she couldn't understand why I did some of the things I did.

I tried to justify myself by telling her I wasn't the same person. The old person died, and I wanted to live right. It hurt my feelings that my best friend had turned her back on me and to be honest I didn't want another one if I had to change. All my life I needed friends. I felt lonely without a person to be with or talk to and now I didn't care if I even had a friend. I had the only thing I needed and as His Word states, He is closer than any brother.

Sad to think that your husband ignores you, your daughter wants to be with her friends all the time and now your best friend who had been so close was deserting you because of your faith. Maybe this was another test I was going through. I'd make it, there is always tomorrow.

I wasn't attending church much anymore, but I thought my spirit was being fed. At lunch, each day I'd come home for forty-five minutes to watch the Christian Broadcast Network with Pat Robertson. After work, the first thing I'd do would be to turn on Marilyn Hickey who was on the Trinity Broadcasting Network. Those programs were my lifeline and helped me cope. After watching them, it helped to ask the Lord questions for me. Each morning I'd let Him lead me through His Word. I was trying my best to rest and be content, but it was very hard.

My only anchor was His two words to me, *"Trust me."*

Things started getting worse for us financially and I was forced to look for another job. I applied with another government agency and landed a job two pay grades higher than the one I had. I was glad I had the new job, but I was afraid Ralph and Rodney would show up on my job high as a kite and cause problems for me. I now worked in an office where Sheriff Officers could visit regularly, and I was in constant fear of Ralph and his brother being found out. Plus, I was told we were under strict rules concerning alcohol and drugs because we handle a lot of money each day.

The Labor Department had been the brunt of a scandal a few years earlier and everyone was afraid to mention alcohol and drugs. It was said that many of the employees there had to undergo lie detector tests and drug screens and I couldn't risk that. I'd be canned instantly if I was asked if I did drugs or if anyone in my family had. Then what would we do? We'd lose our finances, our health insurance, life insurance and be almost destitute.

Because of Rodney's actions, his wife wanted a separation from him. For a while, he moved in with us. He promised to behave and not bring any drugs in the house, but I knew he was lying to me. One day, one of his shady friends followed him into his bedroom. I didn't like it and knocked on the closed door. When Rodney opened, the room smelled like marijuana smoke and I freaked out. I threw both out and told Rodney to find another place. Our lively hood depended on my job and I wasn't going to let him ruin it for us.

Ralph wasn't too happy with me, but he tried to understand. Somewhere along the way, he knew he had to straighten up. He agreed to let me use my influences at work to find him another job. After all, I did work for the Labor Department.

I scraped up enough money to buy Ralph a nice outfit and a new pair of shoes for his interviews. I typed up his resume, so he would be ready when jobs were available. He wanted something to do with his hands. One of my co-workers found a job announcement for a foreman position in a local wax manufacturing plant. The job entailed repairing equipment and she knew Ralph was qualified and set up a job interview for him.

Because of his associations at Gene's Oyster Bar, he had an interview with someone he knew and got the job. Things were finally starting to look up and turn around for us. Steady work rain or shine.

Several months into the new job, Ralph could get another truck, and this made his self-esteem so much better. He was learning to be more responsible and started wanting to do better. I noticed he wasn't getting high as much after work and this made me happier.

SHAKE, RATTLE & ROLL

My little girl was now fifteen and had her learner's license. Every time we would have to go somewhere she wanted to drive. My patience wasn't all that great, but I did what I had to. Ralph also let her drive with him from time to time especially when I had to work out of town.

During that year, my new job had me traveling a lot; two or three days a week some months. It was during those times alone in hotel rooms, I would have the most awesome revelations while studying my Bible. While working in another town, I met a co-worker named Margaret who was just as much into the Word as I was. We had so much fun together sharing our thoughts. She loved the Lord as much as I did, and our conversations got to be somewhat colorful at times. I missed having a Christian friend to talk with who understood me. I hadn't had one since my friendship with Betty. Betty and I lost touch with each other after their family had to relocate. Her husband's job was the main source of their livelihood, so they didn't have a choice but move when he had to go to another plant. That's why they rented houses wherever they went.

After Darlene turned sixteen, she was determined to work. We were shocked when she found herself a part-time job after school. Our rock stepped in once again. Daddy took it upon himself to find her a car, so she wouldn't have to use mine. Like me, Darlene didn't know how to voice her opinion around Daddy and she hated the car he chose for her. That car really was ugly. It looked like a box on wheels. It had no pizzazz. It was just a blue square cube. It had one good feature, it moved and that was all that mattered. She promised us she would pay for it anyway and help me with her insurance, so we were content.

Daddy was in the car buying mood. As he was looking for Darlene a car he was also wheeling and dealing for me a new car. He wasn't happy I was traveling a lot for my job in a car that didn't have enough power to get me out of situations when needed or braking ability to stop on a dime when I had too. Atlanta was a fast and furious town and sometimes you needed speed and good brakes.

One afternoon, Daddy called me at work and asked me to drive over to this car dealership located in our area. I did as I was asked. When I arrived, I saw this beautiful new silver Grand Am and commented to myself that I'd really like something like that. To my joy, Daddy had already made a trade with my old car for that very one. I was very happy. The little car was great, and the payments weren't going to be bad either. Daddy really had a gift when it came to buying cars. This time I can say his choice was right on with my taste.

I loved working at my new job. It made me feel important and valued. I wanted to work hard to show my appreciation. I had a training session scheduled in Atlanta and as I was getting ready the morning of the trip I slipped on a piece of dry cat food in the kitchen and landed hard on my bad knee. I had trouble standing and was very unstable, but I managed to drive myself to the hospital to have it checked out. I was given pain pills and a brace to wear with instructions to stay off my leg as much as possible. I called Ralph and told him what happened and that I was all right.

I was hurting and unstable even with my brace, but I still went to Atlanta because I had a job to do. Those two days were very uncomfortable, and I couldn't rest well. I was thankful to God that I had a co-worker also scheduled for the Atlanta training to travel with me in case I needed help.

When I got home my knee was still hurting so I made an appointment with an Orthopedic doctor. He x-rayed my knee again and was livid with the hospital. I hadn't sprained my knee. I had broken my kneecap. Due to my history with knee trouble, he ordered an MRI and realized I had no ligaments supporting the two large leg bones. Without a stable kneecap, I was in real danger of harming myself badly.

It took six weeks for my kneecap to heal properly and get strong enough for me to undergo ligament replacement surgery. After that surgery, I was given another type of brace to wear and ordered to take therapy starting two weeks later.

The therapy was torture, but I needed it if I was going to be able to work. I was glad Darlene could drive. She took me to appointments and therapy when needed. Our time together then was very special. She was getting older and I tried to use our times together to stay connected and learn where her heart was and if she was truly happy.

"**We** have another entrance inside her mind fellows," Evil said. "We can't make her doubt His love for her brat. We'll cause her to forget His promise to protect this kid and make her do things to ruin their relationship. If she relaxes and trusts in Him, He'll take control and we won't stand a chance. We have to work fast and make the kid rebel."

"**Oh**, no you don't," Preservation said to Evil. "She has a hedge that you cannot break through. Stop or be destroyed!"

*****

I'd begun noticing Darlene was a little too secretive about a boy she was seeing, and it caused me some concern. When I found out why I was not a happy camper. This boy was a known drug addict in town and he was several years her senior. The more I tried to talk to her about him the worse she lied and did things behind my back.

Frantic with worry, I did the only thing I knew and that was to pray. I was reminded so sweetly, by my sweet Jesus that I had given her to Him many years ago, and He had warned me not to focus on what I saw. He saved me from hell's pit, didn't He? I knew He could protect my daughter.

I can honestly say my faith was not very strong and I let my flesh get in His way often. My mouth just wouldn't shut up. If I could plug up my mouth and trust Him things would work out.

One day, Darlene called me from her job very upset. This boyfriend had shoved her around and stolen her car. Upset, I told my boss about her situation. I had known he had been a cop prior to working with the State. Maybe he would know what to do. He and I went to get Darlene from work. He took us straight to the police station, so we could obtain a warrant for his arrest, and press charges for assault against the boy.

Close to midnight, the Belmont police department called our house because they had found Darlene's car in a drug-infested part of town. The boyfriend had abandoned the car and was nowhere to be found. Several days passed before they called to tell us he had been arrested. By then, Darlene was doubting what we had done and wanted to forgive this boy and take him back. She was mad at me when I wouldn't dismiss the charges. She was extremely embarrassed and very upset when her Granddaddy got involved.

She didn't know why he was so adamant about making this boy pay. I had never told her how badly Al had treated me so she didn't understand why Daddy was so upset about her issues. Daddy had made a promise that no man would ever hurt us ever again and even in his old age he was going to make sure that promise was kept. Whatever it cost, he wanted to make this boy pay. He was using him as an excuse to release pent-up guilt over what had happened to me.

The boy called our house all hours of the night. Darlene rigged our phone to prevent us from hearing it ring when he called. She would accept the charges for his calls, so they could talk. I didn't know this was going on until I got my telephone bill. I had acquaintances at the Sheriff's office because of my work. They gave me all the telephone numbers that inmates used. I immediately acted with this ammunition and blocked every one of those phone lines, so he couldn't call anymore.

Christmas at our house that year was a little stressful. My daughter had become one rebellious cookie. She was mad at all of us, me, my Daddy, and Ralph. No one was making her happy. I felt if we could keep her and that boy apart long enough it would give her time for her feelings for him to change. That plan backfired, and it was my plans that were changed.

Shortly after the Holidays, our court dates came due and our case was thrown out of court. The boy's rights were validated. We had no proof that he stole Darlene's car or that he abused her. We had no right to keep him in jail any longer and the court agreed. Now, this boy was free, and my daughter was rebellious. What were we going to do?

"*Trust me!*" I heard my Lord whisper.

I can't explain what happened, but she lost interest in the boy shortly after his release after she got a different job working evenings at the local Waffle House. She was making good money and was associating with a better group of people. Maybe his bad-boy appeal was over.

"**R**eady guys? We must start another plan-of-attack immediately. If we can't make her doubt the kid's protection maybe we can cause her to panic over her husband. Let's try it. Something has to stop her from believing Him." Evil stated.

Preservation said. "When will they ever learn that we can hear them? Angels, start watching for this attack. Be ready for anything."

*****

April 19[th,] 1994 the day God protected my husband from death.

I was just getting into my stride at work when I received a call from Ralph's boss. He informed me Ralph had been badly hurt, they had just called an ambulance to come for him and I needed to come to the plant where he worked immediately. I was so shaken I couldn't stand up. One of my co-workers who had watched my reaction to the call knew I needed help. She ran to get her keys and told her supervisor where we were going then she drove me to the plant where Ralph worked.

When I arrived, Ralph was a bloody mess. He had been crushed between a concrete floor and several large air conditioning units. I almost fainted as I watched him lying there. When he saw me and spoke, I realized he was coherent and my fear subsided. His co-workers at the plant had removed the air conditioning units off him and the ambulance crew was on the scene checking him

299

over. I was ordered by one of the emergency technicians to sit in the front of the ambulance because they needed space to work on Ralph in the back while traveling. Like lightning, we were at the hospital. I followed the crew into the hospital, but I was directed to go to the emergency room information desk to give the hospital our insurance information.

Standing at the information desk I overheard a nurse tell the lady who was waiting on me that Ralph was being labeled in critical condition and needed to be admitted into the intensive care. My emotions went into overdrive and I started to shake so bad I felt I might need critical care as well. I needed to get a grip, but I was scared. In my heart, I cried out to the only one I knew could help.

"Jesus!" I sobbed.

"I'm here." He said.

That is when I told the lady at the information desk that I needed to see my husband. Now! Not later but now! I knew if Jesus was with me I was okay.

I guess they didn't want a scene with a hysterical woman, so they let me in the room with Ralph. He was a mess. His face didn't even look normal. He had a large gash over his brow, his nose was somewhat flat, and his new teeth had been broken. Even in that condition, my silly, sweet husband wanted to make jokes about everything. He would laugh and joke with the nurses as they poked and prodded him. When he saw me, he spoke from his heart, "I need my Mama." I wasn't enough for him then. He needed the one person to come to the hospital he knew really loved him.

The emergency room nurse told me other doctors had to come in and examine him further. She recommended that I call the rest of his family because the emergency room doctor had expressed it was going to be touch and go for a while. Before finding a telephone to call Ralph's folks, I took a few seconds to praise the one in charge, "thank you, sweet Lord, for making sure Ralph was spared." I also asked Him, "Please be with Ralph while the doctors have to do what is needed."

After my quick prayer, I proceeded to call Ralph's mom and dad. I was still very shaken up by the doctor's report so by the time Ralph's mom came on the phone I could hardly speak. "Mom, Ralph's been in a horrible accident. He needs to see you and Dad as soon as you can come to the hospital."

The time dragged by. By this time, Ralph was crying for pain relief. I asked the nurse in attendance, "Why can't he be given any pain meds?"

She was very patient with me and said, "We were told that we couldn't sedate him due to the trauma to his head."

As bad as Ralph was hurting when his mother came in the emergency room, her very presence was like a pain shot for him. She calmed him down a lot.

A short time later we were all directed to a waiting area while Ralph had to go into surgery for his face. It would be several hours before Ralph would be put in an intensive care room. During the wait, we had many visitors come by who wanted to know how he was doing. I appreciated the company, but I needed my other rock, so I called Daddy. He and Joan came immediately.

Darlene still didn't know that Ralph had been injured. She had been trying to call him at work but was not told anything. She needed his help. One of her tires had gone flat and she didn't want to be stuck at work when her shift was over. She was very confused to hear Ralph wasn't at work and I wasn't either. No one told her anything.

I didn't want to leave the hospital. I asked Rodney to go tell Darlene for me. She didn't need a phone call. She needed an in-person visit. I knew from the experience of that morning's phone call what hearing bad news was like. As soon as he explained what was going on, he fixed her flat tire and she followed him straight to the hospital, mad as a wet hen that she had not been called. Over the years, she and Ralph had finally become very close and she was upset we hadn't considered her feelings.

Ralph's parents left the hospital asking that I call them the minute he was out of surgery. Most of Ralph's co-workers left the hospital after a few hours of waiting to leave Rodney, Darlene, Daddy, and Joan to wait with me for news. By the time someone finally came into the waiting area to speak with us we were all very tired and anxious.

Three doctors were standing in the room wanting to speak with us.

The Plastic Surgeon went first. He explained, "I've completed stitching up Ralph's forehead, but I'm not finished. Ralph has several broken bones in his face that include his nose, cheekbones, and a cracked lower jawbone. He will need more extensive surgery to repair them once he is stable enough to undergo complete sedation. I've made proper arrangements with a Dental Surgeon to assist me with some of the reconstruction. The surgery will allow him to eat and breathe again properly."

Next to speak was the Internist who explained, "Ralph's stomach, kidneys, and spleen were severely bruised and I'm having him monitored for internal bleeding."

Then the Orthopedic Doctor told us, "Ralph's back has been partially broken in three places requiring bracing, plus he has two broken ribs. His x-rays show that he may have some brain swelling as well, so we are watching for more signs. Right now, his eyes are not dilating correctly."

All this news was very disturbing, but we were assured he would be in good care. One of the nice doctors recommended we all go home and rest since Ralph wasn't allowed visitors anymore for the night.

Darlene finally convinced me by saying, "Why wear yourself down, Mama. If the staff needs you, we don't live far. We can be back in a few minutes."

One of my co-workers had driven my car to the hospital for me. So, we left even though my heart wasn't willing.

I couldn't sleep. I tossed and turned for hours. I finally got up and watched TV. There was nothing on television worth watching so I turned to one of the Christian channels that I loved to watch. That's when I heard a word that my spirit grabbed hold to. Pat Robertson said on his late-night program, "The Holy Spirit is looking over us to save, protect and provide. Open your hearts and let Him do His job." The rest of the program gave me encouragement. That one sentence helped me enough to sleep a few hours in God's care.

I made Darlene go to school the next day. I used the same tactic on her that she used on me the night before. "If I need you, I'll call you out of class first thing. I promise." I told her.

I arrived at the hospital too early for visitors, but I didn't care. I was content to be only a few feet from Ralph. When 9:00 a.m. came around I couldn't wait. I needed in that room with my husband. I buzzed and buzzed the nurse until I was allowed entrance.

I entered the room after bracing myself for a shock. I knew that he had had surgery on his forehead, but I didn't know what else to expect. He looked like a monster. His face was swollen, black and blue. He had tubes in both arms, a heart monitor, an apparatus helping him breathe, plus a urinary catheter. I wanted to cry just looking at the mess lying there before me.

To my surprise, he was awake and still his joking self. He was watching me as well and told me, "Don't cry. I have a hard head I'm not going anywhere. You can't get rid of me that easy."

304

I told him, "The doctors had me scared. They said you may have a brain injury."

"They stopped worrying about that when I told them my eyes did that from time to time anyway. I was hit in the head when I was a kid while playing softball." He told me.

All I could smell was dried blood. His hair was matted, and his mouth was also a bloody mess. I asked, "Are they going to bathe you? You really stink."

"I don't know. I don't think smelling good is a priority right now. Don't bug them about it, okay." He ordered.

I spent as much time as was allowed with Ralph. When his mother came back to the hospital, we swapped places, so she could visit. She was like a drug to him. He visibly relaxed when she was near.

By the next day, we got good news that Ralph was stable enough to be put in a private room. Now his real grit was going to be tested.

For the first week, I hardly left his side. Some days I even washed my clothes in the sink and laid them to out to dry at night, so I could wear them the next day. I brought my pajamas to change into, so I could be comfortable enough to try and sleep. I knew how it was in a hospital. Nurses couldn't always get to you when you needed them, so I refused to leave him alone very much. The staff had provided me with a reclining chair to sleep in. When Ralph made the slightest peep, I could be right there. He was in a lot of pain and didn't have enough strength to do much for himself. Eating was also an adventure for him. His jaw was not working properly, and he couldn't chew. He ate mush most meals.

After the second day in his private room, he became very uneasy. The doctors said it was probably due to nicotine withdrawal. They gave him a nicotine patch to wear. Being stubborn after he heard that, he had me help him into the bathroom for a smoke when the staff left the room. I didn't care, I wanted him to rest and if he needed a cigarette then he was going to have one. After he got his smoke, he agreed to try the patch, so we wouldn't get in trouble.

The second week he started insisting that I go home at night to make sure everything was okay. He didn't like the fact Darlene was at home so much by herself. I knew Daddy was making sure all was well with the home front, but I couldn't convince Ralph of that. I decided he was tired of being babied so I agreed to go home in the evenings.

After his release from the hospital, he was home about a week before he had to go back for more surgery. This time the doctors were going to repair his cheekbones and jaw, so he could eat properly again. My poor husband had his teeth wired together and his jaws bound shut. He had two buttons on his face next to his eyebrows to keep the tension tight and allow for emergency access if they needed to open his mouth.

Trying to understand him was hard because he could only mumble. I was very frustrated at times trying to help him. The man had to eat so I tried to blend his food into a liquid he could drink through a straw. The doctors left him a small gap in front, so a straw could be inserted to drink. I had no choice but to buy protein drinks and breakfast drinks or blend meat and vegetables together, so he could drink them. That was not fun. He had to eat that way for six weeks.

He lost so much weight I could pick him up if I had too. He was nothing but bones after six weeks and his journey was not finished yet.

Even though he was very weak he still wanted to be part of Darlene's graduation ceremony. She was leaving high school and he didn't want to miss seeing her getting her diploma. We loaded him up in the car and got a seat for us as close to the parking lot and near the football field as we could, so he didn't have to walk very far. He even tried to party with the family afterward but the exertion was too much, and we left Daddy's early.

Soon after the wires were removed, he had to undergo more surgery to his nose. His sinus bones and the bridge of his nose had to be reconstructed so he could breathe through his nose again. He only had to spend one night in the hospital after the Plastic Surgeon reconstructed his nose, but the man looked like he had been in a fistfight. His eyes were black and blue again and he had tubes sticking out of his nose. "When will my husband's torture be finished?" I asked the doctor when I saw him. I was told all that was left was to have Ralph's teeth realigned. Ralph was finished with the surgeries. At the end of the next week, they would remove the tubes from his nose and he would be able to eat and breathe again normally.

I knew Ralph had a life-changing experience. He was very grateful to be alive and eager for us to start going back to church. First, we went back to our old Sunday School class to give it another try. We became very involved this time even though in my heart I knew the real reason we were supposed to be there was hardly ever addressed. Jesus wasn't edified enough in my opinion. The church service was a little better and we felt okay being there.

Just when things started improving, the worst flood in over five hundred years hit Belmont and surrounding towns. Water was coming from everywhere. Darlene got separated from Ralph and me. She had to live in a nearby hotel for a few days across the river from us near the Waffle House where she worked. The Waffle House paid for her to have this hotel room because they were the busiest they had ever been and needed their staff close by. State Law Enforcement and Natural Resource Officers were everywhere from all over the state and the business was hopping due to their twenty-four-hour service to customers.

Darlene, learned to wash her clothes out by hand when she got a break and let them air dry while she slept so she would have clean garments. Somehow, Daddy got her a change of undergarments and something else to sleep in. He was also separated from us due to the raging waters.

Ralph and I were a little scared. He was still weak from all he'd been through and we were afraid we would somehow have to pack up our animals and leave our home behind. The river was close, and the water was approaching the houses just two streets over from us. The only peace I had was our telephone still worked and we could keep in touch with Darlene and Daddy.

The neighborhood was in a panic. The grocery store nearby was empty and now the water was approaching us fast. I begged Jesus to help us, but it seemed like he was so far away.

Little by little over that few days the water seemed to stop rising. We had been spared. My Lord had heard us after all.

Now we had to face what others had lost and would have to go through to recover.

My job at the Labor Department was crazy busy. So many people were displaced and out of work. Ralph couldn't do anything but watch people struggle. He was physically unable to assist with any of the cleanup or restorations and he felt helpless.

CRANKED UP

Ralph had a lot of time on his hands. He was concerned about our future and what he was going to do with his life. The doctors all agreed he would never be able to do physical labor again. Now what?

Worker's Compensation really was great. It helped us keep our bills paid and furnished everything Ralph needed. He was also very fortunate his job had provided insurance for accidental dismemberment and injury. That program provided us with a large payout. But what was Ralph going to do with himself? Daily he worried about not going crazy. He was not a person to sat around doing nothing all day.

To ease the discontent, he wanted us to travel a little. To go somewhere he had always wanted to visit but never had the funds. I arranged to take a week's vacation and we headed to New Orleans.

We stayed at a nice hotel right in the French Quarter. The trolley ran right in front of the building so tourists could go to key places in the town. It was great. We had so much fun. I could tell all the walking and going was wearing him down. It was wearing me out and I hadn't been through the physical hell he had.

When we got home, depression set in. He needed an outlet badly, so he started rambling around town trying to find relief. Just to have something to do he often visited one of his closest friends during the day who worked for a freight brokerage company.

Through this friendship, the boss of the company became aware of Ralph's predicament and offered him an internship.

As I watched him go through this depression I'd often ask the Lord for guidance. When Ralph told me about this job offer I knew My Lord had been working things out for us all along. I must admit it was hard waiting. When Ralph shared his news with me it was a big relief.

Ralph and I agreed that he should give the freight business a try. When we contacted Worker's Comp they agreed to keep paying him while he trained. It was just another confirmation this was a blessing from God. Their weekly assistance would stop as soon as he reached a sufficient clientele and work knowledge.

When he went into their office to train each day and became accustomed to a steady routine, I could travel again for my job. One of the first places they sent me was the Macon office to cover for a secretary who had to use medical leave. I was happy to be reunited with my friend Margaret. She and I could begin our daily talks about the Lord again.

She shared with me how she found a Texas preacher on TV who really got her attention. She felt I would love watching him also. While out of town, I got up each morning to Kenneth Copeland's Believer's Voice of Victory. Boy, did I ever get revelation from that man. Just from those few minutes each morning, his teachings gave me many questions to ask my Lord. Just like the scriptures said, every one of them was answered through study, seeking Him, and meditating on His Word.

311

When I got home I told Ralph about Kenneth Copeland's program and we started watching it together each Sunday morning before we went to our church. I started noticing a change in my husband. He also wanted more knowledge from church services than what we were receiving from ours. We started visiting other churches around town.

I was eager for us to visit the Pentecostal church where I had been reunited with Sunny, but Ralph was a little skeptical. He was unsure about some of their beliefs but went with me anyway. We even took Darlene and his kids with us.

Our first visit they were laying hands on people causing them to be slain in the spirit. This fascinated me but it scared Ralph especially when he heard people talking in a strange way in the seat next to us. When we left, he said he didn't think he could go back to that church. All it did for me was create more questions and I couldn't wait to get alone with my Lord.

I started reading as much as I could on becoming slain in the spirit and about speaking in tongues. I'd never been taught anything about this and I needed to know if I was missing a blessing. While alone with Jesus I asked.

"Lord, is this for me? I haven't heard much about this at church and what I've heard has always been negative. Some have even said speaking in tongues is from the devil. So please show me."

Closing my eyes and opening my heart to Him I achieved real peace in my spirit. I looked up in my concordance the word tongues and read about it being highly desired and no one should deny someone their use of it. What really decided it for me was reading where it said when we prayed with unknown tongues the Holy Spirit Himself was praying to God through us. That the two of you were talking to God together. Wow!!!

I really needed to hear a word from Jesus. So, I said, "Jesus, if you don't speak to my heart about this I'm going to explode. Why am I so anxious about this? Are you trying to tell me something?"

Then like always, I heard *"Yes, Little One I want to use your spirit with mine. It's time to show our enemy he can't use your own words against you anymore. If you allow me to pray with you in a language, he can't understand then you and the Father can agree with my word. Your unknown language will be between you, me and the Father only."*

"**N**o!" Evil screamed. "If she ever learns the power of speaking through Him we are doomed."

A light bulb went off in my head as well as in my heart. I knew I needed this more than I needed breath, so I asked, "Jesus, please help me obtain this ability. I want you and me to be so close only God knows what we are praying. Help me receive this."

Tears started running down my face and my body began to tremble as I opened my mouth for any sound come out. I heard clicks and pops, one after another, click, click, pop, pop but I wasn't discouraged, I knew this was a baby step into something grander so I just clicked and popped on for about thirty minutes.

Each day I started talking with the Lord and then on purpose ending our time together with praying in tongues. I had such peace after that. The more I read the Bible the more revelations I received. It was like everything that I had read before was different to me now. I understood God's desires better so when I prayed in tongues I also thought about what I had read.

During a conversation with God, Jesus asked if he could bless Rachel. "I'd like to prove to her that our prayer language together is a real form of communication, so she can have confirmation in her heart to continue and never give it up."

"I agree, Son; she needs to have a little encouragement from time to time," God answered.

One evening while watching TV with the family a commercial came on showing an African family speaking to each other. They were clicking and popping their words. I jumped up from the couch so shocked to see these people speaking in my heavenly language. Even though I didn't have a clue what was being said they used clicks and pops like I used English. This confirmed to me that what I was doing with Jesus was from God. Didn't the Word say after the resurrection when the 120 were baptized in the Holy Spirit that people from other countries heard them speaking in their own languages? Yes, it did, and I was ecstatic to know I was speaking something from God in an African language that someone else could understand if they needed.

Soon after the TV commercial experience, I continued watching my Christian channels and I was hearing message after message about speaking in tongues. Kenneth Copeland was talking about it Marilyn Hickey was talking about it and so was Pat Robertson. Wow! I felt like I was in a flow with them and all of us were working together with and for God.

My friend Margaret and I were determined to see Kenneth Copeland during the upcoming Tallahassee, Florida Convention that fall. We started making plans. It looked like all odds were against us at first, but we didn't give up. One of her friends in Tallahassee let us stay with her while she had to work. Each day we'd get up and go straight to the Civic Center where the convention was being held. The praise and worship there was wonderful. It felt like we were in a heavenly place amongst hundreds of brothers and sisters. Gloria Copeland's message was also very good, but Kenneth's stole the show. He was energized and full of the Holy Spirit and had a hard time staying still to speak. I didn't mind. My heart hung on his every word.

The last day of the convention was supposed to be great. Gloria was holding a healing service after she gave a lesson on the subject. The weather prediction that morning was horrible, so Margaret and I decided to leave earlier so we could get the Civic Center before the weather got worse. Everything started as usual. The praise and worship were the best yet. Then it was time for Gloria to speak. Satan must have been very upset because ten minutes into her message the building began to shake. The roof was being stripped like someone peeling an orange causing rain to pour onto the people.

I heard people screaming and others speaking in tongues. I decided to side with Jesus and started praying with Him in my tongue as well. A tornado was trying to destroy the place where God's people were gathered, and we needed Him badly. Why not let Jesus intercede? It's hard to explain. I was very frightened but at the same time, I had a sense of peace. Margaret and I ran down the bleachers as fast as we could and were directed to the basement of the building. After several minutes, staff in the Civic Center informed us no one had been hurt but that the building had sustained too much damage to remaining inside. Glass and metal lay everywhere. I didn't have to wonder why people weren't hurt. I knew God had protected us.

Outside I saw further evidence He had been right there with us. Cars were strewn everywhere but mine wasn't damaged at all. As we left the parking lot, I knew I had to get to a telephone to call my family. They were probably frantic especially if they had heard the news about the storm. When Margaret and I found a pay phone that worked in town, we called our homes to let everyone know we were okay. Driving home, I felt like I had been robbed of something very special. We didn't know the healing service was being re-scheduled in another part of town.

Days and weeks went by. Every day I pleaded with God to find me a church with a pastor like Kenneth Copeland in my hometown. I couldn't find peace returning to a church that wasn't edifying my Lord. I started recording daily broadcasts on the Trinity Broadcast Network to watch. Darlene and Ralph had to get over it. I was needy for God's Word and if they wanted to watch TV in the afternoons they could go somewhere else. I needed to hear preaching while I cooked.

After Christmas, I was invited to hear a lady preacher in Columbus. She was holding a three day and night convention very much like Kenneth Copeland's, so I was on fire to go. Joyce Meyer was a small lady but a powerful speaker. She was the female equivalent of Kenneth I was again in a heavenly place hearing her glorify my Lord. More than ever after hearing her speak I knew I needed to be in a church that believed like all of us.

*****

It's time her prayer is answered." Jesus told Preservation. "Send one of your angels to show her the way and make it easy for her to know where to go."

*****

Reading the newspaper one morning at work I came across an advertisement about a new church that was having services in an

317

office of a car dealership. The ad stated, "We believe like Kenneth Copeland and Kenneth E. Hagin." Those few words were all it took to capture my heart, so I read on. The Pastor's name was familiar to me, Ben Sharpe. Where had I heard that name before? I asked a co-worker if he knew this person and low and behold they were good friends. For the next few minutes, I had to hear him tell me all about their musical histories together and how far Ben had come in his life to being so devout. I remembered after our conversation where I had heard the name before. Ben played music in some of the nightclubs I used to frequent years ago. I was amazed that he had changed so much but I knew if Jesus could change me He could change anybody. I was still not sure about trying out a church in a car lot.

Evil had a plan and told his companions, "There is still hope for us to discourage her away from this new church. If we can cause her to have doubt in her heart just because of where it is located, it may cause her to be afraid of going.

Preservation just laughed, "He'll never learn. Angels, make a way for her not to have any fear about where this church is or of whom this Pastor is. Give her a reason to be excited. We'll stay ahead of this evil crew as much as possible."

That afternoon, my co-worker friend played a trick on me. He called me from another extension in the building and told me he had Ben on the line with us. After the introduction, he hung up leaving Ben and me to talk with one another. Ben was such a nice person and before we ended our conversation I had promised to visit his church service the next Sunday. I should have known Jesus had his hands all over this. He was answering my cry for a church and a Pastor that believed like me.

Three days later I kept my promise. I found the little car lot and made my way inside the building. Ben and his wife Anne were very lovely people. They treated me very special as they showed me around before service. The attendance was small. Only about fifteen but the atmosphere was what I needed. As soon as praise and worship began I knew I was in the right place because my heart was almost exploding with joy. Ben played and sang so lovely that it made me weep.

It only took a few words of the message for me to know Jesus was about to be lifted like He should. This man had had an experience with his Savior that possibly could match mine and I knew this by the way he spoke to the congregation before him. I looked around at the people around me and saw what I needed to see. They were not bored or sleepy. They were enthralled. I had a church home. My prayers had been answered. "Thank you, Jesus."

I was excited by the time I got home but my joy was too much for Ralph to absorb. He was still skeptical about his visit to the Pentecostal church to say he would jump right in there with me. He did listen to me as I praised the service. I could hardly wait for the next time.

All this time, Darlene had been dating a very nice guy who seemed to be interested in the little church. When he volunteered to go with me to New Life I didn't know if he was trying to butter me up to win my approval. He was the only one willing to go with me to the service the next weekend. Darlene had to work, and Ralph still wasn't sure. Dennis, like me, loved the service and he agreed to go with me next time. It wasn't long before Ralph couldn't stand it. He had to see for himself. I was glad when he finally attended and liked it as much as I did.

Jesus spoke into Rachel's spirit. *"Little One, it's time that you learn the blessing of giving and receiving. We want to bless you and have our Word back you up when evil tries to invade your life. Tithing and giving offerings give us the authority to rebuke evil away from you."*

I knew Jesus was convicting me about tithing. I needed to support my new church. I was scared and didn't hesitate telling Jesus I was afraid. Ralph and I only had sixty dollars to our name that week after bills had been paid and I still hadn't bought groceries. I asked Jesus to help me do it. When I walked in the church I asked Ben to take my money before I could change my mind. I had to rely on Jesus and not let fear keep me from doing what was right.

It was very hard letting go of all our money when three people needed to eat that week and Ralph didn't get paid for five more days. With the Lord's help, I did it. All week long, I could find things in the pantry or freezer that I could cook so we didn't go without anything to eat at all. After that week's trial, I set a pattern for myself and promised Jesus I'd tithe and would never change. I would tithe at least a tenth of the money I made no matter what.

Ralph would have to learn to tithe in his own time. I wasn't going to press the point with him. My promise was between me and Jesus. He would have to learn for himself. I'd just share with him how it made me feel to know I was obeying God. I knew the Lord would work on Ralph's heart about it and it wouldn't be long before he agreed to tithe with me.

Our little church was outgrowing the car lot. We needed to find a larger space to meet. Ben and Anne sought a place and found an old Community Center several miles from town to buy for our meetings. It was almost twenty miles from where I lived but I didn't care if it was fifty. I would be at the services as much as I could. Darlene and Ralph were going regularly with me and Dennis would show up sometimes. I was so happy my little family was being taught the Word as it was written and not as a fairy tale story. Ben made Jesus appear real to the congregation through his messages and he also made Him appealing, enough as a person to want as a friend.

He shared with us how Jesus had delivered him from alcoholism and drugs. It gave people hope. I knew his message was working on Ralph because he was changing before my eyes.

Even though he was still drinking he wasn't getting totally smashed all the time. Plus, I didn't smell marijuana on him like I had.

Until this conviction, Ralph's drinking didn't bother me because his moods and mannerism never changed. He was always a sweet loving person no matter how much he drank; nothing like Al had been. But after listening to Ben, I knew Ralph needed to stop. Just another issue I had to bring to my Lord.

At our little church, I experienced wonderful things happening to my family. I got to see my husband and daughter both receive the baptism of the Holy Spirit. I also got to see Rodney, Ralph's fun-loving brother commit himself to the Lord. Ben's messages rang true to them and I knew Jesus was working miracles in their lives. Time will tell just what those specific miracles would be.

CHANGE IS INEVITABLE

Darlene and Dennis came to me saying they had some good news. They had become engaged and were trying to set a date to get married. They needed my help to make their wedding plans. I loved weddings. They were a passion of mine. I loved everything about them and always wanted to be involved when someone I knew was having one or planning one.

During the planning stages, Darlene and I got together a lot more. She even invited me to go to a Christian Concert with her and one of her girlfriends at the local Civic Center.

Jesus asked the Father, "I'd like to reassure Rachel that there are babies on the way in her future. May I impress on her heart to specifically request this desire she wants so bad? "

"I'd love nothing more than for that family to be fruitful and multiply. Yes, show her this desire and give her the ability to plant it in her spiritual realm." God agreed.

At the concert, the Holy Spirit came over me in a big way letting me know about another desire I had deep in my heart. I knew about desires and how He was always involved in fulfilling the desires of our hearts. When the lead singer of the concert made the announcement that a love offering would be received I knew I had a chance to plant that desire through the offering. The Holy Spirit

323

confirmed the idea when the singer dedicated this offering time as one to fulfill requests made from the hearts.

One of my deepest desires was having a baby in my life again. My baby maker was dead, but Darlene's wasn't, and I needed to know that my past sins were not being passed down. When I placed my gift in the bucket that was being passed around, I shouted aloud "I want a grandchild!" Darlene looked at me stunned. I told her, "Honey, I want a little delight so much. Now that I know you've found a good mate I've put in my petition. Time will tell."

When Darlene and Dennis finally decided on a date to get married I suggested they have the ceremony at our church. She wanted to get married at our old church, so she could invite a lot of people. Great, they wanted a large wedding. Where was, I going to get the funds for that?

"Lord, please show me how I can get these funds. I want my child to have a wedding she can look back on and be proud of. Help me love on her this way so I can make her day special." I prayed.

Even though I didn't hear a verbal response, I knew my prayer was heard. Jesus loves Darlene as much as He loves me.

I volunteered to travel a lot more for my job because the overtime and travel monies would come in handy. I even took out a mortgage on our house so that I could give my little girl her dream wedding. When the time came, I was ready. I had money for food, her dress, the flowers, the rehearsal dinner, everything.

It was going to be a beautiful wedding. I was happy for her and I loved her fiancée as if he were my own child.

My Daddy did it again. He helped find them a new trailer and had it set up in a trailer park only a few minutes from our house. Another prayer answered. She was going to live close by. I could be at her place in a snap if I wanted.

Darlene called me to come over to their trailer one afternoon after work, so she could tell me something. When I got to their place she was laughing and crying at the same time, so I knew something was up. That's when she handed me not one, but two pregnancy tests. Yes, my baby was pregnant only a month after her wedding. "Look, Mama, you got what you asked for." She told me sniffling. Under my breath, I thanked the Lord so much.

Nine months later after Darlene worked at the Waffle House through the whole pregnancy, she gave birth to a nine-pound baby girl. In attendance for the event were Dennis' mother, Dennis, Ralph and me. It was the most wonderful event I think I've ever attended. Little Elise was born looking just like her Daddy and nothing like her mother. I didn't care. To me she was perfection.

At that point, my life couldn't have gotten any better. I was a grandmother. I had a wonderful husband, a wonderful son-in-law, and a wonderful daughter all because I had my Lord.

Little Elise had been dedicated to God and was now in His care. What more could I ask for?

*****

"She's so smug," Evil said. "I'm going to rock her world myself. I'll see to it that the whole family is tormented and oppressed. If I can't destroy them, I'm going to make their lives miserable through my form of fear and doubt."

*****

Then the news came. A bad report concerning Elise. The doctors had determined she was deaf. No tests were showing that she responded to sound. Panic gripped my heart. Darlene and Dennis were also heartbroken. What to do?

On the way home from the hospital, the Holy Spirit reminded me about the scriptures that I had been studying. How a priest was to be there for you in times of need. They were to be His representatives for us on earth and we were to go to them in times of crisis. So, what did I do? I called Ben as soon as I got to Darlene's home phone.

Crying I told him what the doctors had said, and he immediately told me that we needed to shut up. We were not to even speak about it again. No one, but he and the family were to even be told anything. He explained that we were under attack by Satan and our words would be used against us if we got into an agreement with the doctor's diagnosis. The three of us (Darlene, Dennis, and I) promised we would not talk about it at all. We would do as he said and not tell anybody this news.

For the next month or two, Elise's ears had to be tested; two times she failed the hearing test but on insistence from us they agreed to do one more. This one proved we had our answer to prayer. She responded. Her hearing was perfect, and we could hardly contain our joy.

After we received our good news, Pastor Ben agreed we needed to share our testimony with the whole congregation on how good our God is. The devil had been defeated.

As time went on, Ralph was becoming content as well. He was learning to like his work and our finances were improving. His daughters were coming around more often. What made me happiest was the fact he loved going to church with me. He was growing in his faith right along with me. Plus, he had agreed to tithe his income along with mine.

Evil was livid, he shouted to his companions "We can't allow them to get into agreement. When they start acting as one we will be doomed. How can we stop this madness from happening?

Addiction spoke up, "I'll make Ralph's little problem with me more pronounced, so Offense can have a play and make the house divided. If we can cause them to split or keep Ralph from church altogether then our plan will succeed. Give me time to twist him up and cause things to escalate."

327

Ralph loved our church so much that he would tell his friends about how our church allows even drunks to attend. He sincerely meant it from his heart when he told them, "Look if they let me in on Wednesday's nights after I had a few beers, so Jesus could work on me I know they'll let you in, so he can overhaul you, haha." The only problem was that Ralph wasn't trying hard enough to stop drinking and Pastor's messages were directed to help people quit. Ralph's attitude caused Ben to have issues with him.

It was after we had outgrown our current church building and moved into our new place that Ralph really wanted to get involved more with serving in the church. Ben couldn't have him showing up smelling like a brewery. That was when he needed to speak with me about how he felt.

"Rachel, I need to talk to you about Ralph," Ben said. "I love Ralph, but his smelling like beer during service is not helping our deliverance ministry. You're one of the church's officers and it looks bad when your husband disrespects the deliverance message. It concerns me everyone is looking at this. It may cause someone who is truly seeking deliverance to fail and fall back into a serious problem. I need your help expressing to Ralph that he has to stop."

Jesus spoke with Preservation about what was happening. He knew a serious blow had been made on Rachel's marriage and true feelings and actions were going to be uncovered. "Preservation, I see Rachel's heart is more concerned with how people are going to perceive her than it is on truly helping Ralph to change. Evil has used one of our own to cause her this problem. Do not let Offense drive a wedge between their marriage vows. Help her to see she is focusing on herself rather than the truth. Evil can't win but he sure has frustrated things.

Disappointed in my husband, and ashamed that we were causing problems for the deliverance ministry, I truly agreed with Ben's point and took it upon myself to speak with Ralph about it.

Speaking to Ralph about some issues is like speaking to a brick wall. I tried to explain to him how his drinking was embarrassing me especially when he showed up at church smelling like beer. I asked him to please have respect for the others that were coming who were trying to change for the better and not tempt them by his disrespect.

At one point, I even tried threatening that if I had to move on with God I would. I couldn't let his insistence on drinking cause me to lose my faith. The truth was I was scared it was going to make me lose my respect as one of the church leaders.

*****

Finally, Jesus said to Himself. She sees the truth. Losing respect was making her afraid. She had admitted this to herself and now she can heal.

*****

Shocked at my revelation, I cried out to Jesus. "Please Lord, I'm ashamed of my reactions. I'm more worried about what people will think of me than trying to get Ralph some help. Help us both."

*****

Ralph really tried to stop drinking. It was very hard for him because all his life alcohol had been accepted in his family. His whole family drank to the point of being drunk. Some waited until after 5 pm each day and never drove, but the rest did what they wanted when they wanted so he had a real problem trying to resist especially around them. He loved visiting with his parents, but alcohol was everywhere and being freely consumed so it made it hard to deny his thirst. I can give him some credit, though, I watched him try and he did slow down considerably. By his efforts, I knew in his heart he really wanted to change.

Different forms of ministries were being formed as our church grew. One of the ministries was small home study groups called cell groups. They were designed to be in home church meetings where people could meet and fellowship. Then after the groups increased to a certain amount they would split into another cell, thus the name cell groups.

I wasn't excited about this ministry, but Ben had chosen me to head one up. Yes, me. Shy pitiful me. Why me? I hated speaking in front of people and being watched made me shake uncontrollably. I agreed to do it because apparently, Ben had seen something in me I couldn't, and I trusted his direction.

The first meeting was not fun. I felt sick to my stomach. I was nervous and had no support from Ralph because he couldn't go. I was a lone ranger so to speak. The first meeting was held in one of my attendee's homes and only three people showed up including myself. The next week we had the meeting at our house, so Ralph could be there and only one person showed up beside us.

The third week, before the meeting began, a sense of panic came over me that I was going to fail at this and be an embarrassment to our church. I liked sharing one-on-one with others what the Lord had shown me over the years, so I gained strength in that. Not wanting to be defeated, I went outside on my small deck and took my Bible in one hand and looking up to the heavens professed to my Lord, "I will do this for you, Jesus, even if I have to come out here and preach to your bugs."

As our church grew other ministry issues developed and volunteers were needed to maintain them. One of the services we needed was an Intercessory Prayer Team that would pray for the Pastor and his message before and during each service. I wasn't interested in being part of the team because I was already heading up a home cell group and doing many other things to help. One Sunday afternoon I was sitting at home when I was urged by the Lord Himself to go to one of their meetings.

"What Lord?" I asked.

"Rachel get up and go to the church. I need you to sit and listen. You'll know what to do." Jesus said.

I told Ralph where I was going, and on my way out to my car I heard Jesus say, *"Go back and get your Bible."*

I did what was told and then proceeded to the meeting.

Like I've said earlier, I am not a person who likes confrontations or speaking out unless provoked. When I sat there listening to this person who was supposed to know the Word tell those willing listeners that a clear reference to Satan was my Lord in the Bible, I had to speak out.

"Stop right there," I said loudly. "You are referring to this white horse rider. in this, scripture verse as Jesus, when it clearly says that this imposter is going to deceive many people. Jesus is not a deceiver." Then after embarrassing myself, I showed everyone in the book of Revelations the truth. Jesus would have a sword strapped to his thigh, which represented the sword of the spirit. This guy's reference didn't have a sword. I wondered after that just how many other scriptures were being twisted to fit into Satan's deception at these meetings.

That night I prayed and talked with my Lord a lot. What was going on and why did He have me interfering with this program? After my night of concerns, I went to Ben with them the next day. I shared with him about the previous day's experience and why I was worried our intercessors. In my opinion, they were being taught to focus on evil more than on the power of the Lord.

At first, nothing changed but I made sure I attended those meetings, even if I had a different motive other than to learn. I was there to spy and confront if necessary and the leader knew this. After a few months, he stepped down and left our church. I didn't like being part of causing him to leave but I knew in my heart if I didn't stay on top of some things people may be misled. Of course, I wasn't an expert in the Word and I'll be the first to tell anyone, but I knew when Jesus wanted me to do something. Protecting these prayer volunteers and Ben's message was necessary.

Our little prayer group went on the same way without a leader for a while doing the best we knew how by praying and speaking the word. Everything needs a head to operate and I was approached to be the leader of the group. I was honored just by being asked, but I knew in my heart I wasn't quite ready. So, I asked to be given time to think and pray about it.

I asked the Lord specifically, "Do you want me to be another group leader at church?" Waiting for a reply from Him, I didn't think I was ready for his answer.

"*Yes, but not yet. I'll give you a special sign to show you when the time is right. Your wait will not be long, and you'll have my go ahead before Elise starts school. This sign will instigate a time where your perception of truth from fiction is going to change. Study my Word. Get strong through what you learn. You'll need to get stronger and have your eyes opened to things that will terrify others. Only then will you know I am truly with you in this venture.*" Was His answer.

*****

Overhearing Jesus, Evil pondered what His plan would be for Rachel. Was He going to let this woman see into the spirit realm where she could see him? His reply to her was too vague.

*****

Darlene volunteered to start a school program for our church; Pre-K through 2nd grades. The church bought buildings to accommodate this feat. It was almost two months before it was to start. I knew I didn't have long to wait for my sign. Elise was four and would be in Pre-K so I was anxiously waiting. What would it be? What did Jesus mean by the word 'terrifying?'

Two weeks before school began, I started feeling like I was being encapsulated. I felt like I was in a clear box and was trying to hear what people were saying to each other, but it was difficult. It was very frustrating and felt very strange. Sort of like how a hamster must feel while it is inside a plastic exercise ball. I could see out and walk around but sounds were distorted.

Sunday morning before the school was to start the next day, I went to be alone with the Lord, which was my normal daily procedure. I would study, inquire about what I'd read and then pray. I had a feeling today was not going to be normal. After reading we didn't war against flesh and blood but against spirits, in another realm, I started to shake. Was this message about evil spirits the terrifying part I was warned about? I closed my eyes to

334

summon my Lord. Before I could focus, I heard glass loudly breaking all around me and my spirit started screaming, "Jesus!"

He answered me by saying, *"I'm here, don't fear. I've broken the barrier between you and the spirit realm you'll need to operate in from time to time. From this day on, you will be able to hear and see what is coming against you and your beloved church. The key is hearing unholy words that indicate truth from lies then you'll know what you are up against. You will assist me by standing in gaps where others have no strength to stand. Trust me only during those times and by faith take your position."*

I said, "I don't know if I'm ready. Jesus, I've never liked confrontations, ever, and this means fighting, doesn't it?" I asked Him fearfully.

"Yes, but you will not be fighting people. Instead, you will fight the evil that lies behind people causing them to do and say wicked things. You'll also be used to protect your man of God from distractions and fears. Only know that when you verbally agree to take on this responsibility evil will come at you stronger than it has ever done before." He informed me.

"What? Has evil been after me? What do you mean? I am now very confused. I'm scared Lord. Help me." I begged.

"Look at the scriptures you've just read. Do what it says. Use it like armor and know nothing can prevail against it. You have faith. I know because you've used it often. You have confidence in me and in your salvation. You are faithful in learning from me every day and wanting to apply what you've

335

learned. Now, I've appointed you as an Armor Bearer for your Pastor." He informed me.

"Why me?" I asked.

"No one else is ready in your group. You love this man like a father and as my representative. You respect his calling and you know what his calling means. Yes, you are weak, but you are going to be strong in me." He answered.

While showering that morning, I cried the whole time, I was truly scared. This was not a game. This was a reality. No one in my whole life had put this much responsibility on me. I knew I had to suck it up and take on this call with gratification instead of whimpering like a scared baby. So, I gritted my teeth and said aloud, "In the words of Joyce Meyer, I'm going to do this if I have to do it afraid."

At church that morning, I told Anne what had happened. I knew she thought I was crazy when I told her the spirit realm' barrier had shattered. When Ben got a minute, I explained my experience to him. He seemed excited that I'd taken on the job of Head Intercessor.

I wasn't expecting to be recognized as Lead Intercessor in front of the congregation after the service ended that morning. I certainly wasn't ready to be deemed Ben's personal intercessor to everyone. When Ben made the announcement I just looked at him stunned. I hadn't told him Jesus selected me for that task. How did he know? Duh! Doesn't he have the same Leader as I do? Of course, he was told.

TORMENTED

Evil had another plan to share with his little army, "I'm going to bombard her with information about us and frighten her away. We can't always hear her conversations, but we can poke and prod her into doing things before she gets Him involved. She will be able to hear us so we can turn the tables and make her think she's hearing from Him. We'll use deception against her like we did the other intercessor. Wasn't it this very thing she warned her pastor about before? We'll use it to hurt her this time."

✶✶✶✶✶

"This little idiot demon still doesn't understand that we can see and hear everything, we knew what we were doing before we put her in this position," Jesus said to the Father laughing.

✶✶✶✶✶

"Yes Son, Rachel is ready for the responsibility, but she must go through a testing period before she relaxes enough to let you have the reigns and not take on the burdens alone. Just like before, we must watch and wait until she comes back to us for help. Those same demons are going to torment her for a while, but she will bounce back humbled and ready to let you fight." God said.

✶✶✶✶✶

After Pastor Ben made the announcement at church that I was Head Intercessor, people started giving me all kinds of books on the subject. I read some and skimmed over others which totally confused me.

I understood the part about being involved in another realm's activities but knowing and understanding demon activity was new. I became obsessed with demonic signs and symbols and wanting to be prepared when I had to face people involved in those demonic activities. I had a strong aversion to all things antichrist. I began to express my dislike verbally when I came around someone involved even if they did it unknowingly.

I admit I prayed in the spirit a lot. I was still talking with my Lord regularly, but I was also feeling a sense of distance from Him at times when I would get overwhelmed with the prayer requests and needs of others. I was also sensing a distance within my family. They couldn't understand what I was going through. It wasn't anything they could relate to, so I had no one to with about it. I didn't want to alarm Ben.

I was having weird dreams and hearing suggestions that we were always under attack. It was my responsibility to prevent and intervene before trouble struck those I loved including the congregation I cared about. Each morning found me searching scriptures to fight demons instead of studying and seeking the peace of my Lord. Wasn't that my new job? I thought I was meeting my obligation.

During these times, I was aware Ralph was being tormented about something. He was drinking more than usual and even showing up at church and cell group after indulging. Ralph was no longer trying to slow down his drinking and was always grumpy. Several times during these days of uncontrolled drinking, Ben would call me in his office to complain. I agreed that he had a right to be angry with Ralph about his lack of consideration. He encouraged me strongly again to do something about Ralph because of my position at the church.

I was highly embarrassed again. When I did confront my husband, I attacked him instead of listening. I made it very plain I was going on with my walk with the Lord with or without him. If he got thrown out of the church it wasn't my fault-I had warned him. He embarrassed me and made me look bad. It was all about me, me, me! Not one time was I able to step back and ask him to explain the real reasons for his behavior.

Then it happened! My husband started having chest pains during one of my cell group meetings. What was going on? I called an ambulance at once because Ralph wasn't playing around. I asked my group to clean up and lock up after finishing while we went to the hospital. I called Ben as I followed the ambulance in my car and asked him to pray explaining we were on our way to the hospital.

It was after the doctors examined Ralph and determined he was having a severe anxiety attack instead of a heart attack that I relaxed. He would be fine and was going to be released after his blood pressure stabilized. It was in that hospital room Ralph finally shared with me what was causing him to be stressed out.

339

He said, "I hate my job. Everything about it is against my new beliefs and morals. I must listen to others in the office lie, and fight and fuss about accounts. I'm not like that. I don't want to make money by deception and greed."

"Why didn't you tell me instead of trying to drink your way through your feelings? I think I would have been a little more sympatric and understanding." I said.

"You've been disappointed in me lately. I didn't want to add to your worry. It's my nature to sulk and pout. I drank more just because you told me not too. I'm stubborn that way. I don't like being told I can't do something. It makes me crazy." He shared.

Before I could respond to him a telephone rang. The nurse told us our Pastor and his wife were waiting to see Ralph. I went into the waiting area to lead them back to Ralph's room for their visit. Ben prayed for Ralph, but I could see Ben wasn't happy with him.

Then he asked the question, "Ralph, have you been drinking?"

"Yes sir, I've had a few beers. I can't deny that," he answered truthfully.

Ben looked up at me. I understood another office conversation was coming soon. I wasn't looking forward to it at all. Ralph had been caught again red-handed, in distress after a drinking binge on cell group night. I knew Ben was going to have a hard time understanding. He saw Ralph as a trouble maker who disrespected his ministry. He couldn't see Ralph's heart intent.

Ralph only wanted to help serve our new church. He loved it so much and really wanted to be a good example like Ben. He wanted to be able to say he had overcome and straightened out his life for the Lord. He was doing that little by little in his own way. He wasn't drinking a twelve pack a day anymore but was consuming one or two. He was still a baby Christian and hadn't studied the Bible very much. All he knew was to help others and love them as much as possible. Helping and loving during a service while smelling like beer was not acceptable. He couldn't understand that people smelled beer on him even if he'd only had one that day.

I could not convince Ralph that it didn't matter how many he drank, he smelled like beer because he had not eaten anything before the evening service. He couldn't understand that beer stench also lingered on someone even the next day.

After the hospital ordeal, Ralph and I talked in detail about what was going on with him at the office. I made it a priority to pray daily for God to do something to make him happy. Our Lord had gotten us through other hard times. I knew He wouldn't fail us now.

My office confrontation with Ben didn't come as soon as I feared. His attention was needed elsewhere. Diverting Ben's attention away from us, was a visit from a Pastor from Mexico. The Mexican Pastor visited around town and was invited to attend another patron's cell group to observe how we conducted our home ministries. For about a week Ben and Anne entertained our Mexican guest while our issue was moved to the back burner.

While talking with Ben on the phone I expressed how glad I was my cell meeting had not been chosen for Pastor Horge's visit. I was usually terrified to speak in front of a group. I knew if I had him in my cell group I probably would have freaked out and fumbled it badly. I truly meant what I said but somehow that simple statement was interpreted as hurt feelings by not being asked to host this Pastor. The next time I saw Ben he was furious with me and made no bones about it. He had stewed over that conversation all day and thought that I couldn't understand. I could not convince him I knew why he didn't ask me. Ralph and I would not have made a good impression for the church. We would have been an embarrassment to his deliverance ministry.

We both had to take a step back before we said things we didn't mean. He was angry at me over a misunderstanding. Now I was angry because he couldn't see my husband's heart and how much Ralph truly loved his ministry. We both left the church that day with unresolved issues between us.

My heart was broken. I couldn't believe my Pastor couldn't hear me. What had gone wrong? I really didn't want that visiting Pastor at my cell group because of my fears, but the discussion was totally turned around to attack Ralph again. The mama bear in me was back and wanting to tear something apart. I badly wanted to avenge my husband! I was mad and hurt. I

342

wanted to destroy something to feel better. Only one other person in my life had made me feel this way and it was my Daddy.

Evil was rolling with laughter. "We got her boys. She is strung out with self-pity and she hasn't even thought about Him. Prayer warrior, ha! She is truly a mess and right where we need her to be.

*****

On the way home, I couldn't stop crying as I drove. My mind raced with thoughts of betrayal and accusations that were unfounded. What had happened to cause such confusion? Pray? That was the last thing I thought about doing. I needed an outlet to express my frustration. So, as usual, I turned to food. Cookies, cake, pie, ice cream, nuts, peanut butter whatever I could get my hands on were my pacifiers. Yes, I could destroy something and that something was myself through food.

After eating until I got sick, I was ready to analyze this issue that had loomed over me. I started asking myself questions. What and why had this happened? Then a scripture came to mind. Pride causes a fall. What? Pride. How was I prideful and where had it started?

I knew this coaxing was from the Holy Spirit. He was trying to keep me from condemning myself, so I tried to listen. I couldn't hear Him right away, so I did something that usually worked when I really needed to hear Him and that was to take a shower.

Letting the warm water rush over me, I cried out to my Lord that I realized I had failed and disappointed Him. I wanted release from this pain and anger towards Ben. I wanted Him back. My life was so much simpler before I started serving the church. I didn't want this pain anymore. I didn't want Ralph to be put under a microscope and judged anymore. How could I do these services when I was angry and hurt? How could I pray for a man that judged us so harshly all the time?

In the shower, I let my heart spill out to Jesus, the only one who cared. The only man I had in my life who didn't judge me but wanted my happiness. Daddy always judged me. He hated I was overweight. He hated my eyes didn't do right and I needed glasses. He hated I wasn't an athlete. He was even disappointed that I wasn't chosen first in our high school beauty pageant, even though I scored third place out of thirty girls. It never seemed that I was good enough for him in anything.

My husbands were jokes. Not one of them, not even Ralph, cared about my true feelings. Drake wanted an extension of his mother but with sexual benefits. Al wanted a victim he could verbally and physically abuse. Ralph wanted a beer instead of me and our ministry. Now Ben, a minister who looked past my flaws and seemed to approve of me doesn't approve of me anymore. I decided he wished we would move on to another church.

Then I heard something. It was Joyce Meyer's words coming through a voice I knew as well as my own. My Sunny said, *"You can be pitiful or powerful, but you can't be both."*

Those few words struck a nerve within me and got my attention. I could focus better. I hated being pitiful, weak, and needy. That did it! It woke me from a pity party so could reason with my Lord.

"What do I need to do Lord?" I asked.

Then I heard Him softly say, *"First, focus on me. Then allow your thoughts to be for others place your self-centered thoughts behind you. The men you were judging have issues as deep, maybe even deeper, than yours. That is why they are like they are."*

"How did I fail Lord? What went wrong?" I asked Him sincerely.

"How far do you want to go back Little One?" He asked.

"Is it truly so bad, Jesus, that I have to revisit my whole life?" I needed to know.

"We can view the shortcut version, so you can get my point, okay." He answered sweetly.

"I shared with you not so long ago that you would be terrified due to your new positions. Since you are seeking me now instead of chasing ghosts, I'm willing to help you understand so you can be what we've designed you to be. Do you remember the

time you wanted to play with the farm animals and I told you not to do it without me?" He asked.

"Yes, sir. I was very young. I loved animals and wanted them to love me." I answered.

"Most of your life you've been trying to seek approval from others without me being there with you. What happened when you ran up to the bull?" He prodded me.

"The bull charged at me," I remembered.

By this time my shower was getting cold. I dried off and dressed quickly to resume our conversation. Ralph was off somewhere doing his thing. I was alone in the house to meet Jesus as I desired. I crawled in the bed with my Bible to continue our conversation.

Then I asked Jesus, "Can you show me, Lord, in a way I can truly understand so I can fix my relationships and be happy again."

"That's the problem Little One. You want to fix it but you can't. You should let me do it. All your life you've felt the need to correct yourself. When you couldn't you took on a sense of guilt and shame. The burden you carried was not yours to bear. It was mine. When you progressed, you took accepted a sense of pride which took away the glory due to me. Your life became a see-saw, up and down, up and down, never stabled or set." He shared.

Sobbing, I said, "I'm so sorry."

346

About the time the lesson deepened, Ralph came home hungry and ready to relax. Through the day, he just nibbled. By evening he was famished. That evening he knew something was up when he looked at me.

"What's going on?" He asked.

Learning from Jesus, I mentally asked the Lord, "Is it okay to share with him?"

"*Yes, because you've asked me.*" Was my Lord's reply.

I proceeded to tell Ralph what had transpired after he left church that day and how Ben misunderstood me. Ralph knew he was a sore subject with Ben. But, he also had an issue with him. He didn't understand why Ben never admonished him directly but chose to correct him through me instead. If he was the problem, why wasn't he the one getting chewed out?

I tried to explain, "Ben's deliverance started with Anne's rejection and ultimate removal of herself and his kids. I think Ben thinks if I do the same thing then you would change like he did."

"Threatening and giving me ultimatums are the last things that will make me change. It only fuels the problem. When he wants to talk to you about me the next time promise you'll ask him to talk directly with me. I can't take a bitchy woman. Ask Pam. She threatened, fussed, and fumed. All it accomplished was me leaving her and the kids to drink and drug even more." He said.

"Okay, I promise." Thanks for listening.

"That's not all you're sad about, so give." He said.

"I feel like I've lost a good friend today and what I discerned as camaraderie was fake. My goal was to share Jesus. Now all I do is battle mentally and spiritually. I just need more time to get a handle on things." I shared.

I wanted more time alone with Jesus. We had only scratched the surface of my concerns when Ralph came home. But, I sought rest and felt better after Ralph listened to me.

After eating dinner and watching television, it was time to go to bed. We both had a job to go to the next day. I lay in bed tossing and turning knowing the reason. I had unfinished business. I got up, picked up my Bible and went into the living room to be alone with the Lord so I could truly rest.

Sitting there I asked Jesus if we could continue our discussion. I needed help understanding what He meant by my pride.

Again, He took me through my life showing me when I had taken the credit for things instead of giving Him the glory. When He spoke of my ministry I was shocked at how prideful I had become. I'd become religious by works instead of relying on Him through fellowship.

He showed me how I took recognition for my cell group's growth instead of giving Him the glory for the increase. I bragged my group was the only one that had grown enough to split. I was shown I never once sought Him concerning another in intercessory prayer. I only relied on quoting scriptures. I'd never taken any demonic issue to Him asking Him through His righteousness to rebuke them due to violations against His Word. I was constantly searching out evil but never asking Him to show me where to look. He showed me the many times I had taken unwarranted responsibility and credit and proclaimed, me, me, me or I, I and I, instead of Him.

Ashamed of myself, I promised Him I would try my best not to do that again. I would try as much as I could to include Him in everything. Then I asked Him to show me how to deal with something that was heavy on my heart.

"How was I going to be effective as an intercessor for Ben when I was so angry and hurt with him?"

"The first action you must take is to give Ben your forgiveness. He has dealt with issues deeper than yours that compel him to act certain ways. Your main purpose is to pray for his office, not him directly. His issues are between him and me. The office of Pastor is my business which I gave him stewardship over. Pray that my purpose prevails without consequence. The deliverance ministry is my ministry, not his. He is only the example I choose to use in this area. Profess over him my love, practice patience and forgiveness. Don't go beyond this for a while." He told me.

"Forgive Drake, Al, and Ralph for all their transgressions against you. I'm working on them at their own rate and levels of acceptance. Give me your pain, worries and hurtful memories so

349

I can replace them with my joy. Know if I am willing to help you overcome, I am willing and able to help them. Don't live in 'the what could have been or should have been'. From this moment on, live in what can be with me."

"Listen for words of unbelief and come against them instead of the person or persons delivering them. Then speak my word of blessing over the ones speaking unbelief. This is an intercessory prayer for others. You will be coming against unbelief in lieu of evil for now. Don't look for evil, listen for it. Any words heard, or thoughts received that are not pure, loving or of good intent are not from Me. Listen for them and cast them away."

"Even in embarrassing and trying situations keep me in your heart, mind, and mouth always. Remember the animals and how they are friendly when you are with me. Evil has no choice but to be friendly when I'm near." He shared.

Then I asked Him, "Will I ever be what you truly want me to be?"

"You are human. You will fail often because your instincts cause you to want to take control. But, just like I told Jerusalem while I sat on the mountain looking over it, if you'll be like a little chick staying under my wings or run back as soon as possible then you'll be okay." He replied.

You've lived in darkness for too long, Little One. Start trying to see me like you did when you were young. Live in my light. Don't be self-serving or pitiful any longer."

350

I closed my eyes. Trying with all my might I could only see a bright light. I couldn't see the Sunny I use to visualize as a child. However, the light was soothing and comforting because I knew it was Him. As the night progressed we talked so much I felt like a sponge soaking up volumes of knowledge. Then I heard my alarm clock sounding in our bedroom. I had been out of the darkness and I wanted more of the light.

Wow! I been with Jesus all night and didn't even feel tired. I got ready for work, as usual, trying to heed all I had learned. I had to keep Jesus with me as much as I possibly could. He said I'd sometimes get sidetracked, but I could mentally run back under His wing as soon as I caught myself uncovered.

Over time my relationship with Ben and Anne improved. We were speaking kindly to each other, but I wasn't as trusting as I had been. It kept my goal specialized instead of personalized. Jesus was my only friend and priority.

We'll show her just how hard it is to keep Him close, we'll attack her family. Let Grief have a part in her destruction. With Jason gone her security blanket on earth will disappear. Oh, what fun we are going to have taking what she has relied upon." Evil said.

Tragedy struck! My Daddy got sick then died from heart failure. The one I had deemed my rock on earth was gone. During my

351

sorrow, I turned to Ben and Anne again. Through this pain over the death of my Daddy, our friendship was completely restored. Through his ministry calling, Ben became a father figure to me. Even though he was only a few years older than me he showed me the loving nature of my Heavenly Father.

While we were alone together in his hospital room before he passed into heaven, Daddy made me promise him something. He asked me to do certain things that would be very hard for me to do. When he started talking I immediately called in Jesus keeping Him close to me, so I could have help listening to Daddy's requests.

Sadly, Daddy told me "Honey, I've spent most of the money I had planned to divide between you, JL, and Joan through bad investments and medical expenses. I need to leave what is left to Joan for her welfare. She has been good to me and deserves a good life. Promise you will keep your brother from doing something stupid. There isn't much money left to fight over. It's not worth fuming about." I couldn't speak, so with the help of Jesus, I promised by nodding my head.

I didn't want to hear my Daddy talk about dying. I would rather have him than all his money. But I must admit the news stunned me. Death is inevitable. I knew this day would come but for so many years I believed my Daddy had made provisions for me financially. He'd promised, and I trusted his word. He made a pledge to us before the sale of the farm was final. My security was gone. The only money JL and I were going to receive after his death was from an insurance trust fund he held that Mama secured for us before she died. Twenty thousand dollars was very different from what Daddy had promised. His original plan was to give each of us about one million dollars from the sale of the farm. I had that figure nestled in my brain for so long I had not concentrated on savings of any kind. I didn't need too.

After Daddy passed I kept my promise to soothe JL and my sister-in-law. Wasn't money the root of all evils? It wasn't worth fighting over. The only problem JL had through the whole mess was not knowing just how much was left in Daddy's estate for Joan to keep. Why worry about it? It didn't matter because his Will determined it was all hers regardless the amount.

*****

Watching from heaven, Jesus and the Father discussed what was going to happen next. Rachel had to go through another trial and testing. Reliance on another was a big fear of hers and one she had to get over fast. Remembering that Rachel had placed her life's authority back in Jason's hands after her separation from Al was an issue that must be corrected. She needed to submit to her life into her husband's authority. Fear had kept her from relying on any man except her Daddy and now he was gone. The order of man was incorrect in her life. She wasn't Ralph's authority, he was supposed to be hers.

They planned for one of the angels to give her a vision jolting her out of her rut and making her want to run to the protection of another. But, Evil overheard the angels talking and twisted their vision into a horrible dream that scared Rachel and fueled her fears.

*****

The night before Daddy's funeral, I had a horrible dream. The dream was vivid and so real I knew it had to be an omen of some kind. In the dream, I saw Ralph standing in a boat having the time of his life, fishing away, happy, and carefree. Then I was watching a person sitting in Daddy's lounge chair observing the rise and fall of the stock market. My focus was directed to the person sitting in the chair and I realized it was me. I was skin and bones. My eyes were dark and sunk deep in the sockets. My skin was dry and wrinkled. I was agonizing over what I was watching on the television. The economy's difficulties were tormenting me. Then I woke up.

In Ben's SUV going to the graveside, I shared my dream with him. In the past when Ralph was fishing in Florida, he would always be drinking and doing things I didn't approve of. I was worried I was still going to have issues with him. At the same time in my dream, I was going to be really worried about money for some reason. I couldn't completely comprehend the meaning of my dream, but I knew it was a puzzle I didn't need to solve just yet. I asked Ben to pray for us.

JL tried talking us into investing Mama's money into real estate in Florida. He had made a lot much money buying and selling condos. At first, I agreed until I remembered the dream I had. Now I was worried I would regret the investment because

Ralph would be tempted to do things he shouldn't. I couldn't put us on that path. My heart wasn't into selfishness of any kind.

The day of the funeral, before JL and Kelly went home to California, we agreed to be happy with our inheritances without bickering. He mentioned to me that God was in his life and he didn't really need the proceeds because the Lord had been good to him. He was already financially secure and self- sufficient. Why cause distress? I was glad to hear that he had Jesus, too. Knowing that eased my heart. I knew deep inside after drove away I'd probably not hear or see from him for a long, long time.

After I received Mama's gift, tithes and offerings were donated as Jesus instructed. It felt so good to be used that way. Next, we purchased some property on a lake. There we could eventually build our dream house. It was closer to our church home and close to Darlene and her family.

The last thing I did before putting the rest in savings was to plant a specific seed into God's work. I asked my Lord, "How much do you want me to plant and where do you want me to plant this seed."

"*What is your need?*" He asked me.

"I need to be out of debt. I feel like I haven't been a good steward over the years with the money you've given us. I bought things on credit when I could have waited." I said.

"*Give me all of your debt.*" He said.

"How?" I asked

"Write down everything you owe and to whom on a piece of paper. Then give it to your Pastor with your seed." He answered.

"How much should I give him?" I asked.

"Since it is a large debt, I suggest you plant into his ministry accordingly." He said.

We didn't have a lot left after our land purchase, so I decided on a thousand dollars.

Without questioning myself, I wrote out the check and then made a list of all our debts and where they were held. I gave both to Ben the next time I saw him.

"What's this?" He asked me.

"It's a seed towards a need Ralph and I have in our lives," I told him.

"We want to be out of debt, so we can focus on building our dream house and start living the way we are supposed to." I shared.

He was very grateful and promised to pray for our debt freedom whenever he thought about it.

It had been a few years since Daddy's death and our sacrificial seed against debt. The bills were still with us. Our finances stayed stagnant for a while. Then suddenly we noticed Ralph's paycheck getting smaller and smaller. It was becoming harder and harder to put any money aside towards our dream. In the summer of 2004, we saw hardly any commissions coming in. We had to start living off the trust fund just to pay bills and eat.

As job issues at Ralph's work got worse, by nature he would come home every night drunk and angry. My emotions wanted to rise but Jesus would check me and remind me to focus. During those times, He showed me I shouldn't fuss at Ralph. He reminded me that change was coming, and I was not supposed to focus on Ralph's actions but on the fact that He was working.

I remembered to listen to conversations like Jesus instructed. What I was hearing from all angles were words that were exactly the opposite of words to glorify Him. Whatever financial issues were stalking us, they were not from Him. We were in a war. I kept rebuking the nasty things I heard and saw. I tried to profess what the Word said, but it was hard.

One morning after my time alone with the Lord, I asked Ralph if he would start praying with me for change concerning his job. He agreed. For weeks, we took hands and asked the Lord to change the hearts of the people he worked with and to improve the working conditions. It wasn't long before something happened.

THE WILDERNESS EXPERIENCE

Evil always likes to brag. During their next meeting, he shared the following. "We know Rachel's heart is floundering and scared to trust in any man. We'll make the one she is tied to remind her that men, in general, are worthless and unreliable. She will not want him to ever be her head. Not having any money will translate as no easy lifestyle. The fear of lack will surely seal our deal and she will doubt Jesus ever sent her this mate.

Each week Ralph's working conditions got worse. His paycheck started dwindling down to almost nothing. No matter how hard he tried he couldn't drum up any new customers.

Eventually, things got so bad Ralph's boss agreed he could file for unemployment. His job didn't produce enough money for him to even pay for the gas it took to drive back and forth to work. He had no choice but to try and find work elsewhere. He had no choice but to file for unemployment. At least the unemployment check would be based on what he made the year previously instead of the amount he was bringing home.

Times were hard, and several times Ben and Anne would give us money to help with our bills. It was a shame we had allowed our lifestyle to become adjusted to Ralph's income in the good days of his job. Now, he wasn't even bringing home a third of that amount. Bill collectors called us frequently not making it easy for us to have a pleasant transition.

I guess the stress of what was happening was evident even though I tried very hard not to display fear or concern. Our cell group was so good to us. They would hide money in our house after our meetings. Each time we would find their gifts we would thank God for them as well as His urging them to act on His behalf.

There were no gifts exchanged that Christmas. We didn't have anything to give so we made the kids agree they wouldn't buy us anything either. We did get together to celebrate the Lord's birth at their house.

A few weeks after the holidays we went to the kid's house for some reason. We noticed their neighbor's dog had puppies. We witnessed the little things being neglected and the sight broke our hearts. Their owner wasn't feeding the mother much and the puppies were starving. Darlene told us she had taken upon herself to feed the animals and tried to find homes for the puppies, but she wasn't having much success. The puppies were dying.

So, what does Ralph do? Like someone possessed, he walked into the neighbor's yard to claim one puppy.

"I must have this dog. Look at his little face. He's so cute." He told me.

"I guess it's okay. But you'll have to train him. I don't know how." I stated.

Then the fun began when we took him into Darlene's house for a bath. Elise begged, "Dobbie, name the puppy Fred, okay."

"No, I'm going to call him Derf," Ralph told her.

"NO! Dobbie, please call him Fred." She screamed.

Seeing that she was getting upset Ralph took her in his lap and said to her, "Elise, honey, spell Fred backward. What does it spell that way?"

After she thought about it, she just smiled, "Derf. It's Fred spelled backward. I love it."

Ralph and Derf were inseparable. When the unemployment benefits ended, and Ralph still didn't have any work, the dog was his lifeline.

✲✲✲✲✲

"It's our cue fellows," Evil announced. "Their government help is about to run out and we can ruin this man. He has a problem anyway with self-doubt and worries. We'll let Depression persecute him beyond his limit and Rachel hates when people wallow in pity."

✲✲✲✲✲

No money. By this time, guilt and shame were gripping Ralph hard. He was beginning to feel useless. He couldn't find anything to do to generate income.

Desperation over our circumstances, caused him to contact a freight broker's office in another state asking if he could work for them. Finally, we had hope. Mr. Gardner agreed to work Ralph on commission. He would do the job he was trained for with

Georgia operations based out of our home. We set up a room with an extra telephone, fax machine, and internet service so he could focus on getting his old clientele back. He started doing what he could to move freight.

We were hurting financially with nothing but my earnings to live on and creditors were constantly calling us. Some would try to work with us while others would be ugly. The more Ralph tried to work, the more depressed he got. He hated sales. That was all a freight broker is, a salesman. Finally, in exasperation, Ralph asked God to help him find the strength to work with his hands again.

Preservation told his fellow angels, "It's time we show the devil is a lie. We are going to give Ralph courage enough to try working a physical job again. Not everyone is called to work a desk job and he hates it. Blessings come to those who have faith enough in their prayers to try."

Ralph wanted more than anything to work again with his hands. He resented being cooped up inside, chained to a desk and telephone. When one of our friends at church needed a laborer to help clean a construction site. Ralph begged for the job.

Pete hired Ralph as a day laborer on a trial basis. He knew Ralph hadn't done any physical labor in over ten years. He feared

Ralph wouldn't be able to keep up. But Ralph fooled him and endured each day, slow but steady. Each night he would come home wanting to wash up then eat. Afterward, I rubbed him with a muscle relaxant. Ralph was sore all over due to being so out of shape. But he was happier than he had been in a long time. Pete even let him take little Derf along each day, so he had his buddy to keep him company.

As much as Pete hated it he just didn't have enough steady work to keep Ralph employed. Because Pete had given Ralph a chance, he stayed focused on finding jobs he would love rather than settle for sales. We disconnected everything at the house just sitting there costing us money. We started trying to find other things for him to do.

With Ralph being handy in all kinds of construction we decided to go into business for ourselves. We decided the name of our business would be: Threefold Services. We got this name from Ecclesiastes in the Bible which states a threefold cord was not easily broken. We had Jesus as part of our cord. He would be the center of our new venture, so we proclaimed that it was going to work.

Months came and went. We had very little business come our way. It got to the point we started to fear losing our trucks and maybe even our home. Groceries were being bought on credit cards. Then banks started threatening us because they weren't getting minimum payments. We were in a jam big time. I was beginning to lose sleep at night because I was so worried.

Fear gripped me hard after a verbal fight over the phone with a creditor. It scared me enough to beg Ralph's parents for help. They did but it was only a temporary fix. I felt bad about begging. I couldn't ask for any more help from them. The only other step we could see was to file bankruptcy.

Our cell group meetings every week weren't fun anymore. The stress of trying to deceive people about our situation was mindboggling. Finally, we asked everyone if we could stop our meetings for a while until we could re-group. I loved sharing the Word with my friends but right now, I wasn't resting. The extra expense to hold a group in our home was an issue. We could hardly buy food enough for us let alone for a group each week.

One of my cell group friends gave us a blessing that summer. She asked her apartment manager if he would allow her friends use of the complex's swimming pool. During those few times that I took Elise swimming, I would swim down to the deepest part of the pool and float and I'd commune with my Lord seeking his voice.

"Lord this water is holding me up when I should be sinking. Relaxing and not struggling is the key to floating. Can I count on you hold me up from this financial mess? I don't want to be a failure causing other people to question my faith, wondering just where you've been in my life, or if I am just a teacher of the Word. I want everyone to know I rely on our fellowship instead of stories I read. Please don't let me fail you." I pleaded.

363

"Relax Little One. Know I'm working. Don't doubt." He said.

After another few confrontations with creditors, fear gripped me again. I finally made an appointment with an attorney, so we could consider filing bankruptcy. All the while, my spirit grieved and I felt like such a failure. Plus, depression over this was affecting Ralph. I'd find myself eating the weirdest things to compensate for the stress. I noticed whenever I got a few dollars extra I spend it on junk. It didn't matter what I stuffed in my face. When I'd catch Ralph with a beer I couldn't fuss. His stress reliever was in liquid form where mine was in food.

Finally, the day came to meet with the attorney. I'd gathered a list of all our debts and assets as instructed. We were as ready as we would ever be to cross this bridge. I was glad my Daddy wasn't alive to see us go through this.

Preservation told several angels to protect Rachel and Ralph during the bankruptcy consultation. Not to allow any words or distractions to come toward them preventing the exchange needed between Ralph and Rachel. It was time, per the Lord for Rachel to give her life's authority over to her husband. They were not to allow anything thing or any person stop that process.

Our consultation was an eye-opener. To file bankruptcy, we would have to give up our lake property. We couldn't have any assets and we would not have enough money for tithes after the attorney made other adjustments. Our consultant told us tithing wasn't possible in these circumstances. Every dime had to be accounted towards the bankruptcy process. That's when my husband spoke up and said we needed to think about it. I knew he wasn't accepting her plan of action neither was I. I was proud of him for speaking up.

The second we were in the truck Ralph declared we could not stop our tithe. We decided we would rather do without than deny God our money. We had made it a habit years ago, to tithe before we paid any bills or even bought groceries. It was God's money, not ours. I looked at Ralph and said, "We need to pray."

I audibly prayed, "Sweet Jesus, from this day forward we fail or succeed by your plan. You are our provider. We are finished dealing with the devil. From now on whatever happens is for the best. You promised we would have a good life through your Word and an expected end. We are expecting the best to come from this to give you glory. I also agree I need to place my life under the authority of the man you have designated for me and not fear. I agree with him and I am proud of him. Amen."

When we got home we had five calls on our voice mail from creditors. Immediately I wanted to cry. My mind started to go to places it should not travel. I pictured us living with my daughter and her family using their old beat-up car because my truck was repossessed. My sweet husband reminded me to focus on our prayer.

"Remember, Satan comes immediately. You asked for God's best through this so don't jump into fear, okay." He said.

"Thanks. My mind was going into complete failure mode and I needed a punch of confidence." I responded.

Ralph said, "I need to think. I'm taking Derf to the lake to walk around and sort things out. I'll be back in an hour or so. You go take a nap or something. We are going to be okay."

While he was gone, I needed my sweet Jesus. I was struggling to stay in peace and only He could keep me there. I stretched out on the couch and asked Him to help me.

"Why are you so scared?" I heard Him ask.

"I saw this coming long before you started experiencing the pressure. Why do you think I directed your steps when you had the funds? It was to place a block between you and what was coming." He said.

I was confused for a few minutes until He reminded me of our special offering right after Daddy died.

"Do you remember when you gave Ben the special offering and the list of creditors?" He asked.

"Yes," I responded.

"That was to protect you from them. When you gave Ben the list with a gift, you put your belongings in my care through him. Now wait and see through me, you will not lose anything." He informed.

After our little chat, I must have fallen asleep because it was dark when Ralph came home. He had to wake me to tell me he was home. Not only had I received peace, he was more confident as well.

About a week passed when Ralph received a call from Ben asking him to help build a home for a couple who had lost everything in a fire. When Ralph told me about the job offer, I almost shouted. "It's the fist-size cloud just before the rain. We are about to have our socks blessed off."

In less than a month, we could use the job as proof that Ralph was working. We could refinance our vehicles to manage the payments better.

After that job was finished, Ben asked Ralph to help with building the church's new sanctuary. It was like God Himself was employing Ralph making sure we were meeting financial obligations. With that job, our credit card holders adjusted our payments where we wouldn't have to pay so much. After a year, they would review our credit again.

The sanctuary took several months to complete. Ralph could find other means of steady employment. He was even asked to help build another house for one of the church's patrons whose house was also lost in a fire.

While Ralph was building the house, I was asked to do the flowers for a large wedding. The funds came just in time to pay the taxes on my vehicle. And if God's goodness wasn't enough, the people who owned the new house Ralph helped build gave us a love gift that was just in time to help pay land taxes.

After the work at the church and house were completed, my mind wanted to panic when Ben told Ralph his assistance was no longer needed. Even with all the blessings, my emotions ran off in fear. Faith didn't drive me to Jesus fear did and I began to thank Him for getting us through the mess, so I could ask Him to find Ralph more work.

I realized later what I'd done. Faith and fear couldn't work together. We would have to keep relying strongly on our promises from Jesus to get us through. He hadn't failed us yet so why should we doubt. Two days after Ben told Ralph he no longer needed him, Ralph was offered work with a business development firm that wanted to rebuild portions of downtown Belmont.

Christmas that year was so good. We could buy the kids' gifts and something for each other. I was happy, and I even wanted to decorate the house. We didn't have as much as we did before Ralph left the freight brokerage company, but we were once again able to pay our bills with money left to enjoy our lives. Jesus knew what He was doing. During the Holy Days, I thanked Him a lot more for loving us and seeing us through.

THE OTHER SIDE

Before the New Year, I asked the Lord to join me. I needed time with Him to answer my many questions. I pondered what Ralph and I had gone through. I needed to know what happened and what was expected of me in the future. I still had some fears and needed my Lord's reassurance.

The first question was simple and to the point. "Lord, what happened? I spoke your Word. I taught others about the blessings of first fruit giving. Instead of seeing an increase, Ralph and I almost suffered a financial disaster."

As usual, my Lord would answer me by asking questions. Simple questions that would make me think before I answered. The first one was easy enough to answer. He asked. *"How many years did you respond with an emotional answer of lack without thinking about your future? How many years did you depend on your own methods and strength to get by? Weren't they many?*

"Wow! I hadn't thought about that, but you're right. I was always worried about making ends meet. I had no problem voicing my concerns or worries with others. It was years before I started changing the way I talked and tried not to worry." I said.

He replied. *"Your professions of lack were spiritual seeds that were going to grow. You didn't worry before about your future because you were counting on an inheritance from your father. Before he died you could only worry and profess a need, or give for the moment letting a spirit of lack rule over your situations. No matter how long you've tried to ignore them, the old words of lack were still growing, waiting for a time to trip your faith. After your father passed over, your fear for your future gave the old seeds strength to grow faster, as if they had been fertilized."*

He also continued, *"Don't fear. My Word also must grow and be tested for people to trust it. You were teaching others from a lack of experience. The revelations you received from my Word needed to be tested for you to put faith into action. Pressure from a trial will cause a person to use their faith or fail in fear. You and Ralph had victory because you believed my Words. Your seeds of faith were planted prior to the trial. During the trial, they operated for others to witness. People trying to cope with their financial needs are curious about how you survived this awful experience. Now, you are a witness proving my Word is truth. There is a constant battle over territory and you are the one who determines who wins.*

Do you understand?" He asked.

"I think so," I responded. Then I stated, "What you are telling me is that if a person stays in fear it gives that fear strength to take over a person's life. But if we rest in your Word and act on how much you love us then our faith can cause fear to die out. Am I, right?" I asked.

"In a sense, you have the revelation." He laughed. *"Little One, I need you to keep on trusting me fully and try to relax. Remember I have good plans for you which include an expected end. What are you expecting? Is it success or failure? If you*

370

honestly trust me, you'll know in your heart what is in your future." He said.

I was curious then, so I asked Him another question. "You said there is a battle going on for territory. What did you mean?"

"Everything in heaven and earth belongs to me. For you to share with me, you are caught in the middle of a battle between the demons of hell who want you to suffer and the angels of heaven who are assigned to minister your good. Your words allow one or the other power over you to harm or to help. That is why it is so important for you to trust my Word and agree with it. Your earthly inheritance depends on how much you trust in me." He answered.

"I thought I knew all of that. Wasn't I using my intercessory prayers to come against the spirits of darkness? What am I doing or praying wrong causing these evil beings to still be around? Plus, I need to know if I'm still being influenced by these evil things?" I asked.

"Yes, you are praying against darkness! But, no one is free from their attacks. They are always in the secret realm trying to kill, steal, or destroy people. That is why speaking in agreement constantly with my Word, gives strength to the angels who have been assigned to watch and take care of you and keep evil at bay." He stated.

"This makes me angry." I shared.

"Good! Righteous anger is good when you know what you are truly fighting." He responded.

371

"I want to be a better intercessory prayer leader. I want to help other people understand what we are up against." I told Him.

"Good again! But, you must truly believe evil beings exist just as much as you believe I exist. Are you ready for this?" He asked me.

"I thought I already did believe evil existed. Are you trying to warn me or disclose something new?" I asked.

"Both," He said. *"Remember this! The world is trying hard to make people believe in fantasy, so the truth of pure evil will not be believed and fought against. But it is as real as you and me. A force to be reckoned with at every turn."* He said.

Continuing He described how to fight. *"Listen to people's words. When you hear people speak words of fear, doubt or condemnation know a demon spirit is whispering to them urging the utterance. Demons want the evil seeds from their words of destruction to have a place to grow. You can immediately come to me in prayer for the people, so I can rebuke the words. Stand in the gap for those who do not know what they are doing. Be like the ones who tore off the roof of Peter's house to get a crippled person to me. That person could not come to me on his own. He needed the help of others. You do the equivalent for others through prayer. Bring them to me."*

"Should I confront the person when they speak words of fear?" I asked.

"*Sometimes it will be necessary. Most of the time it would destroy your fellowship with them by condemning their speaking over and over. Just know if they understood, they would not allow evil to cause them to speak untruths. There will come a time when the two of you can discuss correct speaking. That will determine when their faith can operate with yours.*" He answered.

Then, He asked me a question. "*What has just transpired between us Little One?*"

Confused, I said "I don't know. What?"

"*Are you still fearful?*" He asked.

"No! Why is that?" I asked.

"*When you came to me for answers, your heart was troubled about what happened to you and Ralph. You were still afraid. Then, your focus changed to wanting to help others. You've stumbled across a key to overcoming fears.*" He said.

Grasping His meaning, I replied. "When I start to fear about something concerning myself, I need to change my thoughts towards helping others. Is that the key to stomping fear?"

"*One of them, yes.*" He said.

"Terrific!" I replied.

"Will you help me be a better intercessor? To discern when others are being influenced? Will you also help me be more aware of when I'm being influenced by evil?" I asked Him.

"If you wish. We'll take it slow. The kingdom of darkness isn't going away soon. Together we will fight it better." He promised.

I asked Him one more question. "Lord, there was something else that happened during our financial trial wasn't there?

"A shift occurred that was needed for you. The two of you truly became one in spirit on the day Ralph put his foot down. Up until that day he was just playing along. You were the spiritual head of your house. When forced to choose between me and financial ruin his spirit man took over and agreed with yours. He took back his God-given authority over his family. He and I are one sharing the duty of taking care of you. He is your head the way it is supposed to be and I am his. Until that time, you were afraid of letting any man have authority over you but your father. When he passed over, you were uncovered so to speak. Now you're not." He said.

"I felt a shift, but I could not quite put my finger on what happened. I've noticed him praying a lot more and making decisions. I used to be the one always taking authority. It's a good feeling. Thanks for telling me." I said.

From that day on, I was more focused on the spirit realm than I had ever been. I listened to how people spoke and knew almost instantly when to call Jesus, so He could rebuke or give grace. He was always with me. It wasn't hard to ask if He also heard or if I was right on track. We became a team. I also noticed after a while I'd get a chance to help those close to me change their speaking, so it didn't sound holier than thou all the time.

About a year after Ralph took on his new job with the developer he revealed his unhappiness about his changing duties each day. I asked him, "Honey, do you want me to start looking for a job change? You know I have access to job announcements at work. It won't be a problem."

"I went to work with this guy to do repairs and maintenance. Now he has me cooking in his restaurants. I swore I'd never go into the food service business again. So please, start looking for me." He answered.

Soon after he made his request known, I located a job that perfectly suited him. I sent in a resume for him. Within days the employer called him in for an interview. My God is so good! Not only was the job something I knew Ralph would like, it was a job with someone he knew from his volleyball days. The guy hired him on the spot.

Later the Lord showed me how refusing fear when Ralph wanted to change jobs then submitting to his desire allowed a blessing to flow towards us. He showed me when we allow fear and doubt to come in our hearts His control is taken away causing His blessing to be pushed aside. The curse seeps in to cause havoc.

Things were really changing for us. We still didn't have a lot of money, but our attitudes were better. We could enjoy life.

Darlene, Elise, and I could go to the beach for a few days. As I was soaking up the sun, I heard the Lord whisper, *"Get by yourself."*

I stood and told the kids I needed to go to the room for a while but for them to stay. I'd be back.

In the room, my soul was uneasy. I took off my swimsuit and got into the shower. I could hear the Lord speak to me clearly sometimes while taking a bath, so I decided that was where I needed to be.

"What is it, Lord?" I asked.

"It's time for a financial adjustment." He said.

"What?" I asked.

"You are in trouble and you need to pay off debt soon." He said.

Then He was gone. That was the extent of our conversation.

✳✳✳✳✳

Evil said, "We've got to keep her guessing boys. Don't let her operate in faith. Keep her worried."

✳✳✳✳✳

Always watching Preservation just laughed. "My Lord knows what's up and He has blocked their plans. They still don't know just how much Rachel loves Him and follows His lead."

*****

I knew our time for paying off our credit cards was near. They had given us only a year of grace to get our debt in order. How could that be the trouble I thought? The rest of our trip I pondered what to do to speed up this process.

When I got home I told Ralph about the need to pay off the credit card bills. We both decided to ask if our mortgage company would work with us refinancing the house and adding the credit card debt to the mortgage. When we contacted them, we were met with questions and barriers at every turn. It seemed they were in control instead of us. We decided not to do business with them approaching another lender instead.

As soon as we decided to go with a different lender, obstacles disappeared, we had no problem extending the loan, getting a fixed rate instead of an adjusted rate or getting the extra money for the credit card debt.

As soon as we got the money we paid off that bill and felt relief immediately.

About a month later we heard on the news that our old mortgage company was being federally investigated for urging people into adjustable rate mortgages. Soon afterward, the mortgagees' adjustable rates caused them to face foreclosures due to extreme adjustments. Adjustment changes made their expected payments increase beyond the means to keep up. We were headed in that same direction before Jesus diverted us from that problem. We were facing the same trouble until we reacted quickly to His warning.

After hearing that news story, I started thanking the Lord so fast that my head was swimming. I couldn't believe we were faced with losing our home. He truly looks out for us. "Jesus, you are so good!" I kept telling Him over and over.

"You are now equipped to help others." He said.

"You have something you need me to do?" I asked Him.

"Yes. You and Ralph have been through what so many people in this nation and in your community, will be facing soon. Give them encouragement by telling them how you fared and what to expect. Give them hope. Show them how to stay focused. Keep praying them through and start listening even harder when their words overtake their hearts with fear. Remember our teamwork." He said.

Layoffs and business closures were overwhelming the Labor Department. I was certainly able to hear people speak in fear. Not only were they speaking in fear they were angry and hateful. So many demons attacking each day made my spirit weary. I was taking on their pain and it was oppressive.

Then Dennis lost his job with the local tire plant. It pushed my daughter into a panic. She was one person I could talk to and confront about this fear. No way was this demon of lack going to destroy them. She witnessed how Ralph and I prevailed. She knew firsthand how the Lord saved us. She needed a spiritual swat.

It's been hard for them, but the Lord promised the wealth of the wicked has been laid up for the just. Not only is Dennis getting unemployment he is also getting a full college scholarship that will pay for gas as well as books. In a little over a year, he will be equipped with an education working with something he loves which is computer science.

The prayer needs at church were mainly focused on two areas, financial blessing, and healing. It was evident that both types of request were tied together. The stress the people coping with was causing sickness to overtake their bodies. A few times I even had to ask the Lord to rebuke words from Ben. The financial needs coming against the church seemed enormous and his focus would get diverted to the lack of funds coming in instead of on the Word.

She is so worried about everybody else that we have access to her now. The stress from others is heavy on her and has opened a door for us to attack her health. Let's move quickly before she starts inquiring from Him what to do."

During this time of constant prayer petitioning Jesus to intervene for the hardships, I started putting on the pounds. I was using food to comfort my own stress and feeling horrible all the time. I was very weak in my body I could hardly get around. I knew not to focus on it and keep prodding forward.

While having, my teeth cleaned, the intern told me my blood pressure was too high and I needed to have it checked. I'd never had problems with my blood pressure before. I just ignored her comment that day and went right back to work thinking nothing more about it until I could consult the Lord.

When I got home, I felt my spirit being pulled again. I went to take a shower listening for the Lord.

"What is it, Lord?" I asked.

"*Little One, it's time*." He said.

"Time for what?" I replied.

"It is time for you to be how I see you. Little One. It will help you be an example for others. Plus, if you know a curse you can fight it." He said.

"Okay, but what are you asking me to be? I don't understand." I said still confused.

"The generational curse that has kept you from being my Little One must be stifled or broken so Darlene and Elise can live unhindered. You must try and surrender your need to feed and start living a healthy lifestyle for me and for them." He said.

380

Crying by now, I answered Him, "Okay Lord, I'll try but I've never been able to keep the weight off. You know the extremes I've gone through to be small. All of them failed. What do you want me to do that I haven't tried before? What if I succeed and then regain the weight?

"Shame has no place in this. Realize your body will always fight your mind so it can be pacified, satisfied, and pampered through food. Especially in times of stress. If you fail to overtake your fleshly desires, we will forgive you. This demonic curse has haunted your family for centuries and it needs to be weakened. Don't focus on losing the weight so you'll look good. Focus on doing it for me. Remember, this demon is causing obesity to attack, Darlene. Get mad at it! Be determined to eat healthy foods that God talks about in our Word. You will be able to eat any of them by focusing on the energy they give. You'll lose the weight." He explained.

I was mad! I never considered that a demon was causing me to be fat. I thought it was me and my desire to overeat. After my shower, my mind raced, and I turned on my computer typing in "energy from food" and the response was all about calories. I looked on the computer for information about the number of calories I needed to stay healthy and lose weight. I started the very next day counting calories of everything I ate. When I'd get close to twelve hundred calories for a day I'd quit eating.

The weight came off extremely fast and I was ecstatic. I was enjoying what I was eating. Fancy that! I would eat sweets, oven fried chicken, potatoes, bacon even bread and continued to lose weight. I had to teach myself different methods of cooking. I was having a lot of much fun! I followed the computer's advice eating mostly vegetables and fruit with lean meat most of the time to maintain control and stay under 1200 calories, and I found ways to eat my sweets.

*****

"**I**'m tired of playing with this girl. It's me and her now, one on one. She'll know that I'm real and my weapon of pain will sting." Evil screamed.

*****

As mad as I had gotten with the demon of obesity he got angry right back at me. Out of nowhere after church on a Wednesday night, he struck me. It felt like I was being stabbed in my stomach with a red-hot poker. My whole system shut down and seized up. I was in so much pain that I could hardly tolerate it. I couldn't throw up nor have a bowel movement. I felt like I was literally dying.

All night I tried forcing myself to vomit just so my system would quit cramping. I'd sit on the toilet gagging in agony which upset Ralph. Now evil had our house in an uproar just where he wanted it causing Ralph and me to be at odds.

I started crying and telling Jesus I needed Him. I didn't hear Him speak but, I heard a soft voice singing next to me. I tried

382

to focus on that lovely music and voice knowing it was Him trying to comfort me through the night.

Just before dawn, my emotions broke. I was hurting so bad I begged Ralph to take me to the hospital. Relieved by my request for help, he called our insurance nurse for clearance to go to the emergency room. Then he drove me to the hospital nearest our home.

Seeing me in that condition, the nurses started checking for heart problems first then taking me in for x-rays. Tests had to be run for a doctor to know what to do. After all the tests were done and a doctor finally came in to talk with us, she was clueless. Nothing showed up on x-rays or heart tests. What did the doctor do? She gave me pain medication and muscle relaxants then sent me home with orders to follow up with a stomach specialist. Money flushed down the toilet so to speak. Nothing that was done helped me. They only gave me meds to alter my mind and force me to sleep.

The next day was a repeat of the night before only this time I was dopey. I still gagged and had severe cramps in my stomach. I had to call in sick from work again. My boss was so sweet. She advised me to take the rest of the week off to recuperate. By Sunday, I was better but very weak. I'd been in a fight and knew it well but, I didn't let my enemy keep me from church and praising my Lord.

I remember the key Jesus and I had discussed once. Focus on others and your problems go away. That was just what I intended to do. I was going to pray and focus on as many people that day as I could.

*****

"No! No!" was all Evil could say.

*****

After several days, I was still shaking up from the battle. I called a doctor friend from church to request a referral to a specialist for my stomach. My God is so good. He blessed me by convincing Dr. Kenna to take my case herself. Now, I had a doctor I could honestly relate to without worrying about having my beliefs persecuted.

My visit with Dr. Kenna was truly God's gift. She tested me for everything she could think of and found I was extremely anemic. I asked if my diet was the cause. She didn't know. For me to be extremely anemic something had been going on in my system for a long time. She was worried I was bleeding internally. All this time I thought the reason I was feeling bad was due to obesity. Now, I knew I had a blood disorder that could be treated.

I started scanning the computer for symptoms of anemia and was shocked to find many of my symptoms. Anemia was causing high blood pressure problems and was the reason I was cold all the time and the source of my heart palpitations.

Even though I was undergoing treatment for anemia I had to submit to upper and lower G-I tests to determine if I was

384

bleeding internally. No point taking a drug to stop anemia without finding the source of the problem. To be honest I was curious and a little fearful considering what I had done to myself so many years ago, to lose weight. What if this was a result of the stomach by-pass surgery?

I didn't stray from following my diet plan though I struggled in the face of evil. I knew my old enemy wanted me to fail. He would cheer when I fell off the wagon like he had done so many times before. I even stayed on my diet while on vacation with the kids at the beach. I was truly proud knowing I had divine help on my side this time.

Jesus knew Rachel's problem. She was not following God's Word. Instead of eating organic and healthy foods for energy, she was determined to eat what she liked just in smaller amounts and under a certain caloric range and it did play into her anemic problem. Counting calories was not His plan. The demon was still in control and would continue to plague the family. At least Rachel knew she had a demonic monkey on her back and it was not a character flaw in herself.

Returning from vacation, I underwent the tests. Both upper and lower GI tests determined no problems at all. I was relieved even though the tests cost me a bundle. I decided my peace of mind was well worth the cost. When I went back to see Dr. Kenna, she advised all I needed was iron supplements and a precautionary medicine to relieve stomach seizure. I didn't need drugs to make me sleep or pain meds, I just needed a stomach relaxant to be used when necessary.

Each follow-up visit found my blood count improving as weight steadily reduced.

I thought I lost weight, so I could be an example for others so, every time I'm asked about my weight loss I explained I lost weight from counting calories. But, in the back of my mind, I felt it wasn't how Jesus wanted me to lead. I did the best I could. If I was mistaken, I knew Jesus would correct me.

CATALYSIS

I was trying to be a good example in many ways. So, when Jesus asked me to investigate an issue, I could not resist Him. It was during the fall of the year and I noticed the young girls in our church totally obsessed with certain popular books and movies. Not only the girls at church, but some of my friends at work were really into these same books and movies. My curiosity was piqued. Jesus told me people would be intrigued more from fantasy more than from the truth. I asked Darlene if she had read the books. She told me they were great, and she thought I'd like them even though they were about vampires.

"What could all the fuss be about," I asked myself. I even checked with my spirit to discern if I had a sense of revulsion. I felt no warning keeping me from them.

The first thing I did was to study the author of the books. I noticed ideas for them came from a dream she had. Okay, I know how dreams influence people. Now, I'm really intrigued. I went to the library and checked out the first book in audio form since I like listening to books while working or cooking.

It wasn't long into the first book before I knew what the entire obsession was about. Even though these books were written about vampires most of the references were Biblical.

Jesus' saying was true. The Word draws peoples' attention no matter how it is presented. While listening, I started hearing references describing the main male character of the book. Words the author used came from "The Song of Solomon" in the Bible.

This revelation obsessed me! Not with the book, but with trying to find a way to tell young girls how these books used the Bible to create a leading man. It wasn't a vampire but our Lord that was causing them to swoon and drool over the stories. Jesus is loving, unselfish and an immortal.

I tried hard to share this revelation with the Youth Minister's wife, but she hadn't read all the books yet. She intends to read them but as a new mother who is trying to finish school, she hadn't had time. I was frustrated because this information needed to be shared with the young girls but not through me. I was a grandmother to them and they weren't interested in what I had to say.

I finished listening to all the books before watching the movies, of course, they would provide a gorgeous young man to play the leading man. Thereby making young girls everywhere go crazy for him and not Jesus. I'm crazy at this point and obsessed with explaining this to Elise. I wanted to show her what she was missing, but she couldn't hear her Nana when she discussed Jesus. Fantasy was blocking the truth from her and she couldn't understand what I was trying to say.

"Jesus, I need your help! I can't stop thinking about what is happening to this younger generation. They are focused on the wrong thing and don't even know it." I explained.

"That is the way of the world. Satan will try and stop anything that even hints of me. Don't you know that?" He said.

"How can I dispense this knowledge? It is like a fire inside of me that must be put out and I can't do it alone. No one wants to listen and I'm beginning to sound like a crazy person trying to share what I know." I told Him.

"*Haven't you heard the scripture that says where sin abounds grace much more abounds*? He asked me.

"Sure, but what does that have to do with showing these girls how the author wrote the books about a vampire using you as an example," I said.

"*If you can't get someone to listen to you and volunteer to tell these girls what you've seen and heard, then you do something that will get their attention.*" He said.

"How?" I asked puzzled.

"*Write your own story and tell them about me. Show them how I've helped you overcome evil and what you've lived through in the process.*" He shared.

"My story, I'm ashamed of my story," I said really confused.

"*Why? Your story shows salvation from me over and over. It shows how much I love you and how beautiful life can be with me.*" He said.

"Lord, as much as I want these girls to know you, I don't want them to know what I've done. That's not being a good example. I've killed and been immoral. Letting others know what

I've done would cause me too much shame. May I please take these awful secrets to my grave? I'd want to crawl under a rock if my church family found out how I acted. I'm not like that anymore. I really don't want to do this!" I said troubled.

"*Do you really want these girls set free?*" He asked pointedly.

"Yes Sir, but I'm scared," I said sobbing.

"*Why?*" He asked.

"There are so many reasons. In my younger years, I was such a klutz just stumbling through life and not very popular. I did stupid things trying to win friendships. I wanted a boyfriend so bad I almost sold my soul a few times. As an adult, I lived an immoral and unhindered lifestyle. I know now that it was because I was lustful and searching for true love through sex. But even after I found you again, I still didn't raise our girls to do right and have good moral values. All of them sought after men like I did. Our youngest is still out in the world chasing every guy who winks at her."

"Jesus, to be honest, I'm not a writer, I have problems with grammar and sometimes even spelling. I know it's ironic since I work as a secretary. Me, trying to write books is too funny."

Most of all, how can I tell people about myself where they will not want to reject me? I don't want to be hated." I said.

"*I know everything you have ever done or thought of doing. Part of my plan was humbling you enough to die to yourself for the*
390

benefit of others. People will love your honesty. Don't worry about writing, I'll have people willing to help you with grammar and spelling. Young girls and women who have been through hard times need to know I'm always here. Just do this to show off our relationship." He said lovingly.

"Think about the victory. If you could spare one girl the pain and worry of a lonely and guilty life, don't you agree it would be terrific? Think of the help you'd be to others. This is the example I want. Show them how to have a relationship with me." He urged.

At that moment, He gave me an idea. One person's fantasy was another one's reality. I could write my story in a fictitious manner with supernatural elements. I could grab this generation's attention using the fantasy they crave while explaining the truth.

✳✳✳✳✳

With Jesus' help, people will know THE PLAN He had for me was to write and share His love. I'm was to tell every horrid thing I can remember about myself. Explain the outcome of bad decisions so my daughter, her daughter, and any other young girl wouldn't have to experience what I went through. The great part would be expressing how the love of God got me through hard times and wicked mindsets.

I'm not perfect. I still fail Jesus in a lot of ways. I have fears and doubts plague me every day. But, I know He will help me through the confusion. To know Him is a wonderful experience. Jesus' loving nature is always available and through it, you can dream big and live a happy life. He will help you fight fear and He will give you a purpose for living.

His Word and His promise to give us a good life will encourage everyone to begin their quest to find His plan for them.

THE END.

EPILOGUE

I can happily say the Youth Pastor of our church understands why I was obsessed with the vampire books and movies. He is using some of the books' references to explain moral values.

If the vampire books get resurrected because of my book, I'll be happy about that. One thing remains, books and movies die or become uninteresting, but God's Word never will die because the true immortal one, Jesus lives forever.

About the Author

Raven H. Price, is a Christian fiction writer who uses romance mixed with fantasy and supernatural events to intrigue her readers. She also enjoys devoting her time inspiring and encouraging people to believe in themselves and trusting in a loving God.

She is happily married to her husband, Ralph W. Price, III, and they live in Leesburg, Georgia with four cats. Since she is a cat lover, her Twitter handle is 'roaringpurr.' Her Facebook author page @Roaringpurr, is devoted not only to her books but as an outlet to encourage love, respect, and acceptance for all mankind.

Please consider leaving a review on Amazon by clicking on this, thank you.

www.ingramcontent.com/pod-product-compliance
Lightning Source LLC
Chambersburg PA
CBHW060148260626
47160CB00001B/168